FEATHERS IN FLIGHT

D. R. Cassady

ISBN: Paperback: 978-1-7361395-8-5
eBook: 978-1-7361395-9-2

ACKNOWLEDGMENTS

I want to thank B. J. Myer-Bradley for taking the time to read the manuscript, point out my goofs, and make suggestions to improve the story. His input has been so valuable. I am also grateful to each of you for taking the time to read Willow's story. I hope it will bring light and inspiration. I welcome your feedback at:

dwain.cassady@dwainwrites.com.

After you are done, please leave an honest review on the site from which you purchased the book. Thanks again and enjoy the read!

FEATHERS
IN
FLIGHT

Chapter 1
May 20, 2023

Sitting on the deck watching the river flow by is fitting. My life is in a beautiful transition, flowing from past to present to future. I tried to stay in the now, but past and future pulled in both directions.

It's graduation day! Mom and Dad rented a bungalow on the Tennessee River for the weekend. The coffee tasted extra special. I woke up early and just caught the sunrise. The sun still hid behind the trees and mountains to the east.

My heart swung between relishing the past four years, being excited for the future, and dreading the changes that were coming. With our state championship in high school, Will and I both received tennis scholarships to the University of Tennessee. We were the top two in mixed doubles on the team, but third and fourth in singles. The competition was fierce at this level, but we both held our own.

To be honest, I'm still surprised at Will's major. After flipping around a few times, he finally decided to go with the pre-veterinary program. He'll be staying here, at the University of Tennessee, to finish his training as a vet.

Therein lies the angst. Will is staying here, and I'm moving to Atlanta to go to seminary at Emory University. Thinking about being separated from him is frightening. This will be the first time in twenty-two years that we haven't lived in the same place. I hope I can handle that. Life flows on, unstoppable, just like the river.

The sound of footsteps in the kitchen drew me from my thoughts. Will opened the door. "You're up early."

"Yeah. I'm surprised I woke up before the alarm. It's a good day for brooding."

"I hear you're graduating from college today."

"Funny, I heard the same about you."

"I've already showered, so it's all yours."

"OK. It's time to quit pondering and get moving."

"I'll wake up the parents."

I gathered my things and turned on the shower. *College was so different from high school. I have been openly lesbian and most people are OK with that. I was even welcomed in the student ministry group for our denomination... A refreshing change from Roger.*

The steam dragged me from my thoughts and into the shower. *If I don't quit daydreaming so much, I'll miss graduation!*

Wrapped in a towel, I hustled to the bedroom to dress. Romeo and Sophie were sleeping on the bed. Sophie looked up as I walked in. After our first year of being required to live in the dorms, Will and I got an apartment together. We brought the gray twins with us. It seemed fitting that human twins should have twin cats.

I half expected to see Taz. *It's hard to get used to her being gone.* My parents had to put her to sleep four months ago. She had cancer. I stopped in front of the mirror. An eddy of sadness disturbed the joy of the day.

Dad was still against me being homosexual. *It's been over four years, and he still hasn't come around.* He is mostly silent, expressing disapproval with grumps and huffs. *I'm going to put all of that aside and be happy today!*

Mom, Dad, and Will were in the kitchen eating breakfast. "Good morning!" I chirped in my happiest voice.

"Good morning!" Mom and Will echoed back. *Come on, Dad! Even you can be happy today.*

"Good morning," he added.

"I can't believe we have two college graduates today! And you're both going on to even greater heights! I'm so proud of you!" Mom gushed.

"It is an awesome day!" Will said.

"Will, you have great things ahead for you. Willow, I wish you wouldn't throw the next three years of your life away. You could still do something worthwhile with your psychology degree. You'd be a great counselor."

Here we go again. That has been Dad's mantra for four years. He had such a duck fit when I announced I wanted to major in religion that I changed to psychology, figuring that would help me in ministry just as well. It would also help if I decided to go into counseling or chaplaincy.

"Dad, how many times do we have to go through this? I feel like God wants me to go to seminary. I know you think lesbians have no business being alive, but apparently God thinks differently."

"Please, let's not argue. Today is supposed to be a happy day," Mom pleaded.

"You're right. Let's bury the hatchet," I said.

"Well, you know we're not paying for seminary," Dad continued.

"I know. And you know that I have already looked into the process of arranging loans. Let's quit talking about this. Can't you be happy you have two of your offspring graduating from college on the same day?" *He thinks he can talk me out of seminary, but I will win this battle.*

"And our tennis skills paid for that," Will added a jab.

"Two honor graduates! You'd better hurry or you'll be late," Mom said.

She was right. We were required to be there at nine o'clock to get instructed and lined up. "OK, I'm officially in hustle mode!" I said. I finished breakfast and went to put on makeup.

"I'll be waiting impatiently," Will called as I left the kitchen.

We arrived just a couple of minutes late. "I think that's close enough to count," I said.

"You had me sweating," Will answered.

"I'm glad we get to sit together,"

"Me, too. It's only fitting we go out side by side."

"I'm going to miss you next year."

"Hey, none of this sad talk! Atlanta's only three and a half hours from here. We'll be able to visit."

I went quiet, knowing Will was trying to steer me toward happy. "Chin up," he said as friends came to greet us.

We marched in to "Pomp and Circumstance," which was punctuated with whoops from the crowd as their loved ones appeared. I settled into my seat next to Will and braced myself for a long ceremony.

"Do you think this will really last two and a half hours?" I whispered to Will."

"Looking at all these people who have to walk across the stage, I'd say definitely."

"I predict some severe fanny fatigue is coming."

Will laughed, and we tuned in to the opening remarks.

My mind resumed brooding as the speaker droned on.

I think the river is a fitting symbol for my life. It's always moving, always changing. I have been a river the last five years, flowing from not really fitting in my own skin in high school to graduating from college as a new person. It's OK being gay.

That's quite good! It could be my new mantra: It's OK being gay!

For some reason, I pictured a feather floating by in my mental image of the river. It reminded me of Grace. *I wish you hadn't died. We could have been such good friends. But I learned a lot from you.* I no longer cried when I thought of her.

Remembering her brought joy and warmth. *Grace, part of me still wants to swim even if I was meant to fly. There are so few of us gay folk. It's like always flying into a headwind. There are birds that swim, you know. Penguins are quite at home in the water.*

It was like I could hear her voice, that scratchy old voice that I miss, "They can swim, but they can't fly."

I'm about to fly! I'll walk across that stage, announced as a Summa Cum Laude graduate! Will settled for Magna Cum Laude, sacrificing a few grades for fun. But he is going to fly, too. He'll make a great vet.

We stood for the turning of the tassels. After we were presented as the 2023 graduating class of the University of Tennessee, applause exploded and mortarboards sailed. I didn't toss mine very high because I wanted to make sure I got it back. *I put a lot of work into decorating that thing!*

Will launched his high into the air and it sailed four aisles over. He hopped over chairs to retrieve it and got back just before they marched us out, giving me a quick hug. "We did it!"

"Yes, we did!"

Chapter 2

Wednesday, May 24, 2023

I woke up and stretched, disturbing Romeo and Sophie. It was 8:23. "I slept late," I announced to the two cats and hurried out of bed. *Why do I feel guilty? I hope Will isn't up, yet!*

I threw on shorts and a t-shirt and went for breakfast.

"It's about time, sleepy head," Will said, putting down a muffin.

"I see you beat me by a long time," I jutted my chin at his muffin to let him know I saw that he had just started eating.

"It's nice to sleep in. I think I'm still recovering from sleep deprivation during finals."

"Me, too. That was tough. You'd think they'd give us a break our last semester."

"I can't believe I have four years to go!"

"I only have three," I smirked.

"You're going to school for seven years so you can live a life of poverty. That's just not right."

"There are things more important than money."

"That's true, but I think I'll enjoy a bit of the green stuff."

"Hey, you can help me pay for my student loans since you'll be making so much!"

"Believe it or not, I had already thought of that."

"I was just teasing. I'll manage. Somehow."

The prospect of signing up for student loans to cover tuition and living expenses was staggering. The tuition for Candler School of Theology would be a little over $26,000 a year, and that didn't include books and living expenses. I had gotten some scholarship money and had applied for a work-study program.

"I'm going to be one indebted puppy by the time I'm through. I'll probably owe over a hundred thousand."

"That's scary! But you are doing what you feel called to do, so it will all work out. Try not to stress out over it."

"Who says I'm stressed out?"

"Your thumbnail for one. It's tired of being chewed."

"I'm glad you can still read me like a book. Oh! I'm supposed to meet with Pastor Stevens at ten thirty. I'd better get moving!"

I had come to look forward to my meetings with her. She was good at helping me explore my sense of calling and what I had to offer as a minister. We also talked about the Bible's passages on homosexuality. I had been able to share what Grace taught me. I couldn't be sure, but I think she was beginning to come around to the idea that homosexual people could be acceptable pastors.

I knocked on her office door. I could hear a muffled voice then, "Come in."

She had her finger held up and a phone to her ear when I entered. I turned and studied the books on the shelves. *She has so many commentaries. I wonder how much those cost? I'll have to look that up.* My financial worries zinged. Books are expensive, and apparently seminary involved a lot of them.

"If you see something you want to borrow, just let me know," Pastor Stevens said. I had been so absorbed in my thoughts I hadn't noticed she'd ended her call.

"Thanks! I'd love to look through one of your commentaries."

"As long as it's not one I'm preaching on in the next three weeks, you're welcome to borrow it."

"To be honest, I was wondering how much they cost. The finances of going to seminary are getting scary."

"It's a lot more expensive than when I went. Did the scholarship come through?" She took a sip of coffee and frowned. "Cold."

"They've promised fifteen thousand a year."

"That's a nice chunk. I'm embarrassed to say, but Roger is still blocking the idea of the church providing you a scholarship. He convinced enough people, and they voted it down. Politics is the least enjoyable part of pastoring, in my opinion." She looked irritated.

I had no comment on Roger. I was drawn to the commentary on Romans and pulled it out. "Are you preaching on Romans soon?"

"No, you're in luck."

"Thanks," I said, sitting down and wanting to open the book more than talk.

"I see you brought the book we've been discussing. Did you finish it?"

"I did."

"In what direction do you feel your calling is leading you now?" She pushed back her brown hair and leaned forward.

"I believe I'm being led to pastor churches, but I still flirt with the idea of counseling. Sometimes I think that is just my parachute."

"Your parachute?"

"Yeah. I think it's an option if I can't get ordained."

"I see. I think you'll make a great pastor. I'm a little concerned about the committee meeting coming up, though. We'll be proposing to recommend you as a formal candidate. There are nine people on the committee." She was looking over a piece of paper. "I'm sure of four positive votes. I don't have a good read on the other five."

"I hope my own church will at least open the door for me to try." I was running my finger over the corners of the pages nervously.

"I do, too. The talks we have had and your certainty about your calling have convinced me that there is no reason a homosexual person couldn't make an effective pastor. I plan to talk with the five questionable folks before the meeting and encourage them to support you."

"I'm so grateful for you. You have been such an encouragement to me over these last four years."

"Thanks. It's a joy to work with you. If… no, *when* we get you through the church committee you will have to meet with the district committee. That may be difficult, too. Are you prepared for possibly not being approved?"

"This whole journey has been an exercise in managing rejection. I'm getting quite good at it, I believe."

"What will you do if they turn you down?"

"I think my first move would be to change denominations. There are churches that will welcome me. I could be United Church of Christ or maybe Episcopalian."

"It's good to have options. But first, we're going to fight to open doors here."

"That's my plan! I'll bring the commentary back Sunday. Thanks for letting me borrow it."

"You're welcome."

Driving home, I thought back on some of our conversations over the last four years. Pastor Stevens had asked me as many questions about my sexual orientation as I had asked her about ministry and the process. I laughed when I remembered her asking me how I felt when I first kissed Liia. That memory also brought a wave of sadness. Liia's family moved back to Sweden last summer. Her grandparents needed care in their old age. *I still miss her.*

Two gray cats were curled up on my bed, one at the head and one at the foot. Romeo was snoring as I walked in. Sophie looked up then went back to sleep. *I don't think I would enjoy sleeping as much as you guys do!*

Sitting on the bed, I crossed my legs and flipped the commentary open. I noticed the author was Paul Achtemeier. I flipped to the discussion of the passage in Romans 1:18-32, the one that Grace had shown me.

The reading was technical and dry, talking about grammar. Then it got interesting. The author was saying that Paul sees the things he lists as signs of God's wrath for people turning from God to idolatry. *What if we don't turn from God, and our homosexuality is still there?"*

Chapter 3

*T*he time has come. *I have to buckle down and apply for that loan. Ugh!* I had exhausted every avenue I could find to apply for grants. None were available to "a person like me." As soon as they found out I was homosexual, the door shut.

I pulled up the FAFSA form, created my account, and started filling it out. *I don't see any other option.* I was in the middle of entering my personal information when I heard a knock.

Opening the door, I saw a sheriff's deputy standing there.

"I'm looking for Willow Grier."

"That's me." *What could this be about?* My nerves tensed.

"I have papers to serve for you. I need to see your identification and will require a signature."

"Am I in trouble?"

"I'm afraid I don't know the contents of the papers."

"I'll get my purse." I left the deputy waiting as I hurried to my room. I pulled out my driver's license on the way back.

Handing him the license, I waited nervously. He studied it, comparing the picture to my face, then took a picture and handed it back.

"Sign here, please."

I took the envelope back to my room. My hands were shaking as I opened it. "What in the world could this be?"

Will popped into my room. "What was that about?" He looked like he had just awakened from a nap.

"It was a deputy bringing me this envelope."

"That can't be good. What is it?"

"I haven't opened it yet."

"Well hurry up!"

The heading on the paper said, "Probate Court." I started reading, and Will looked over my shoulder.

"Holy cow!" Will said.

I was struggling to comprehend the words on the page but kept reading.

"What does this mean?"

"I think it means you're a rich girl!"

I flipped to the second page and there were numbers.

"Holy cow!" Will said again.

"Does this mean what I think it means? Am I really inheriting Grace's estate?"

"That's what it says! You might as well exit that FAFSA form."

I started from the top and read again. The court had spent four years probating the will, looking for family members that might contest it. Finally, based on a note Grace had stuck in the envelope and the fact that I took the cats, the court had concluded that I was the rightful inheritor.

"You get the house and the five hundred and seventy-six thousand dollars in her account! I can't believe it!" Will gushed.

I stared at the paper. My hands were cold and clammy. "Is this for real?"

"It looks like you have seminary covered and then some!" Will was excited. My mind was still trying to comprehend.

"They say no good deed goes unpunished, but that's not the case this time!"

My heart finally registered the reality enough to generate a smile. "I have money!"

"You have lots of money! I wonder what the house is worth!"

"Wow!" I leaned back in the chair, and a warm, tingly feeling flooded my body. A wave of sadness chased it off. "I wish you had gotten to know Grace. She was an amazing lady."

"She must have been, and she obviously appreciated your kindness."

Doing the twin thing, Will had read my mood shift and changed his tone to match.

"No more of that!" I closed out the FAFSA application and stood up to hug Will.

"Why don't you want to tell the parents?" Will asked, doing the twin thing again.

"Who said anything about not telling them? Yeah, you're right. The thought ran through my mind to let them think I'm still going in debt to pursue my dream. Especially Dad!"

"Sweet revenge! But you'll worry Mom sick."

"Yeah, I guess I'd better tell them. I can't believe it! I'm rich!" I forced myself to stop jumping up and down.

"You could always split it with your brother."

"We'll see. I'm sure I could spare a dollar or two."

Will studied the instructions. "You have to appear at the courthouse in order to collect your inheritance."

"That's scary! Want to come with me?"

"I wouldn't miss it!"

Wednesday, June 7, 2023

"I was hoping you'd come away with a check." Will was as disappointed as I was.

"I should have known it would take time to process everything. At least I know the money is coming. I hope I get it in time to pay the lawyer fees for transferring the house into my name."

"If not, I'm sure the parents would loan you the money."

"I'm not going to dwell on that. I need to celebrate! How about a stop at Bellini's?"

"Are you paying?"

"Of course!"

I was watching the server make my dark chocolate cherry gelato when I heard, "Willow!" and the sound of running feet.

By the time I turned, Myra grabbed me in a hug. "Myra!"

"I can't believe I ran into you. I was thinking about texting you before I came!"

"You should have! Did you get valedictorian again?"

"No, but I graduated. That's what counts. It's so good to see you. I still miss you a lot."

"Same here."

"Hmm, hmm," Will interjected.

"You're right. I owe you a hug, too," Myra said.

"I've got big news," I said.

"Tell me!"

"You'll have to wait till we get our gelatos!"

"Well?" Myra asked after we sat down, her eyes expectant.

"I am suddenly rich! I'll have the money to go to seminary without having to borrow my life away!"

"That's great! But how?"

"Grace left her estate to me. I just went through probate court today."

"That's amazing! You deserve a break like that!"

"It's a big relief! I had just started the loan application when it came."

"You should have bought my gelato!" Myra teased.

"What's up with you?"

"I've been accepted into the PhD programs at Vanderbilt and Georgia Tech. I have to decide which one to take."

"Yay! Go to Georgia Tech! We can be together in Atlanta!"

"That is tempting."

"Excitement!" Will said with a grin.

"I wonder how far apart Georgia Tech and Emory are. Maybe we could live together."

"Now you're really tempting me! I'll let you know. I'm still evaluating the potential of the two programs."

"Any romance news?" I asked.

"I had some dates and one not so serious relationship. You already know Kyle and I broke up the first year of college. What about you?"

"After Liia left, I haven't hooked up with anyone."

"I'm sorry about that. You two were close."

"It still hurts."

"You sure are quiet, Will," Myra observed.

"I've learned to just sit back and relax when two women get to talking."

Myra smacked him on the shoulder. "I guess that's the truth, though," she laughed.

Chapter 4

Sunday, June 11, 2023

Sitting on the bed, I rubbed along Sophie's back. "I can't believe I'm this nervous," I confided to my little gray friend.

"Meow." She stepped on my leg and rubbed against my chin.

"Thanks. You do know how to reassure a soul."

It was 7:00. The meeting was in thirty minutes. *Tonight I find out if the church will recommend me as a candidate for ministry.* I wiped my cold, sweaty palms on my pants.

OK. It's time to go. I looked in the mirror, checking for wrinkles and cat hair. *That looks OK, but I need to wipe the petrified off my face!*

My heart was doing laps as I walked into the conference room that doubled as the church library. I was ten minutes early, so I scanned the books. *I should check out something to read.*

"There's our girl!" startled me.

"Hey, Ms. Johnson. How are you?"

"You have to call me Molly. I'm excited. We haven't had anyone from our church go into the ministry before!"

Molly was a forty-something brunette. *I believe she will be a "Yes" vote.*

"Thanks. I'm excited to be starting seminary this fall."

"Have you found a place to live, yet? It must be scary going off to a new town on your own."

My nerves stretched a little tighter. "I haven't started looking, yet. I am nervous about the move but trust it will all work out."

"It will. God has a way of opening doors."

Pastor Stevens and the other members of the committee filtered in. Most came by and congratulated me.

"May we pray?" Pastor Stevens said. "Dear loving God, we are grateful for all of your generous blessings in our lives. We are thankful that you have placed your call on Willow to minister in your church. Please guide us as we consider recommending her as a candidate for ministry. In Jesus's name we pray. Amen."

I gripped the seat of my chair. Joseph Jernigan, sixty-something and balding, was the chair of the committee. He began the meeting. "You should all know that our business for this evening is to consider recommending Willow Grier as a formal candidate for ministry. Her process starts with us, which is fitting since we know her the best."

I can't tell if he is for or against me. He's hard to read.

He continued, "First I want to commend Willow on her willingness to answer the call she feels God has placed on her life. That is laudable.

"Secondly, and I trust you are all already aware of this, we have the unusual situation that Willow is homosexual. Currently, our denomination will not ordain an openly homosexual person."

Bob Clayborne interrupted. "Since that is the case, I don't see any point in this meeting. Why should we recommend someone as a candidate for ministry when they won't ordain her?"

"I agree," Cheryl Simpson said.

"On the other hand, we don't know what the church's position will be in three years when Willow is ready to be ordained. I believe we should approve her candidacy since she feels called to do this," Molly added.

Pastor Stevens had warned me to expect some contention.

Joseph resumed, "That is why we've been entrusted with this task. We have to sort out the pros and cons as well as Willow's readiness for this step. I think it would be helpful for us to hear from Willow before we proceed with the discussion."

My mouth went dry.

"Willow, please share with us your calling and how you are currently feeling about pursuing ministry."

I swallowed to get my tongue loose enough to speak. *I've rehearsed this. I can do it.* "Most of you were here four years ago when I shared how God called me during Youth Sunday. It was at the lowest point in my life. I had run away to avoid going into an institution that tries to force people with different sexual orientations back into the heterosexual mold. God felt so real and close. I'm sure it was the Holy Spirit there with me.

"After four years of college, I still feel very strongly that God wants me to go into the ministry. During my calling, God told me to trust that God would open the doors for me. This is the first door that I have come to, and I'm trusting you will see fit to open it and give me a chance."

"I think Willow framed our decision beautifully. We are deciding whether or not to open the door of possibility for her. Let's take a moment to discuss your thoughts about the matter."

I white-knuckled the seat of my chair again.

Wendy Adams was the first to speak. "I agree with Bob. Since there is no path forward, I don't see any point in recommending Willow. It would just set her up to be hurt in the next step."

"On the other hand," Tom Baldwin said, gesturing toward me with his right hand. "If God is the one starting this process, who are we to say no? I believe if this is something Willow wants to pursue, and God has told her he will open the doors, then We need to join hands with God and approve her."

"I don't mean to offend Willow, but I think we need to stand in line with our denomination's stance on homosexuality. We shouldn't be recommending a person who is not in line with church teaching as a candidate for ministry. This just isn't right." That was Cheryl.

"I'd like to hear Pastor Steven's opinion," Joseph said.

"I have been meeting with Willow for four years now. We have discussed her sense of calling, her gifts for ministry, and the obstacles she will face," Pastor Stevens began. "At first I was torn between the church's stance against homosexual pastors and the need to support one of our own members. As I have gotten to know Willow and come to understand the sincerity of her calling and the gifts she will bring to the church, I have come to totally support her.

"I believe God will do as God promised and open the doors for Willow to serve as she progresses toward that time. I fully believe the time has come for our church to be more open to people of differing sexual orientations. Willow could be the trailblazer to help that happen."

The room was silent. I tried to read the faces after Pastor Stevens' words. I forced my hands to release their death grip and relax. Something came over me, and I suddenly felt calm. *Thank you, Lord.*

Joseph broke the silence. "Is there any more discussion?" No one spoke. "OK, could I have a motion that we vote on the matter of recommending Willow as a candidate for ministry?"

"I so move," Molly said.

"Second," Tom said.

That's a surprise. Does he just want to get this over with? Take the vote before anyone changes into the "Yes" category?

"All in favor of recommending Willow as a candidate for ministry, raise your hands," Joseph said.

I didn't look, keeping my eyes on the floor. It wasn't because I was afraid of the results. The calmness held. I think I didn't want anyone to feel I was pressuring them. The calmness seemed to also come with a message that God would take care of things.

"All opposed."

"Thank you very much for participating in tonight's meeting. We are happy to recommend Willow as a candidate for ministry. I trust she will have the whole church's support as she proceeds along this journey."

I was grinning. When I looked up everyone was looking at me. *They're waiting for me to say something.* "Thank you so much for your support. I promise to do everything I can to become an effective pastor."

All but two members clapped.

Chapter 5

Tuesday, August 1, 2023

It's move-in day! I'm excited, frosted with nervous! Thanks to someone dropping out and canceling a lease, I was able to rent a basement apartment in a house on Oxford Road. *According to the map, it's right across the street from campus. I'll be able to walk to and from class! That should save commuting and give me more time for studying.*

I carried the last box to my Rav4. The old Jeep was barely hanging on, so I traded it after getting the check from Grace's estate. The white Rav4 wasn't new, but it was a lot newer than the Jeep.

We had already loaded Will's old Prius. He insisted on coming with me. He wasn't moving into his apartment till August fifteenth.

"I'm glad you're coming with me."

"You are quite welcome. Besides, I need to know how to find my favorite sister!"

"We're loaded and ready to go," I called as we went back into the house.

Mom came out of her office. "You take care of yourself and be careful." She gave me a long hug.

"I will."

"You be careful, too," she said, hugging Will. "If it doesn't look like a good place, tie her up and bring her back!"

"I have rope in the car," Will laughed.

I punched in the address on Oxford Road, and we were off on my Atlanta adventure. My favorite set of songs came over the speakers, but I was more tuned into my thoughts than the music.

Orientation begins on August eleventh. That should give me time to get my bearings. I wish Myra hadn't elected to go to Vanderbilt. I would have a built-in friend.

There are eleven days of orientation. I can't imagine what they have planned for that long. It seems a bit excessive.

Will's going to stay for a week. We'll have a big time! I wonder what seminary will be like.

My thoughts meandered along random paths as I drove. The GPS app took us to Chattanooga then down I75. I started seeing signs for a town called Dalton up ahead, and it looked to be a promising lunch stop.

The expressway sign showed a Chick-fil-A coming up, so I called Will.

"I'd love some Chick-fil-A!" he confirmed.

Sitting down for lunch, nervousness began to take over. "What if this place is a dump? What if I don't make any friends? What if I'm miserable?"

"All highly unlikely scenarios," Will said. "You saw pictures of the apartment online, so you know it's not a dump. It's not a luxury apartment, but it's not a dump, either."

"You're right. I just have the 'sailing into the unknown jitters.' This is going to be an exciting segment of life."

Will looked at his phone. "You have one hour and thirty-seven minutes till you meet your new life."

"OK, let's hit the road. I'm glad we're getting in before rush hour. I hear Atlanta traffic is horrible."

The GPS led me to the house in which my apartment was located, confirmed by the number on the mailbox. The drive led downhill to the back. Nerves started threatening the excitement as I drove down.

"What's that?" I asked Will, pointing to a device below a grate in the concrete.

"Hmm. Judging by the pipe leading out, I'd guess it's a sump pump."

"That doesn't sound good."

"It's probably just for emergencies."

"Great."

The sump pump was underneath a covered concrete patio. "This will be a nice place to sit and read when it's not so hot," Will observed.

"I hope the AC is on," I said, checking my phone for the code to open the door.

"Snazzy! You won't have to worry about losing a key!"

Cool air wafted to my face as I opened the door, a welcome sign.

"That feels good!" Will said as we entered the apartment, leaving the heat and humidity behind.

I hurried through the apartment, checking out the bedroom, the den, kitchen and bathroom. "At least it's clean! The bed looks like a canoe!"

Plopping down on the soggy mattress I said, "This has to go!"

"Rich women can afford to do things like that!"

"You try it! I'd rather sleep on the air mattress."

Will's lips curled into disgust as he settled onto the bed. "You're right! That has to go."

"Once the mattress is replaced, I think it'll be OK," I assured myself.

Sweat rolled down my neck as we carried in the boxes and suitcases.

"I'm glad it's shady back here. I can't imagine unloading in the sun," Will said.

It was four o'clock by the time we got my stuff in the house and enough boxes unpacked to survive. We plopped on the couch and drank down our sports drinks.

"I don't think we'll be needing the rope to tie you up."

"Yeah, I believe this place will do for the next three years. Hey, let's go look around campus before they close it down."

"OK, but then you have to treat me to supper."

"Deal."

We walked up the driveway, and I said, "Oh no!"

"Yep. There goes all of your money!"

The Barnes and Noble campus bookstore was right across the road from my apartment. Like moths drawn to light, the next thing I knew we were in the bookstore.

"Oh no!"

"Yep. Books or coffee. Tough decision," Will responded, eyeing the Starbucks coffee shop on the first floor. "You can always claim the coffee is in the name of improving your studying."

We meandered through the books, working our way up to the merchandise section on the third floor. "The store will be closing in fifteen minutes. Please make your final selections and go to the check out," sounded overhead.

"Do you want a t-shirt?"

"Maybe later. I don't want to rush," Will answered.

We exited from the top floor. "Wow!" I said, struck by the beauty of the campus unfolding before me.

"Nice!" Will observed.

"I wonder where the School of Theology is."

"The app shall guide us." Will was already typing to locate the building. He studied the phone then pointed. "That way, I believe. Let's follow the red brick road."

We came around a building, and I could see a cross cut out of a piece of concrete reaching toward the sky. We drew closer, rounded the corner of a building, and there it was. I grabbed Will's arm and stopped. *Why am I tearing up?*

"What's wrong?"

"I have no idea. Seeing the building was really moving. I'm not sure what I'm feeling. It's like my whole future lies within those walls. There is the place I'll be shaped into a pastor."

Will tugged on the door once we reached it. "Locked. It looks like your future will have to wait."

Chapter 6

Friday, August 11, 2023

Nervous didn't begin to describe what was going on in my body. *Orientation begins today at ten! I'm going to meet fellow students!*

This was the first time I had thought about my homosexuality in a while. *Will they accept me? I don't have to tell anyone right off. Don't ask, don't tell is the strategy Pastor Stevens recommended.*

Will left two days ago. It would have been a lot lonelier were it not for Romeo and Sophie. *They're good company!* I put down treats for the two hopeful kitties then hit the shower.

I considered my two options for getting to the theology building. *Up the hill and up the stairs to the top floor or turn left, walk down to Eagle Row, turn right and come into the bottom floor. Decisions, decisions! I'll take the easier route today. Wait, there is a third route!*

I elected that one since it was already hot. Entering the bookstore, I rode the elevator up two floors then leisurely walked to the theology building.

Though I was ten minutes early, I could already hear the buzz of conversations coming from the auditorium. *I still wonder what we could possibly do for orientation for eleven days. That's a lot of orienting!*

Walking in, I was greeted with the presence of what seemed like a hundred people. My nerves zinged a little harder. A registration table sat at the front.

"Good morning! I'm Jason, a middler. It's nice to meet you. In case you have yet to figure it out, you are juniors, second year students are middlers, and the high and mighty third years are seniors."

I shook his hand. "I'm Willow, a newbie."

"You're whom we're all about today!" He directed me to the registration table and shepherded me through signing in and getting a name tag. Then he was off to meet another newbie.

Scanning the room, I was happy to see a rainbow of skin tones. *There are more women than I had expected. That's nice.* A group of three women were chatting off to the side of the main group. I was drawn to them.

"Hi, I'm Willow," I said as I walked up.

"Hey! It's nice to meet you. I'm Inaya. I'm guessing you're orienting with us."

"What gave you that idea?" I laughed. "I love your accent!"

Inaya was from India and drop-dead gorgeous. *I hope I'm not blushing.*

"Thanks," she said.

"I'm Shani, and I'm clueless about what we're going to be doing."

"Me, too," I answered, and we laughed. Shani's hair was in long braids that hung to midback and her skin was ebony.

"I'm Avery. Welcome aboard." She extended her hand. I shook hands with her then the other two. My heart fluttered as I shook Inaya's hand.

Avery pushed her jet black hair behind her ear. She had kind blue eyes and pale skin. "I confess that I'm quite nervous," she said. "It takes me a while to get to know people."

"Well, you have made an excellent start," Inaya bubbled. "I think we're going to get quite close over the next three years."

"With eleven days of orientation, I think they're going to make sure of that," I offered.

We all laughed. My nerves were beginning to calm.

"Could I have everyone's attention?" Jason boomed over the crowd. *That must be his preaching voice.* "Please take a seat, and we'll get started."

He waited till we sat down. "Welcome to Candler School of Theology. You are the class of 2026! We're glad you are here and trust that the next three years will both enrich and shape you, sharpening you into the person God has called you to be.

"I'm Jason Maddox. I'm what they call a middler and part of the Student Life Committee. It is our job to help you feel welcome, get you connected, and familiarize you with the process ahead of you.

"You see a lot of new and different faces around you. We pride ourselves on the diversity of our student body. That makes the Candler experience richer.

"OK, we're going to divide you up into groups of ten or so. Each of you has a sticker with the name of a tree… Don't look yet!... The sticker is on the back of your name tag. Nope, don't look! Resist the temptation!"

I wanted to look but resisted.

"Here is your challenge. You have to get together with the other people who have the same tree, but you have to do it without saying a word."

How are we going to do that?

"Most of you are looking at me like I've lost my mind. You've never even met these folks and you're supposed to figure out what's on the back of their name tag without talking? Oops, I almost forgot another rule. You can't show the back of your name tag. That would just be too easy.

"So, draw on your creativity, figure out a way to communicate without words, and go find your group mates. Everybody peek at the back of your name tag without letting anyone else see. Ready, set, go!"

I stood up and looked around, trying to think of a way to communicate that I was an apple tree. Someone across the room was signing. Inaya appeared to be trying to make a letter with her fingers. *That's it! I can spell out apple with my fingers!*

I started trying to form an A by putting my index fingers together. It worked when I used my middle finger to make the crossbar. Holding up my hands, I saw Inaya had the same configuration of fingers.

I jumped up and down, waving my A so Inaya could see it. She grinned. I made a P then realized it would be backwards to Inaya, so I reversed it. She did the same. We confirmed that the rest of the letters matched. *We're both apples!* I was glad she was in my group.

Now just eight more to go! Avery and Shani had picked up the finger formation and both signaled O's. I shrugged my shoulders and pulled Inaya along to hunt other apples. I used my pinkies and ring finger to form the A this time, so it would be more obvious to someone looking at me.

With people weaving through the aisles and hopping on and off chairs it seemed like total chaos. Before long, the laughter couldn't be contained. We had found four people when the idea struck.

I pulled Inaya and motioned for the other two to move to the side of the room. I moved Inaya's arms over her head, then leaned in and made the crossbar with my forearm. Another member waved his arms and pointed to the A. Within a minute, the other six people had joined us. We shook hands and high-fived.

"Can I have your attention, please," Jason called over the chaos. "I see you have formed your groups. I'm going to pair each group with a middler, and you're going to have a chance to get to know each other and learn more about the upcoming orientation and beginning classes. Please follow your group leader when I call your tree."

Our leader took us to a nice sitting area on the third floor. It looked out over a patio with table and chairs. *That will be a great place to study when the weather's nice.* We pulled some chairs around so we were sitting in a circle.

"Look at this wonderful group! I'm Bryce and am excited to welcome you to Candler. We're going to get to know each other a little bit today and then try to answer some of your questions. It takes a long time to really come to know a person, so today is just the tip of the iceberg. You will have that time and a chance to delve deeply into each other's beings as you move through your time here.

"Let's share a little about ourselves. As I said, I'm Bryce Ogletree. I'm from Reno, Nevada. I love to write poetry and play tennis."

Maybe there will be some chances to play tennis here!

Bryce, brown hair and brown eyes, looked to the man sitting next to him. "Your turn. Tell us a bit about yourself.

My nerves tensed a bit. *It seems like we don't have to go deep at this point. Ugh! I'm so tired of trying to decide at every point whether or not to share my real self. Don't ask, don't tell was Pastor Stevens' advice. I feel like an undercover agent having to live out a fake identity.* I tuned back into what the person was saying. His name tag said Johnny McBride. *I'm next. Just the simple stuff.*

"I'm Willow Grier, obviously," I said pointing to my name tag. "I'm from Hawksville, Tennessee. I love playing tennis, too. I played for the Tennessee Vols in college. Maybe we could play sometime." *That was easy enough.* I relaxed into the session.

Chapter 7

*S*o far Inaya is my favorite. She seems to be everyone's *favorite. She's so nice!* It was too early for the bookstore to be open, so I had to climb the hill and stairs to get to school for the first day of class.

I was thinking about the people I had met so far in orientation. *We are an odd assortment. Avery is always so serious. So is Shani. She's all into liberation theology and already seems to know a lot about it. Johnny is a brooder, very quiet. I don't have a good read on him yet.*

Inaya and Avery were chatting when I walked into the classroom. "Good morning! Ready to start?" Inaya chirped.

"I'm as ready as I'll ever be," I answered.

"I'm looking forward to learning all I can," Avery said.

Shani joined our group. Ever since we met at orientation, we seemed to gravitate to each other.

"Good morning! How are the Four Musketeers?" Glenn Parks, a tall lanky guy with an afro, greeted.

We laughed. "So we already have a reputation?" Inaya asked.

"You do seem to stick together," Glenn observed.

Professor Augenstein entered the classroom, and we took our seats. *I can't believe seminary is actually beginning! I have so much to learn!*

After class Shani, Inaya, Avery, and I settled onto a couch and chair in the sitting area on the third floor.

"Which setting did you guys get for Contextual Education?" Inaya asked.

"I wanted the one with the refugee children, but I got the Toco Hills place with the old folks," Shani answered.

"I think we all wanted the refugees," Avery laughed. "I got the state prison. I can't believe they want me to spend an hour driving back and forth."

"I asked for the refugees, too, but got the youth detention center," I said. "How about you, Inaya?"

"Don't hate me, but I got the refugees."

"They're splitting up the Musketeers! It's a conspiracy!" I laughed.

"Do you really think so?" Avery asked. She could be quite gullible.

"No, they couldn't have figured out that we're hanging out together yet," Shani said.

A couple of second year students were sitting a little behind us. I was dragged away by their conversation.

"You might as well give in. It's going to happen."

"That's beside the point. It's the principle of the matter. We have to fight to maintain biblical integrity."

"I don't see it that way. I believe if God created a person and wants them to lead in the church, then who am I to stand in the way. I'm pretty sure that's in the Bible somewhere."

My interest was piqued. It was like I had a radar that could sense what they were talking about. "I see things. I know things," popped into my mind. It was one of Grace's loveable odd sayings. *Is that what I'm doing now?*

"The Bible is clear that homosexuality is against God's teaching," the first guy continued.

"It's not so obvious if you read it carefully. Anyway, the Bible's primary guiding principle is love. We are called to do the loving thing."

"What if the loving thing is to steer people into the right path?"

"You're impossible!"

"We should go for coffee. We have time. It's only nine forty-five." Inaya's words drew me back to my fellow Musketeers. I think it was the word, "coffee," that got my attention.

"I'm in," I said. We donned our packs and headed toward Starbucks. *The battle is still going, even here. I wonder what these three would think if they knew I'm lesbian. Don't ask, don't tell is a lonely strategy. When do I start telling folks?*

Thursday, August 31, 2023

They said they wanted to stretch us out of our comfort zones. Well, they're succeeding. I was so nervous going through the security check at Metro Regional Youth Detention Center I forgot to take my phone out of my pocket. I jumped when the alarm went off. I jumped again when the guard ordered me to stop.

"Turn around."

I obeyed.

"Cell phone," he said with an irritated expression. "Go around and try again."

I put the phone on the conveyor belt and walked through again, passing this time.

"You will want to leave that phone in a secure place," the guard said as I stuffed it back in the pocket of my khaki slacks and smoothed my white blouse.

"Yes, sir," I said.

"There are kids here who can take it out of your pocket without you ever knowing. Down the hall. Fourth room on the right."

I found a conference room with two other first year students, Bryce, who had been my group leader that first day, Professor Bowen, and a lady I didn't know.

"Hey, Willow," Samantha Bennett said. *She looks nervous, too. That makes me feel better.* "Everyone calls me Sam."

"Good afternoon, Sam. How are you?"

"A bit nervous but looking forward to getting started with this."

"Me, too. I set off the alarm coming through security. Not exactly the beginning I had in mind."

"Just a minor detail. At least you're here, and these kids need a caring presence in their lives," the lady I didn't know said. She extended her hand, "I'm Chaplain Michelle Stancil. It's nice to meet you."

"Willow Grier," I responded. Chaplain Stancil was tall and fit looking with a stern demeanor and soft eyes. She wasn't to be trifled with, but I sensed she could be caring. The spiral curls of her black hair hung just past her shoulders.

It was 3:27 when the other four students of our group arrived.

"Cutting it close, aren't we?" Johnny McBride teased.

"We had trouble finding it," Glenn said, looking relieved to be there.

Glenn Parks, Enrique Sanchez, Anthony Mason, and Luna Padilla completed our group.

"Let's get started, shall we?" Dr. Bowen said.

Between Dr. Bowen and Rev. Stancil, they went through an orientation, explaining what we would be doing and how the program worked.

"Why are we coming late in the afternoon?" Anthony asked.

"It gives them a chance to finish their school work without interruption," Rev. Stancil explained. "Today we are going to meet some of the crew. Dr. Bowen, Bryce, and I will introduce you to several of the inmates. Then I want you to hook up with one and get to know them.

"Remember, in every interaction we have with these kids we need to leave them with a sense of hope that life will get better, that there are possibilities that can open up. Right now, they think incarceration is all they have in their future."

I don't know why I wasn't panicked at that point. I had a sense that I might be able to make a positive difference in a person's life, and that excited me.

Rev. Stancil called for a guard to unlock the door. *OK, a nervous zinger hit when I realized I was about to be locked in.*

Johnny, Samantha, and I ended up with Bryce.

"How's your Spanish?" he asked. "Some of the inmates are Hispanic and don't speak much English."

"Hablo muy poquito," Samantha said.

Johnny and I just shrugged our shoulders.

"Alright, then."

Bryce introduced us to several students. "OK, pick out someone and see if you can get to know them."

I looked around. There was a blond headed guy sitting off by himself. I was drawn to him because he looked alone.

"Hi! I'm Willow."

He looked at me with sad, soulful eyes but didn't respond.

"How are you feeling today?" A long pause.

"Down."

"What's got you down?" A long pause.

"Today's my one year anniversary."

"Oh?" I sat down across the table from him and waited for an explanation. *He's too young to be married, isn't he? So what kind of anniversary?* He offered no explanation, so I encouraged him to talk. "What is the anniversary?"

He looked at me, and I could see nothing but sadness in the expression. "It was one year ago today that they stuck me in this hell hole."

He looks thirteen or fourteen. Do I ask what he did to get stuck in here? I don't think that's the right track. Hope. What can give hope? Ah! "How much longer do you have before you get out?"

A shadow of darkness clouded the sadness. He clinched his fist and stared a hole through me. I waited. And waited. *OK, this is getting weird. Do I ask another question? Keep waiting? Walk away? Why is he staring?* I decided to give him time and looked around the room. I don't know if he decided I wasn't going away or sensed that I really wanted to know, but he finally answered.

"My sentence is twelve years. It depends on the parole board. They could release me early."

"No wonder you're feeling down. That's a long time." *Oh no! That didn't sound very hopeful.* He resumed staring at me. *Maybe he's trying to decide if I'm genuine. I have to find something positive in this. That's the instruction.*

"That's two years short of my current lifespan."

"So you're fourteen?"

"Yeah."

"Will they keep you here the whole time?"

"No."

"Oh?" I waited again. *Waiting seems to work for this guy.*

"Somewhere between sixteen and eighteen they'll transfer me to the adult prison."

That sent a shockwave through my soul. *He looks too young and vulnerable. That can't be good.*

"That sounds scary." *I shouldn't have said that. It doesn't sound hopeful.*

"It is. This place is bad enough. I can't imagine what they'll do to me there."

"Is there anything you like to do here? Anything that helps lift your spirits?" *I was fishing for that hope thing.*

"I write poetry."

"Oh! I'd love to read your writing sometime."

"No you wouldn't"

"I wouldn't?" Silence. *I'm getting more comfortable with this waiting thing.*

"They're dark. Most people turn me into the psychologist once they read them."

That's spooky. What could they say? He's staring at me again. I need to say something.

"Would you pick out one and share it with me sometime if I promise not to turn you in?"

More staring. I looked around and noticed all the other Candler students were gone. *I didn't hear them leave. Do I need to go?*

Confusion swirled. *Am I expected to leave the room when everyone else does? I don't remember them saying anything about that. I feel like I'm making a connection with this guy.*

He was still staring. I decided to wait and looked him in the eyes. Without a word, he pulled a piece of paper out of his back pocket. It was compressed flat with wrinkles ironed into it. *He's had this a while.*

He looked from me to the paper and back. I waited. He tossed it on the table then covered it with his hand. "OK."

I reached and gently pulled it from under his hand. Being careful not to tear the fragile paper, I unfolded it and read.

HELD

Held
Tight bonds
No release
Water
Covers with threat
Life dwindles
Dreams never to be
Oh to see the sky
And fly

This corporal cage
Will never release.

-Alecs Taylor
 9/22/22

I was stunned. I flashed back to the dream I had had almost five years ago and remembered it vividly. *Why do I feel compelled to share that with him?*

"You're right. It is dark. It sounds full of pain."

"Yeah."

"It reminded me of a dream I had several years ago. I wanted to hang glide and soar, but people kept throwing me in the water to swim. I thought I was going to drown."

He looked at me with curiosity. I waited.

"You're odd."

That wasn't what I was expecting. "How so?"

"Everyone else tries to tell me everything is going to be OK. You seem to actually listen."

"Yeah, I'm odd like that."

"Thanks."

"Thank you for sharing something so special. I hope I can talk with you some more."

"Yeah."

I sensed it was time to leave. He had had enough. I walked toward the door with no idea how to get out. I noticed Rev. Stancil looking through a window. The door magically opened as I approached.

"Wow! You were talking with Alecs!" Rev. Stancil hurried over.

"Yeah. We had a good talk, I think."

"That's the longest anyone has talked with him since he's been here. He must trust you!"

"I don't think there was anything amazing about it. I just listened, Rev. Stancil."

"Please call me Michelle."

She looked back through the window with concern. "He seems to be OK."

"Why wouldn't he be OK?"

"He usually gets agitated when one of us tries to talk with him."

"Oh." *I hope I haven't sent him into a raging fit.*

"Look at him! He looks calmer than I've seen in a while. What did you tell him?"

"I didn't tell him anything. I just asked questions and listened. At the end, he showed me one of his poems."

"Really?"

"I had to promise not to turn him into the psychologist."

"Does he need to be turned in?"

"I don't think so. It was about his feeling trapped. It seemed more about being trapped in his own body rather than in here."

"You figured all of that out already? We will definitely have to have you talk with him some more. He may be your special project this semester."

Chapter 8

Our group was responsible for leading a meditation for the youth at the detention center today. *I'm hoping to have a chance to talk with Alecs again. He has been on my mind all week.* We had met and decided to base the session on Ephesians 2:8-10.

Johnny thought we should be talking about repentance and forgiveness. "Obviously they need that, or they wouldn't be in detention," he had said. I was learning he is quite zealous about saving the world, even though he is usually quiet.

Verse ten kept banging around in my mind. "For we are what he has made us…" *I like that thought. I am what God has made me, created for good works. Lord, help me do a good work today.*

It was a thirty-minute session, so we decided each team member would take 3 minutes to talk. I listened as Sam, Johnny, and Glenn gave their take on the passage. Then it was my turn.

"It was verse ten that captured my attention. The thought that 'we are what he has made us, created in Christ Jesus for good works' spoke to me on two levels.

"First, it is comforting to know that I am how God created me to be. Even with all my flaws and differences, I am what I am created to be. That tells me each of us is special in God's sight since we were created this way. Even with pimples and character flaws, we are God's carefully formed creations.

"Secondly, we are created for good works. That is life's purpose, and the greatest good work is love. We can do good works wherever we find ourselves, even in this place.

"You look like you don't believe me. Have you ever offered a listening ear or a supportive shoulder when another person here is having a hard time? There's a good work. Have you ever gone out of your way to make a new person feel welcomed? There's a good work.

"God created each of us to be whom we were created to be and to use our wonderful selves to bring good into the world."

I sat down and Enrique got up. I rubbed my clammy hands on my pants. *I'm glad that's over!*

After the meditation, I found Alecs sitting in the same spot as last week. "Hey," I said.

"Hey."

I sat down. "How are you feeling today."

"Down."

"Are you always feeling down?"

Silence. He stared into my eyes. Building on last week's experience, I waited and watched.

"Did you mean it?"

"Did I mean what?"

I thought I saw a wave of exasperation in his face. *Am I supposed to know what he is talking about?* I did the waiting thing.

Finally he said, "What you said… something about being created the way God wants us to be."

I could have sworn he wasn't paying attention during the meditation.

"I certainly did. I think God created you and me just the way God wants us to be."

"That's easy to say when you're normal."

"Is anybody normal?"

"You know what I mean," he snapped. A flash of anger registered in his eyes.

A light came on in my heart. The painful poem, the sadness, the questions. He's not normal.

"Are you talking about sexual orientation?"

Staring. Waiting. Waiting. *I'm going to take that as a yes.*

"No, I'm not 'normal'," I said with air quotes. "I'm lesbian."

His eyes lit up. I waited. Then I felt led to ask, "Are you 'normal'?"

I waited, watching him process. He stared. *The next move is yours.*

"No."

Do I push for more? It can't hurt to try.

"Would you be willing to tell me about it?"

His eyes hardened and his right index finger scratched the table then balled into a fist. *Did I send him over the edge?*

I was about to leave when he said, "Trans."

I was expecting gay. I need to refer to him as her from now on, I guess. I started to confirm that being trans is still being created as God wanted her to be then decided it would be better for her to make that affirmation.

"Do you think what I said applies to being trans?"

"Your dream was about being gay in a world that wants you to be straight."

She remembered the dream. I'm surprised. "Yes, I think it was."

"No."

"No?"

She's going to wear me out with this waiting!

"God can't love me."

"You'd be surprised what God can do. I believe God loves you and created you just the way God wants you to be, trans and all."

Alecs left. Not in body but in spirit. I could see it in her eyes. Our talk was over. One more thought struck as I got up to leave.

"Alecs, I'd love for you to write another poem and show it to me next week. I'll see you then."

I wasn't sure she'd even heard me as I left the room. Michelle was waiting.

"Another good conversation?" she asked.

"I think so." I almost told her she was trans then thought she may not want me to share that. *I want to earn her trust.*

"That's great! I'm glad he is opening up to you."

"Why is he in here? What did he do?"

"He nearly beat another boy to death."

I must have had the proverbial "deer in the headlights" look. She continued. "He… well I guess you might as well know if you haven't figured it out already. Alecs is trans, and the appropriate pronoun is she. She was being bullied at school for being trans. Some boys cornered her after school one day, and she totally lost it. Unfortunately, one of the boys was a baseball player and had his bat bag with him. The boy recovered but does have a head injury that will impact the rest of his life."

"Wow! I can't believe she would do such a thing."

"There's a lot of dark anger in that soul."

Chapter 9

I walked into Systematic Theology and found Avery, Inaya, Shani, Johnny, and Glenn grouped together. Johnny and Glenn had become part of our Musketeer group. *I'm pretty sure Glenn has a crush on Inaya.*

They got quiet as I walked up. "Talking about me? I hope it was good!" I said.

"Good morning!" Inaya bubbled. "Did you get your paper done?"

We had weekly papers due on Fridays discussing one of the theologians we had studied that week. *Nice deflection. I still think you were talking about me.*

"I did, and still got in bed by midnight. How about you?"

"Of course."

Inaya always had her assignments done at least a day early. She was irritating that way. Professor Mallard Jones entered the room, and we took our seats.

After class, the Musketeers gathered in the break area for coffee.

"So far Irenaeus is my favorite," Inaya said. "I like his theology.

"Me, too," I agreed.

"So, is it true?" Avery asked. She was looking at me, and a sinking feeling wormed its way into my heart.

"Is what true?" I asked. *I think I know what's coming.*

"There are rumors going around that you are gay."

Time froze. *Do I lie or let the cat out of the bag? Don't ask, don't tell just went off the rails. They're going to find out sooner or later. Might as well be now.*

It felt like I had stood there for an hour before I said, "It's true."

"It's about time you told us," Inaya said. "I can't believe you were keeping such a big secret."

"I don't blame you," Shani said. "I think it would be scary coming out in seminary. Don't worry, you're still OK in my book."

"Thanks."

"Yeah, we won't think you have cooties or anything," Inaya laughed.

I noticed Avery and Johnny were quiet. Glenn had wandered over to talk to someone else.

"I'm curious. How did you find out? I have been afraid to tell anyone. My pastor advised me to follow the don't ask, don't tell policy."

"Glenn said he heard it at the juvenile detention center."

A flash of anger burned. *Alecs.* "That makes sense. There's an inmate there I've been talking with. I told her to try and establish rapport. Well, my secret's out now. We'll see what the fallout is."

"Fallout? I don't understand." Inaya looked puzzled.

"Let's just say church and homosexuality are like oil and water. They don't mix very well."

"You're right," Inaya said as she put her arm around my shoulders. "Churches do get into an uproar over sexual orientation issues. I want you to know that I support you."

"Me, too," Shani said.

Avery just smiled. Apparently Inaya caught her reluctance. "What do you think, Avery?

I could see the gears churning. *Is she trying to decide what she thinks or find a way out of this awkward situation?* A tense expression formed on her face.

"I'm sorry. I just can't condone homosexuality." She walked away.

Johnny was silent as usual, and no one asked what he thought. *I'm pretty sure he thinks along the same lines as Avery.*

"OK, with that out of the way, does anyone want to get together this weekend? We could work on our Old Testament papers," I said, trying to lighten the mood.

"That sounds great!" Inaya said.

Johnny nodded. "I'll be there."

I was surprised Johnny still wanted to be around me. "You're welcome to come to my apartment. It's just across the street from the bookstore.

"That works for me. Will you text us the address? I'll work on Avery," Inaya said with a wink.

"Thanks. My apartment is in the basement. You'll see it when you come to the back of the house."

"Why don't we show up about two then get dinner together?" Inaya added.

"That would be fun."

Johnny nodded.

Back at the apartment I sat at the table and tried to write a colloquy paper for Systematic Theology, I kept watching the clock. *I wish Will would hurry up and get out of class!*

The clock stubbornly climbed toward three o'clock. *I have to wait till 3:30 to give him time to wrap things up.* The minute 3:30 struck I called him.

"How's my favorite sister?"

"I'm OK. How are you?"

"Doing great! I have a date tonight!"

"Someone you met in vet school?"

"Yeah. You'll never guess her name."

"Sandra," I said with a grin.

"How did you know?"

"It's the twin thing."

"So to what do I owe the pleasure of a call on Friday right after class? Something's up."

"I got outed today."

"Oh. How'd that happen?"

"There is a kid at the juvenile detention center that I've developed a relationship with. I told her, and apparently she told someone and they told someone. Some of my friends asked if it was true today."

"And you told them?"

"Yeah. I'm tired of hiding."

"How'd they take it?"

"So far only one of five has disowned me."

"Hey, that's pretty good!"

I was silent. There was a disconnect in my soul. *My brain knows Will is right. An eighty percent favorable response is good. Well, technically I still didn't know what Johnny or Glenn thought but still... My heart wants to please everyone. Having Avery turn on me hurt.*

"It's going to be OK," Will said, apparently discerning my consternation. "You're too wonderful of a person for things to go bad."

"Thanks. I miss you."

"I miss you, too."

Saturday, September 16, 2023

Saturday I ate lunch, made sure the litter was scooped, and straightened the apartment. This would be our first gathering off the school grounds. I was that familiar mix of excitement and nerves. *I hope everyone has a good time. I hope it's not awkward since they know I'm gay.*

People tended to go overboard either way when they found out I was lesbian. They would either gush approval or negativity. It took a while for folks to settle down and treat me like… just me.

"You two behave yourselves," I instructed Romeo and Sophie just before two o'clock.

"Meow," they both said.

"I see. You know that's extortion." They had moved to the spot where they usually got their treats. "I guess treats in exchange for good behavior is a worthwhile deal."

Inaya knocked on the door at 2:01. "Hey! I brought you some flowers! Thanks for hosting us!" She grabbed me in a hug. *She's going to be a gusher.*

"Thanks for the flowers! Let's get them in some water." I didn't have any vases, so we had to use a tall water bottle.

"Perfect!" she said. "So how are you doing?"

"Fine, thanks. I'm looking forward to our afternoon together." I set the flowers on the center of the table. "How are you?"

"Doing well, thanks! I meant, how are you doing after being outed. I want you to know that I support you and believe that God created people with differing sexual orientations to make our world a better place."

A gusher! "Thanks, Inaya. I haven't seen anyone since yesterday. So far everything is the same."

A knock on the door revealed Glenn and Johnny. Shani came a few minutes later. We managed to spread out around my kitchen table. I noticed Glenn sat next to Inaya. I offered a supply of drinks and chips. Laughter and grumbling about the assignment punctuated the tapping of keyboards.

The only dark cloud was Avery's absence.

Chapter 10

Thursday, October 12, 2023

We gathered in the conference room at the youth detention center before leading the meditation for the day. Michelle pulled me aside.

"I have some bad news."

"What is it?"

"There was a fight. Several of the guys attacked Alecs."

My heart sped up. "Is she OK?"

"She's in sick bay. She has a broken rib and a busted lip. We are keeping her away from the community for a while."

"Can I see her?"

"I was hoping you'd want to. She needs someone."

We had taken to having prayer before the sessions, so I sat down. While Luna prayed, my mind wandered to Alecs. *Why would they do this to her? Well, I know the answer to that. Hatred is fertilized by difference. People want to stomp on others who are not like them.*

I remembered back to the first talk I had with Alecs after she had outed me. I told her about how the word of my homosexuality had spread around the seminary.

"Are you ashamed?" was her response. I knew that was a test. If I had not been able to look her in the eye and say, "No," honestly, I felt sure her sense of self-worth would have crashed.

Apparently I had succeeded because she had been opening up more and more to me.

I missed the "Amen" but looked up when I heard chairs scooting. Luna and Enrique headed off together. They were leading sessions in Spanish.

"Hey, guys. Can I beg off of the meditation? I need to talk with Alecs."

Sam looked at Glenn. "Sure, we can cover, but we'll miss your words of wisdom."

"Thanks."

I followed Michelle to the sick bay. Alecs looked up. Michelle had failed to mention the black eye. I crossed to the bed, and Michelle disappeared.

"Hey."

"Don't look at me!" she answered. I was surprised.

"You don't look that bad," I tried to reassure. She turned away.

"What's wrong, Alecs?"

"I hate how I look."

"You're black eye will heal. It's not the end of the world."

"That's not it."

I studied the side of her face I could see. "OK, you'll have to explain."

She rolled over and stared a hole in me. I waited. *We haven't had to do this waiting game as much lately.* "I'm afraid you'll have to explain," I finally caved.

"How would you feel if you started growing a beard?"

I could see misery on her face. I could also see the beginnings of facial hair around her upper lip and chin. It was peach fuzz, really, especially since it was blond. "I see. That would feel odd to me."

"All that I've been working toward is unraveling."

"What do you mean?"

"They stopped my puberty blockers."

"Oh. Why would they do that?"

"It's Georgia's stupid new law. They decided to treat trans people as if we're not human."

"You're kidding."

"No."

"You mean Georgia has a law that trans people can't take puberty blockers?"

"Yeah. It started in July."

My heart got heavy as I thought about what the future held. *While Alecs feels like a girl and wants to be a girl, her voice will deepen and she'll grow a beard.* "That sucks." *Oops, that wasn't very professional of me.*

"Yeah."

"How are you feeling?"

Silence. *Are we drifting back into that?*

"Scared."

"How is your rib?"

"Sore. It hurts when I move."

"I'm sorry this happened."

"Yeah."

"Why did they attack you?"

"They found out I'm trans."

I stiffened and sat down in the chair next to the bed. "How did that happen? I haven't told anyone."

"I told them."

"Why would you do that. It's not safe, obviously."

"They were making fun of you for being gay."

My heart stopped. *She was defending me?* "I'm sorry, Alecs. You shouldn't put yourself in danger for me."

"Yeah."

She grimaced as she reached for her back pocket. Pulling out a folded paper, she looked me in the eye before offering it. I gingerly took it from her hand and opened it to read.

HIDE

Heat, dry
Pitiful soil
Force the plant
Alone to toil

Life is fight
Fight is life

Hard is the day
Cold is the night

Heat, dry
Pitiful soil
Hold the seed
Deny the spoil.

-Alecs Taylor
10/12/23

A tear wormed its way out. "Alecs, that's beautiful. Sad, but beautiful. You nailed how it feels to deal with our differing sexual orientations and identities. Sometimes it seems best to hide. Maybe someday we won't have to."

"Yeah."

I sensed a deep sadness in her. It was going to be hard living without the treatment. It would be hard living in this prison anyway. I scoured my mind and heart to find something hopeful to say.

"I'll walk with you through this dark time."

"Yeah."

I hadn't noticed the anger rising in my gut while I was with Alecs. By the time I found Michelle, I was boiling. "How can they do that to her?" I fumed. "How can the state just up and stop a medical treatment she has been on?" *Oops, that may have been confidential.*

Michelle looked around. No one was nearby. "Step in here, please."

She closed her office door. "That was close! We can't talk about medical issues with anyone not involved in Alecs's care. Since Alecs told you, it's OK."

"So, what's going to happen? Is there any way we can petition the state to resume her treatment?"

"No. The law is final. Any doctor that prescribed the medicine would be risking their license and possible jail time. It's not going to happen."

"That's just not fair! How can they treat him... I mean her that way?" I was angry. *There has to be something I can do.*

"Our current government believes they have the right to determine how parents raise their children. And they have the power to do it."

"This is going to kill Alecs. I think she's more down about losing the medicine than about being beat up."

"Oh no. That's not good."

"Why do you say that?"

"Suicide is a big concern for these kids."

"So that's the plan. The state hopes to get rid of them by pushing them toward suicide! That is just sick! Is there nothing we can do?"

"What do you think a future pastor has to offer?" she asked, a stern look on her face and her arms crossing.

This is a challenge. What do I have to offer? I searched my mind. "The only thing I have is love and compassion."

"Love is the greatest force in the universe. We have to love Alecs through these next three and a half years. Then she can resume her treatments and work toward becoming the person she wants to be. It won't be easy, but you appear to be the person God has chosen for that task."

My body was heavy as I left the detention center. Sadness filled my veins with lead. There was also a fiery anger in the pit of my stomach. *Poor Alecs. I'm just starting to get the knack of using the right pronoun for her. How would it feel to have your whole identity stripped away like that? I just can't imagine.*

I understood the source of the sadness. It was from Alecs's predicament. I thought I understood the source of the anger: the government shouldn't have the right to treat her this way. But there was something else brewing in my gut. It finally surfaced.

How dare Michelle lay the responsibility for Alecs's future on me. That's too much! That's too scary!

Chapter 11

Saturday, November 4, 2023

Saturday afternoon study sessions at my apartment followed by supper were becoming a tradition. It was one of the perks of living across the street from campus. Plus it inspired me to clean regularly. Romeo loved the company and made the rounds for petting. Sophie usually greeted people then disappeared.

Johnny was the first to show today. He was ten minutes early, and I was still putting away dishes.

"Hey! Come on in."

"Hey. How are you?"

"I'm good. Just finishing putting away some dishes. How about you?"

"Doing OK, thanks."

He set up his laptop in his usual spot. I expected him to study while I finished, but he talked.

"Umm, has anyone caused you problems since you… were outed?"

"Not really. Avery still avoids me, but she doesn't cause any problems."

"That's good. Did you come out in college, or was this the first time?"

"Actually I came out in high school. It was brutal, but college was a breeze. Well, except for living in the dorm that first year. That was stressful, especially the showers."

"How was high school brutal?"

So many questions! I guess I might as well share, though. "People went absolutely nuts. I had three guys sticking nasty anti-gay notes on my locker and car. One of my best friends turned against me. My youth minister outed me to my parents, and they threatened to put me in an institution to make me straight. Those were the good ole days."

"I see."

We were interrupted by a knock on the door. Inaya, Shani, and Glenn arrived.

"What's up amigos?" Inaya chirped.

"Johnny and I were talking about my adventure with coming out in high school."

"Do tell. Inquiring minds need to know," Inaya smiled.

I stiffened a bit. *This wasn't how I saw today going. It's getting easier to talk about, though. And this is my crew."*

"OK. Do you want the long or short version?"

"We do have to study at some point," Glenn pointed out.

I proceeded to recount my experience, including the bit where I ran away. I shared how I felt called into the ministry and wrapped it up with my current relationship with my parents. I left out the part about inheriting Grace's estate.

"So your dad still doesn't support you?" Inaya asked. "That's tacky."

"It does still hurt. Dad thinks seminary is a waste of my time. You should have seen him when I came home from college with the sides of my head shaved! It was fun just to watch. I wish I had a video." *I'm glad my hair grew out before I got to seminary. It would have been a bit much.*

"Still, my parents are one hundred percent behind me. It must be hard. What kind of support do the rest of you have?" Shani asked.

"My mom is totally supportive," Glenn said. "Dad disappeared when I was a kid. I never hear from him."

"That's even worse!" Inaya said.

"Mine have been in prison since I was three. I grew up with a family of foxes. They're incredibly supportive," Johnny deadpanned.

We eyed him then burst out laughing. Shani through a chip at him. "I can't believe you said that!"

Johnny grinned. *I believe that's the first nonserious thing he's ever said.*

"That was bad. Really bad!" Glenn grumped. "It was so bad it makes me want to study."

Glenn was our little group's drill Sargent, always calling us to task.

"OK, but we can't study all the time. Getting to know each other is productive, too," Inaya said.

We opened books and laptops and settled down to study. After about an hour, Inaya, who had curled up on the couch to read ahead for next week, asked, "How is everyone's Con Ed placement going?"

I looked up and caught her beautiful dark eyes. *I wish she were gay! I have to quit thinking like that!* "Mine has me stressed out."

"How come?"

I leaned back trying to decide what I could and couldn't tell them. "You remember me telling you about Alecs."

"Yeah."

"I found out a couple of weeks ago that she had to stop taking puberty blockers because of a new state law. She's really down, and I'm afraid she might become suicidal."

"That's scary."

"The chaplain at the detention center expects me to be the one to keep her from doing that."

"No pressure or anything," Glenn said. "It's hard to get used to calling a guy 'she' or 'her.'"

"I still slip up sometimes."

"What are you going to do?" Shani asked.

"All I know to do is listen and try to convince her that she will be able to resume treatment in three years and two months."

"Thirty-eight months is a long time for a teenager," Johnny pointed out.

He sure is talkative today. Maybe he's coming out of his shell!

We studied until the dreaded weekly task of deciding where to go eat. We ran through various styles of food till pizza seemed to hit the spot. I offered to drive, and we were off to Athens Pizza.

"The waiter is flirting with you," Shani said to me.

"No he's not."

"I guess you missed him eyeing you while you were looking at the menu," she pointed out. Glenn and Inaya nodded.

"If he is, he'll be sorely disappointed," I said.

I don't know why I've never asked this before. I guess I assume I know the answer. "I'm assuming not, but do any of us have a boyfriend or girlfriend? Anything serious?"

"Not me," Glenn answered.

"Nope," Shani said.

Johnny shook his head. We all looked at Inaya.

"Not anymore." A shadow of sadness crossed her eyes.

"What happened?" Shani asked.

"I was dating a guy. When I told him I was going to seminary, he ended the relationship. He said he didn't think women should be pastors. I really liked him, but I guess it was better to find out early."

"Why do people have to make things so hard?" Shani asked. "If we could just accept each other for who we are, life would be a lot better."

"Amen to that," Glenn said.

The waiter brought out the pizza. He actually touched me on the shoulder and smiled as he placed it on our table. "Is there anything else you need?"

"I could use some more iced tea," Glenn said.

"Coming right up."

"You look like you've seen a ghost," Shani grinned. "He didn't bite you or anything."

My eyes must have been the size of saucers.

"He's going to ask you out before we leave," Inaya said.

"Usually I seem to have a 'no guys, please' signal radiating. He must have missed that."

"You are cute, you know," Glenn said.

"Thanks. You're not making this any easier." I would have punched him had I been able to reach him.

"Relax. It's no big deal. When he asks, just tell him, 'No thanks.' If he persists, you can always tell him you're a lesbian," Shani said.

"Great," I grumped. This was the first time a guy had flirted with me since college. I was out of practice with the brush off.

When he brought our checks, I noticed a note at the bottom of mine. "I'd love to talk to you sometime. If that's OK, please leave me your number. Thanks, Chet."

"That's creative," I said and showed my crew the note. "I think I'll write '1-800-NOPE.'"

"That's a little harsh," Inaya said. "How about, 'No thanks?'"

"OK, if you insist."

When Chet returned, he scanned the note and said, "Oh. Are you seeing someone?"

"No," I answered.

"Well why not give me a try? I'm not a pervert or anything."

OK, I have to end this thing. "Look, I'm lesbian."

"Oh."

He backed up so quickly, I thought he was going to trip over the next table.

"I feel bad for him," Inaya said. "He seems like a nice guy."

"True, but there's no future there," I reiterated.

I suddenly missed Liia. Loneliness stung my heart. *I so enjoyed talking with her, making out with her. I wonder if I'll ever find anyone else.*

"Someone needs to run to the car and grab an umbrella," Glenn quipped.

What is he talking about? Everyone else looked puzzled.

"Don't you see the dark cloud hovering over Willow?"

"Sorry. I was flashing back to my high school sweetheart. I still miss her."

Chapter 12

Monday, November 6, 2023

Between classes, I headed to the break area for coffee. I had been up late trying to finish a paper that was due this morning in Systematic Theology. My eyelids were heavy.

"I need more caffeine," I said to the coffee machine, oblivious to the fact that a group of five students had surrounded me. After it had brewed, I pulled out my cup and noticed the disgruntled faces.

"Sorry. I'm done," I said, thinking they were in as much need of caffeine as I. I started to move away, but they blocked me from getting through their line.

"What are you doing here?" Gregg asked in a challenging tone. He was a junior I had met briefly at orientation. I didn't really like him, and we haven't spoken since. Being sleepy, I didn't realize this was a challenge.

"Sorry that my getting coffee was such an inconvenience," I said, countering his rudeness. He and the others still didn't move.

"I'm not talking about coffee."

I don't like where this is going. "What are you talking about then?" I said as I stiffened my spine. *I have a hot cup of coffee if I need a weapon. I can't believe I just thought that!*

"I mean what are you doing in seminary? Homosexuals aren't fit for ordination. You're just wasting a spot for a legitimate student."

I picked Avery's face out of the group and gave her a piercing look. *Should I just push through or stand my ground?* "I have every right to be here, and it's time the church saw the light and realized that just because my sexual orientation is different from yours doesn't mean I can't be an effective pastor. I'm here because God called me to be here. I'd appreciate it if you'd quit harassing me and let me through." I turned my glare from Avery back to Gregg.

They still didn't move. "Is this a vigilante group? Are you about to tie me behind a car and drag me through the campus? Is that your idea of Christianity?" My voice was rising.

"Hey! What's going on here? Leave her alone!" Shani shouted in an authoritative voice, startling at least three of the group. Gregg continued to glare as he and the others walked away.

"What was that about?" Shani asked.

"I'm not sure what they had in mind. They had me surrounded, and Gregg was challenging my right to be here." My hands were shaky, and I had trouble holding the coffee cup still.

"Are you OK?"

"I'm angry. What gives them the right to harass me like that? I've done nothing to them. I can't believe Avery was in the group!" My voice was loud, matching the intensity of my feelings.

I was so focused on Shani that I hadn't noticed Avery had returned. "Now what!" I lashed out. She took a step back but didn't leave.

"I'm sorry," Avery said. I tried to rein in the rage. "They said they wanted to witness to you. I assumed that meant talking about your homosexuality and what scripture has to say. I didn't realize they meant to threaten you."

"They witnessed alright! They witnessed to being street thugs filled with hate." *OK, you have to calm down. Hyperbole won't get us anywhere.* "I apologize. That was spiteful."

Shani and Avery laughed.

"What?" I was exasperated.

"Street thugs is a perfect description of their behavior," Shani said. "I think you nailed it, so don't apologize."

"Yeah. It's funny to think of a group of seminary students acting like thugs," Avery said. "I wish I had spoken up in your defense. I think I've learned a valuable lesson today."

I looked down, and my coffee was no longer shaking. "Thanks, Avery. If you want to talk about homosexuality and scripture someday, I'd love to... But not with those creeps surrounding me."

"It's a deal. How about a Bible and Starbucks soon?"

"I'll look forward to it." At that moment I knew exactly what I wanted to do. *I'll mark my Bible just like Grace marked hers.*

Thursday, November 9, 2023

Alecs was to be moved back into the community Monday of this week. I jogged into the detention center, anxious to find out what had happened. *I hope she's OK. They'd better leave her alone. Her ribs were still hurting last week.* My mother hen nature was flaring.

I sought out Michelle. "Well?"

"So far no incidents. She does seem more down than usual, though."

"No taunts or attacks, then?"

"No. We prepared the others with some sensitivity training."

"I bet that was well received!" I snarked.

"Yeah, but we had to try."

I thought we would never finish with the Bible study, or Meditation as they liked to call it. Alecs had stopped coming before the attack. *I think I'll invite her today. Maybe that's all she needs.*

Alecs was back at the usual table, sitting alone. I saw a desolate spirit in her green eyes, and it pained my heart.

"Hey, Alecs."

"Hey."

"How does it feel to be out of sick bay?"

"The same."

I sat down across from her. "Before it slips my mind, I'd love it if you came to Meditation next week."

"Why?"

"I would just feel good to have you in there."

"No. Why would I go?"

What can I say to that question? "It would be something to do."

"I meditate here."

"I see. What have you been thinking about today?"

Silence. I looked over my finger nails as I waited. Glancing up, I saw her sad green eyes fixed on a spot on the wall. *Is he... Ugh! It's so hard to get that straight in my head... she trying to decide whether to tell me or just off in her own thoughts?*

Finally she turned her eyes to me. "Futility."

"You've been thinking about futility?"

"Yes."

"In what way?"

"Living is futile. Why bother?"

Michelle told me to watch for suicidal thoughts. Is this one or is this just Alecs? I probed. "Why do you say that?"

"Truth."

"Truth? Are you talking about life in general or your life?"

Wall staring. I noticed my heart had sped up. *I'm anxious about her response. What if she is suicidal? What could I do?* I had drifted off into my own thoughts and didn't notice Alecs was looking at me.

"Us."

"Us?"

"Those of us who are different. For us, life is futile. You know. It happened for you."

I was caught off-guard. *Does she know about the incident at school? I'll have to ask.* "What do you mean, 'It happened for me?'"

"I think you were attacked recently. It shows in your eyes."

"How could you know that? I was cornered by a group of students this week. They said I shouldn't be in seminary, that I'm wasting a spot for a legitimate student."

"You want to be ordained, but the church won't. The future shuts down. Futile."

"You're a deep thinker. But what if I can change that future and convince the church I am worth ordaining? That's worth fighting for."

"What if you can't?"

"It's a risk I'm willing to take. If I can't, I'll have to change denominations."

"My future can't change. It is already sealed."

"What do you mean?" I had a crushing grip on the table leg. I tried to relax so Alecs wouldn't sense my stress.

"I can't be who I am. Why live?"

I cringed. *Do I try to talk her out of these thoughts? Express concern? Argue? What do I say next?* It was my turn to be silent as I rummaged through my brain for adequate words. Alecs apparently sensed my struggle and gave me space by looking at the wall. *Grace!*

"Can I tell you a story?"

She looked at me like I was crazy. "OK."

I straightened in my seat. "When I was in high school and my parents found out I was gay, they wanted to put me in a facility that forced people to be straight. I ran away. After a couple of days living behind a factory, I got run off by a group of thugs. Things stopped working out after that, and God led me to an old lady whom I had befriended.

"She took me in. After a shower and some food, she began to teach me about the Bible and homosexuality. As the conversation went on, I discovered that she was lesbian, too. She had a life-long partner. They figured out a way to make it work in a world that was totally against gay people."

"How?" *So she is paying attention!*

"They told everyone they were roommates. No one questioned it, and they were able to live out their lives together."

"I can't just pretend. I need to change. I need medicine to do that. I'm different."

"Yes. The point is that there are ways to make things work. Grace and Joy had to present a lie to the world to get what they wanted. You have to wait."

"Wait?"

"Wait."

I could see Alecs was considering this. She found that spot on the wall. I looked to see what was there. It was just the wall. *She's inside herself. The wall is her blank page.*

"Too long."

"It's thirty-eight months till you can resume your treatment. You'll be eighteen then." *I hoped months sounded better than years.*

The corners of Alecs's lips turned up in a slight smile. *Maybe I got through!*

"You're worried about me."

"Yes, I am."

"You have a kind spirit."

I had a death grip on the table leg again. *Those sound like words of parting.* "Thanks, Alecs. I care about you. Please don't do anything drastic. Give the future time to open up. God has a way of opening doors that we never expect."

She glanced at the prison door, and the irony of what I'd said crushed me.

"How?"

"How?"

"How can I wait? The law closed my future. My now morphs into agony. Waiting only makes it worse. I will change into a body I detest."

"Let's wait by fighting."

She looked at me from somewhere deep in those green eyes.

"Let's write letters to the legislature. Let's write letters to the newspapers. Let's start a social media campaign. Let's tell the world what is going on with trans people so we can build some compassion and understanding. Grace said it might be time."

I wasn't sure what I saw in her eyes. A flicker of hope? Amusement? *Am I grasping at straws?* I decided to wait.

"Maybe."

I let out a long breath. "OK. When I come next week, I'll have a letter ready to send. I hope you'll have one, too."

Silence.

"You'd better be here when I come next week!"

Chapter 13

Saturday, November 11, 2023

The sun created an orange and gold dance in the trees as I walked across the street to meet Avery at Starbucks. I stopped at the end of the driveway and watched, enjoying the moment. It was 9:27, so I couldn't linger long.

"Good morning, Avery," I said. She was just coming off the stairs as I walked into the bottom floor.

"Good morning! How are you?"

"I'm fine, thanks. And you?"

"Doing great. I can't believe how beautiful the weather is. The leaves have been spectacular!" Avery was from Florida and has been marveling at the wonders of fall.

"Fall is my favorite time of year. I love it when the leaves change and the air gets crisp," I said.

"I can see why!"

We chit-chatted while ordering then found a table. I sat the Bible I had marked with sticky notes on the table and took my first sip of the caramel macchiato I had ordered. "Yummm! So delicious!"

"Wow! This is wonderful!" Avery said. She had ordered a brown sugar something with a name that took about three minutes to say.

I wonder what exactly she wants to talk about. How do we get started? I took another sip and steeled myself for an argument.

"I see you brought a Bible," she said.

I was nervous about talking with Avery concerning something so personal and important to me. I guess it was the nerves that started me talking. The next thing I knew, I was rattling on, telling her my story of running away, being called into the ministry and ending up at Grace's house.

Avery pushed her black hair behind her ear as she listened. When I finally took a break after telling her about going to hide out at Grace's house, she said, "You had a dramatic senior year."

I laughed. "Yeah, I guess it was. How about you? How did you end up coming to seminary?"

"As far as I can remember, I've always known being a pastor is what I was meant to do. I do remember one service during which I felt like I really just wanted to go to the altar and pray. During the closing hymn, I did that and, kind of like you, had a communion with God during which I knew God wanted me to be a pastor."

"That's neat! It must have been a special moment."

"It was. OK, I'm curious." She took a sip of coffee then leveled her blue eyes on me. I gripped my coffee cup, a little tense.

"How do you reconcile living a homosexual lifestyle with being a pastor?"

I sipped my coffee to give time for a response to develop. "Honestly, I have never thought of it as a lifestyle. God created me homosexual. I am attracted to females the same way you are attracted to males.

"As for lifestyles, I think mine will be similar to yours. I will try to live a life faithful to God, love my neighbors, care for my church, and if I'm fortunate enough to find a spouse, be faithful to her, too.

"My sexual orientation is a biological thing. It's in my DNA."

"I see." She punctuated her response with coffee. *Coffee is good for slowing down conversations as well as waking us up.* "I never thought about it that way. So you don't see homosexuality as being sinful. You see it as part of the created order."

She's a deep thinker. "That's a great way to put it." I drank more coffee and let her think.

"I know we are all sinners, but the Bible singles out homosexuality as being incompatible with a Christian lifestyle. How do you make sense of that?"

She seems like she really wants to know rather than put me in my place. "That's one of the liberating things Grace taught me before she died." I opened my Bible to the first sticky note. "She showed me how the places the Bible mentions homosexuality aren't as condemning as people want to think."

I showed her the passage in Leviticus. "Well, that's Leviticus. It's the old law that Jesus replaced with the new covenant."

I moved on to the New Testament passages. "You probably already know that it was Paul who mentioned homosexuality. His references were in lists of sins people committed when off their rails in reckless living."

I showed her the passages, and she seemed to consider them thoughtfully.

"Hmm. I see what you're getting at. You're saying that being homosexual is not the issue. The real issue is how one lives one's life."

"That is what I think. If homosexuality is part of the created order, as you said, then we are like everyone else. We are responsible for living a loving and faithful life in as Christ-like a manner as we can."

I took a drink of my coffee. It was room temperature but still tasted yummy. *This is going better than I expected.* I watched as Avery flipped through the passages and scanned them again. She seemed deep in thought, so I just enjoyed the coffee and waited. *Alecs has taught me how to wait and let others have space to form their thoughts. She's given me a new skill.*

I was lost in that thought when Avery said, "I think you have changed my perspective on homosexuality. If God created you that way, then it can't be wrong. God said that all God created was good, though I do wonder about mosquitos."

We both laughed. "You've given me a new thought today, too. I like the idea of being part of the created order."

She looked out the window for a moment, and I thought I saw joy in her eyes. "How is your Contextual Education going?" she asked when she turned back to me.

"It's intense. I'm at the juvenile detention center, and there's a trans guy who got beat up. The state has stopped her puberty blockers, and I'm afraid she's suicidal. She has taken to me, and the chaplain there expects me to keep her alive."

"Wow! That's a lot of pressure."

"She'll talk to me but hasn't been willing to talk with anyone else. I feel responsible for her."

"Willow, you can't control what another person does. All you can do is be there for them and love them."

"I know, but I still feel a lot of responsibility. What if I screw it up? What if there is something I could have said or done that would have made a difference, and I didn't?"

"Take a breath. It's OK. All we can do is the best that we can."

"Thanks. I really stress out between Thursdays. I'm always wondering what's happening and if she'll be there when I get back." Another sip of coffee was in order. "How is your placement going?"

"It's a lot duller than yours. The drive is endless, and the inmates are grumpy. I have connected a little with one lady, but I think she is just trying to get on my good side so she can ask me to smuggle something in."

"I'm sorry. It doesn't seem fair that some of you have that long drive. Of course, if I leave a little early and hit rush hour, it takes me forever to get home."

"True. At least my drive gets me out of Atlanta's traffic. I'm curious about this trans... person. You said this was a guy, but you call him her and she. Which is he or she?"

"Alecs is male by birth, but she identifies as female. She was taking puberty blockers and planning to transition to female, surgery and all. So she likes to be called by feminine pronouns."

"That would be hard to get used to."

"Yeah, I still slip up sometimes. It's easier when I'm talking to her because I just use her name or the you version." I took the last sip of coffee and scowled at my cup.

"What's wrong?" Avery asked.

"It's empty!" I shook the cup for effect. She laughed.

"I guess that's the signal it's time to get going. There are too many papers to write."

"That's the truth! Hey, the Musketeer group gets together at my apartment on Saturday afternoons to study. Then we go out to eat. Why don't you join us today?"

"Where is your apartment?"

"See the gray house?" I pointed out the window. "It's down that driveway in the basement."

"That's convenient! Actually, I'll probably get more done if I study alone."

"How about meeting us for supper?"

"That does sound fun. OK, text me the when and where, and I'll join you."

"Great!"

Chapter 14

Thursday, November 16, 2023

Michelle pulled me aside after Meditation. Alecs didn't come. Worry crashed my heart. *She can't tell me she's dead!* We sat in her office, and my palms got clammy.

"Alecs isn't doing so well."

I let out a loud sigh. Michelle raised one of her eyebrows.

"I'm sorry. I was afraid you were going to tell me she was dead."

A smile lit her face. "I see. No, she's still with us, but her mood is darker. She's been writing letters to lawmakers. They are dark, too."

"That's something we talked about doing last week. I was hoping it would give her some motivation to fight and keep living."

"Good idea. I just want to let you know I think you are doing an excellent job with Alecs. The connection you have made is what ministry is all about to me. Also, if Alecs doesn't make it, please realize that it's not your fault. You're giving her all you can."

My heart had a cold chill. *She thinks Alecs will kill herself.* I didn't want to ask, but I had to. "Do you really think she will commit suicide?"

She paused and looked out the window. Sadness seeped from her eyes. "You have probably looked at the statistics. Over three quarters of trans people assigned male at birth have considered suicide and over a third have attempted it. With Georgia's new… I have no words to describe it… law, I expect the rate to go up. Maybe that's what the legislators are after, I don't know. But Alecs has a lot more pressure than the average trans person. It pains me to say that her odds are pretty grim."

"Yeah, I've been worried, too." My heart sank even lower.

"OK, then. Go and love on her for as long as we have her. That's all we have to give, and hopefully it will be enough."

I took a moment to shift the gears of my heart. *OK, Alecs, we have a mission to try and convince the legislators to roll back this horrible law. Let's tackle that.* With that thought I walked in and found Alecs in her usual spot.

"Hey, Alecs!" I tried to sound cheerful.

"Hey."

"How are you feeling today?"

"I've written ten letters."

"Wow! You're ahead of me. I've just written one, but I plan to send copies to several people. To whom did you write?"

"Governor, Lieutenant Governor, ACLU, and several legislators."

"Wow! Writing to the ACLU was a great idea! I'll add that to my list. Who else could we include?"

She looked past me out the window. *I'm getting good at this waiting thing. The silence no longer feels uncomfortable. It's just part of our relationship, like a third person sitting with us.*

"No one will listen." I jumped when she finally spoke.

"I'm sure they won't listen if we don't try. If we try, we might could help trans people all over the state. What we're doing is bigger than just us."

My mind raced in the silence that followed. *I have to find something to make life worth living.* I noticed a shift in Alecs's eyes, and I didn't like what I saw. She slid a piece of paper across the table.

Broken

The spirit lifts
To give a try
Now it breaks
Into a cry

With talons sharp
Darkness looms
This broken soul
It now grooms

A dead weight
Time is long
So appeals
Darkness' song

-Alecs Taylor
11/13/23

"Oh Alecs." The tears didn't ask. They just poured. "Please don't. We have to fight, not just for you but for trans people everywhere." I wasn't sobbing, but there was a steady river running down both cheeks. Through the liquid I could tell Alecs looked perplexed.

She took my hand. Tears fell out of her eyes. "You actually care about me. Don't be sad. I'm nothing."

"You're something to me," I choked through the tears.

She released my hand, wiped her tears, and laughed.

I wiped mine. "What's so funny?" *I hope that didn't sound as angry as it seemed.*

"We're pathetic."

It was my turn to be perplexed. *Pathetic!* I pictured us being viewed by camera from above. I laughed, too. "Pathetic," I echoed. Then I noticed people in the room were staring. I ignored them and tried to focus on Alecs. *I hope this won't prompt the other inmates to attack again. I have to pull myself together.*

Two thoughts collided, one hopeful and one frightening. *I'll start with frightening then move to hopeful.*

"Alecs, I'm worried. Next Thursday is Thanksgiving, and I plan to be home with my family. I won't be here." I tensed, not sure what to expect.

"Mom will probably visit."

"That's good. I'll be back the next Thursday. Please be here."

"I'll try."

"That's all I can ask. I know this is a hard time in your life. I'll walk with you through it as best I can."

"Thanks."

"Now, another thought. Would you mind if I send that poem with my letter?"

"Why?"

"It may help people to see how desperate they have made you."

"I want to keep it."

"I could take a photo and then copy it onto paper."

I could see she was considering. "OK."

Even though I was driving home, my mind and heart stayed at the detention center. *I don't think I can take it if she kills herself! What else can I do?* "Lord, I can only leave her in your hands. Please lift her spirit and give her hope."

Saturday, December 9, 2023

I was scrubbing the toilet with a vengeance. The stress was high. Two finals and a paper to go. *I need to let up on this poor toilet brush before I break it!* The crew was coming for our usual Saturday study and supper. I had neglected cleaning for too long.

Thank you, Lord, that Avery has rejoined our little group. And thank you that Alecs is still hanging in there. Now, please help me calm down!

I'm as stressed about not seeing Alecs for four weeks as I am about finals. I had already decided to go by and see her before leaving on the fourteenth. *I could come back a little early, which would make it three weeks.* Michelle told me not to worry about it, but I just can't seem to help it.

I was standing with the toilet brush in my hand having zoned out into my thoughts when a knock on the door startled me. *Someone's either early, or I'm late.*

On the way to the door, I glanced at the clock: 1:43. *Ha! I'm not late!*

"Hey, Johnny!" *Shoot, I forgot to put down the toilet brush.*

"Hey." *He looks tense. It must be finals.* "I see you're busy. Sorry I'm early."

"That's OK. Come on in, and I'll put this away."

He sat at the kitchen table in his usual chair. "I'm a bit stressed with these finals," I said as I deposited the brush in the bathroom."

"Me, too."

He was staring at me like he might explode. "Are you OK?"

"I don't know."

"You'll make it. These finals are tough, though."

"It's not the finals."

I sat down, puzzling over what might be going on. "What is it, then?"

"Can we talk?" *I think that's what we're doing.*

"Sure."

"It's hard to say it."

"No pressure. I'm listening."

"I… I… I'm gay." *Wow! I wasn't expecting that!*

"I see." *OK, I have to have more than that to offer.* "I was much happier once I came out… At least after all of the initial turmoil."

His jaw clinched. *I probably shouldn't have added the bit about turmoil.*

"Turmoil?"

"Yeah. I got a lot of backlash the first few months. Remember? I told you. Parents, friends, and church went ballistic…" A knock on the door interrupted me.

Johnny's eyebrows scrunched together. "Please don't tell anyone. I'm not ready yet."

"Your secret's safe with me." I paused on the way to the door. "This would be a good group for testing the waters, though."

Chapter 15

Sunday, January 14, 2024

Hugging Will goodbye drew a few tears. Even after being separated for a whole semester, living away from my twin still hurt. Will had another week before his classes started. I was going back to Atlanta to participate in the MLK march.

Christmas break had been… interesting. It was good being with family. Dad had restrained himself and said I was wasting my time going to seminary only twice. He did manage to dampen our time together with a grumpy attitude. He just shook his head when I told them I was going to participate in the march.

On my way to Atlanta, I thought back over meeting with Pastor Stevens last Sunday. When I told her about being outed, she said, "I hope that doesn't get back to the ministry committee."

I told her I was tired of trying to keep secrets. "This 'don't ask don't tell' idea is not going to work for me."

"You will risk ordination if they find out," was her answer.

"I'll have to trust God to open the needed doors."

The spark to stop hiding my sexual orientation came from a visit to Grace's house. *Well, technically it's my house, but I still think of it as hers.*

I had given it a good cleaning, which took all day. Then I met with a real estate agent. It was time to let it go, so I put it up for sale. We had agreed that closing would have to be the week of spring break or after spring semester.

This is a season of letting go. I'm letting go of Grace's house and letting go of don't ask don't tell. It's time for me to take flight.

Goose bumps flowed down my arms at that thought. With a smile, I turned up the music.

Monday, January 15, 2024

The bus dropped us off a block from the conference center. I was excited to be a part of the Martin Luther King Jr., Day march. Our whole Musketeers group huddled with the crowd.

After a rousing speech from someone I didn't know, a lady stepped up to the microphone and gave us directions.

"The police have informed us that there are counter-protestors lining the street where we'll be marching. It is their right to do that in a free country. They will likely be shouting some ugly words.

"Our best strategy is to ignore them. Treat them like they are irrelevant. In the spirit of Martin Luther King, Jr., remember that nonviolence is the weapon. Please do not engage with these people verbally or physically. Let the slurs run off your backs and let justice roll down like water! Let's march!"

OK, I'm a bit nervous. I wonder what will happen.

We began marching, and as soon as we got to Auburn Avenue, I saw them. People lined the sidewalks behind barriers the police had set up. We turned the corner, and I looked down the road at that sea of white faces. Our group was mostly black with swirls of white and brown. *I've never understood why skin color can be so controversial.*

The song, "We Shall Not Be Moved," flowed from the front of the march. I joined in, moved by the scene. *Equality, love, and peace is flowing like a river through hate and bitterness. What a powerful contrast!*

There were ridiculous signs along the way spewing racist comments. Several people held signs that said, "Donald Trump for President! He'll send all of you back to Africa!"

One particular taunt caught my attention. "Hey, white girl! You dirty skag! Get out of that nasty chocolate! You belong here with us!"

I looked into the crowd, and the person doing the yelling was looking at me. My nerves tensed. "Yeah, I'm talking to you!" I wanted to lash out, but I remembered the call to ignore them. I walked on, but the taunt kept flowing along the road, the words getting uglier as we went.

"You're doing great! Keep ignoring them. That's the most irritating thing you can do," Glenn said.

"I'm trying, but it's hard not to respond."

Glenn linked his arm in mine on the left. Shani did the same on the right. "This ought to get under their skin!" he said. I straightened my spine and walked on feeling like I was defying one of the ugliest parts of our nation.

Bam! Something hit me in the back of the neck, and I was suddenly soaked. Looking down, I saw an open water bottle. There was a scramble to my left. Two police officers were handcuffing the man. He glared at me and shouted something I couldn't understand.

We walked on without a word. Glenn and Shani had gotten some of the spray. It was cold walking wet in the forty degree weather. *The man had made his hateful statement, but it didn't stop the march. Justice and equality will overcome.*

Thursday, January 18, 2024

Alecs has to still be here. Surely Michelle would have called had something happened. I was nervous as I parked at the detention center.

I found Alecs in her usual spot. There was a light in her eyes that I had not seen before.

"Hey, Alecs."

"Hey."

"How are you feeling?"

She pulled an envelope out of her back pocket and slid it onto the table.

"What's this?" I asked.

She tapped it with her finger.

"It's OK for me to look at this?" When she nodded, I noticed the return address was the ACLU office.

"Ah hah!" The letter explained the light in her eyes. It expressed appreciation for her letter and stated that lawyers from the ACLU are looking into options for challenging the Georgia law. It ended with, "Keep the faith! We will do all that we can to fix this."

"That's great, Alecs! Your letter made a difference!"

"Maybe. Nothing has happened yet."

"The ACLU is good at this kind of thing. Of course, it will take time. We'll have to be patient." She cast her eyes to the floor.

"On a lighter note, I got hit with a water bottle during the MLK Day march." She looked up at me with a smile trying to tug the corner of her mouth up.

"So you think that's funny? I was wet, and it was cold." She actually laughed, and a flood of hope and relief flowed from my heart. *Maybe she will be OK.*

We finished our conversation on light notes. Alecs asked about my Christmas vacation, and I went through how we celebrated, fearing it would make her sad. She seemed to enjoy hearing about it.

Somewhere between getting up from the table and getting to the door, a flash of anger hit. *Why does she have to stay in here? She's such a nice person! She doesn't deserve a twelve year sentence.*

I turned and waved to Alecs before leaving. Then I hunted down Michelle.

"I can't believe you got Alecs to laugh!"

"It was a good visit today. I guess you know about the letter from ACLU."

"I do, and I hope they can do something about it."

"Is there anything we can do about her sentence? She doesn't deserve twelve years for defending herself. There has to be a way to appeal." Michelle was signaling for me to quiet down.

"Unfortunately, Alecs pled guilty and refused to appeal. She thought she deserved the punishment."

"That's just not right. What if I can talk her into appealing now?"

"I'm a chaplain, not a lawyer. I have no idea."

"Is there a lawyer we could talk to? We have to try!" Another gesture to quieten down.

"Don't say anything to Alecs about this. I'll reach out to the lawyer for her case and see what he says."

When I left, joy and hope had replaced the nervousness. It was a happy ride home.

Chapter 16

Saturday, January 20, 2024

Crystal clear sky, bright sunshine, and fifty-seven degrees added to my excitement. I finished stretching my hamstrings and stepped onto the court. *This is going to be fun!*

Members of the team were milling around. I stepped up and introduced myself. "Hi, I'm Willow."

"Hey! It's nice to meet you! I'm Susan." She seemed to be sizing me up. "I didn't know you were on the team."

"I'm not. I volunteered to help out with practices."

"I see. I'm the captain of the team, and I hate to be blunt, but are you good enough to compete with us?"

"I played for Tennessee, so I imagine I can hang in there," I said, feeling challenged.

"I appreciate your being willing to help out. I'm Alyssa. Don't mind Susan. She's protective of the team."

"I totally understand." I noticed Susan was eyeing my Babolat racquet. I had splurged with Grace's money. "Who do you want me to play with today?"

"We can volley," Alyssa offered.

"Great! I'm ready if you are."

"I need to stretch first."

"OK. I'm a first year theology student at Candler. How about you?"

"A theology student who is good at tennis. That's an interesting combination. I'm pre-law. A junior."

We chatted till she was ready and volleyed to warm up. *She seems quite good. I'll have to exert myself.*

"Are you ready to give it a go?"

"Sure. You serve first."

She hit a wicked serve, but I returned it right past her. The game proceeded, and she caught up to me at Deuce. Her serve pulled me to my backhand. As I swung I heard a grunt. The woman from the next court was flailing right at me. *She's going to fall!*

I had to make a quick choice: jump out of her way and back to our game or catch her. I elected to catch her. Grabbing her in a bear hug, I steadied her onto her feet.

She let out a few expletives. "I think I sprained my ankle! Thanks for catching me, by the way!"

"You're welcome."

She started limping away, then returned. "I'm Mellie. Nursing. I haven't met you."

"I'm Willow. First year theology. Nice to meet you."

"Why are you here?"

"I played for Tennessee in college and offered to help with practices. I've been missing the game."

Her blue eyes were intense. *She's a competitor.* She tightened her pony tail, thick blond hair spilling over her shoulder, while she scrutinized me.

"Nice racquet. You may have to take my spot on the team."

As she limped off, she said, "Let's get together for coffee sometime so I can pay you back for catching me."

That was a surprise. I had gotten the impression she didn't like me. "Sure," I called.

Turning my attention back to Alyssa, she asked. "Do I get that point or shall we replay it?"

I was feeling confident. "You can have it. I'll take the next three." And that's exactly what I did.

Monday, January 22, 2024

She's late. I hope she hasn't stood me up! It was 7:40am, and I was sitting at Kaldi's Coffee in the student center waiting for Mellie to show. I had just stood to go order when a clanking sound drew my attention. Mellie was hopping in on crutches.

"Sorry I'm late. These things slow me down."

"Did you break it?" I asked, eyeing the boot on her left leg.

"No, it's a sprain. The doc said I need to stay off of it for two weeks, except for walking around my dorm room. A little weight-bearing is good for it."

"How long are you out of tennis?"

"He said light practices in four weeks and hopefully back in six."

"That's a long time!"

"It would have been worse had I crashed on the court. I might have broken a wrist if it weren't for you!"

"I'm glad I was in the right spot at the right time."

"Me, too. Coffee's on me. What will you have?"

Waiting on our orders, she asked, "Have you thought any more about filling my slot on the team? They could really use you. I saw you beat Alyssa, and that's hard to do."

That's really tempting, but I don't know if I can spare the time. She apparently read my hesitation. "It's just for six weeks. It will only be three or four matches. Please! We need you!"

"I do have one more year on my eligibility," I said, yielding to the temptation. *She's actually quite cute. Stop that!* "I may not be able to make all of the practices, though."

"I'm sure the coach would be willing to cut you some slack in order to get that much talent!"

She was grinning, and I couldn't resist. "OK, I'll give it a try."

She grabbed my hand. "Thank you so much!"

My hand tingled at her touch. We spent forty-five minutes drinking the coffee, then had to hustle to class.

That evening I had to call Will. I couldn't wait till our usual Sunday talk.

"Hey, Will!"

"Hey! What's up?"

"I'm on the tennis team!"

"You're what? I didn't think you were going to do that."

"I wasn't."

"What happened?"

"I volunteered to help with practices just to get some playing time in."

"That doesn't qualify as being on the team."

"The first practice, one of the players sprained her ankle. She crashed into me, and I caught her. Anyway, she'll be out for six weeks, so I'm going to fill in. I'm excited!"

"That's great! I hope you don't flunk out, though!"

"Me, too! I had to share the news with you!"

"I'm glad you did. It's always good to hear your voice. I hope this doesn't take the place of Sunday's call."

"Of course not! I just needed an extra contact with my favorite brother."

"I miss my favorite sister, too."

Tuesday, January 30, 2024

"As you can see, the history of Christian thought provides a rich resource for helping navigate the issues we face today," Dr. Jones explained in his lecture. "I want you to break into groups of about ten, identify a current day issue, discuss how the theologians we have been studying speak to the issue, then write a thousand word paper on that. The paper will be due next Tuesday. Let's get to it."

Our group coalesced around the five Musketeers, Gregg, Ian, Melissa, Joseph, and Beverly. *Great! I wish Gregg would stay away from me.*

"Any ideas?" Joseph asked. He was a practical soul and always serious.

"The role of homosexuals in the church is a hot topic right now," Gregg offered.

I should have known he'd bring that up. I tensed, hoping this wouldn't lead to an argument. *Maybe he'll stay civil.* I noticed Johnny's brow knit, bringing a crease between his eyes.

"It may be hard to apply old theology to that, though," Beverly said.

"I think we need to work at it though. If we can't find support for it in the past thinking of the church, then maybe we should continue considering it a sinful lifestyle," Gregg countered.

I wanted to stay out of the discussion, but everyone had turned to me. *I hope this doesn't come back to haunt me.* "I think that's a good idea. Let's see what we discover as we ponder this." The crease in Johnny's brow got deeper. I felt for him.

"Augustine obviously thought homosexuality was a sin. He details that in his interpretation of the destruction of Sodom," Gregg offered.

"But before Augustine, the destruction of Sodom was interpreted as being because of the abuse of the stranger," I countered. "I think that is a more correct interpretation."

"So you consider yourself above Augustine?" Gregg said with a lift of his nose.

"No, but I do consider his interpretation wrong."

"Let's calm down," Joseph pleaded. "Maybe this isn't the right issue for us today."

"I say let's go with it and see where it takes us, if we can be civil about it, that is," I countered, glaring at Gregg.

"I think it's obvious that none of the early theologians had a favorable view of homosexuality. That is a more modern phenomenon," Melissa said.

I'm sure she's right. I hoped to find an inroad, though. Johnny looks defeated. "That can't be the end of the matter," I said.

"Let's see you come up with something different, then," Gregg stated smugly.

"I'll do just that," I said, accepting the challenge.

Chapter 17

Saturday, February 10, 2024

The Musketeers had gathered for our usual Saturday study session.

"I can't believe this paper is due on Valentine's day," Shani complained, flicking a few wandering braids over her shoulder.

"It's just another day to me," I replied. The sorrow of Liia leaving had faded to just a gentle twinge.

"Has anyone found anything to support homosexuality? All I've found condemns it," Inaya asked.

"I found some articles about John Calvin that suggested he was homosexual, but his doctrinal statements still condemned it," Glenn offered.

"I read about that, too," Johnny said. "Some people have written that after his marriage ended he brought several young men into his house to be their mentor."

"It's highly likely some of the early theologians were gay just by the law of averages, but there was such hostility against it they wouldn't have admitted it or written to support it," Inaya stated. "So far, we have no case."

"The only thing I found was the idea of adelphopoiesis," I said.

"What it the world is that?" Glenn asked.

"It's a ceremony that unites two men in a 'brotherly relationship,'" I answered, making air quotes. "But scholars differ as to whether there could be any homosexual relationships involved."

"I hope you can spell that," Shani quipped.

We all laughed, and I spelled it out for them. Keys clicked as everyone did a search.

After a moment of silence, Johnny groaned.

"What's wrong?" Inaya asked.

"We still have nothing," he said, tipping his chair back. "There is nothing to support homosexual behavior. Maybe it is really wrong."

Our eyes met, and I could sense the angst in his soul. This was an existential issue for him, and only I knew his struggle. I was feeling it, too, but it wasn't as raw for me. I tried to find some hope.

"OK, we know homosexuality existed. We know it was condemned by the church fathers, even if some of them were gay. There are glimpses of potential gay arrangements, but nothing can be proved. So our argument has to be one of progressive understanding or revelation. The early church fathers considered women as property, but that is no longer the case. Maybe we can argue the same kind of update needs to take place with regard to sexuality issues," I suggested, looking at their faces to see if they were buying it. Johnny was looking at the floor.

"That's a pretty weak argument, but that may be all we have," Avery observed.

"I'm sure Gregg will tear it apart," Glenn said.

"What's wrong, Johnny?" Inaya asked.

A tear worked its way down his cheek.

"Yeah, it's just a paper. As long as we make some kind of argument, we'll be OK," Shani offered. "We don't have to settle the matter forever."

Johnny looked up, and the weight of the world seemed to be crushing down on him. I held my breath when I realized what he was about to say. The long pause was hard.

"This is important to me," he said. "I'm gay, so it really matters."

The entire group leaned back in their chairs as if a sonic wave had hit them.

"I didn't see that coming." Glenn was the first to respond.

For some reason, his comment struck us as funny, and laughter circled the table. Johnny looked bewildered.

"Thank you for trusting us with something so important," Inaya said. *She's going to be a great pastor. She always seems to know just what to say.*

Johnny looked at me, and relief morphed into a smile.

"Wait! You knew?" Shani directed to me.

"I did."

"Why didn't you tell us?" Avery asked.

"It wasn't mine to tell."

"There's our argument!" Glenn exploded. "If God is calling people with different sexual orientations into the ministry, then who are we to go against it? It's just like Peter said about baptizing Cornelius' family. When God takes the lead, we have to follow!" He was already jotting notes before anyone could respond.

"Yeah, you're still OK with us, even if you were raised by foxes," Inaya said, punching Johnny on the shoulder.

"Thanks! That's a relief!"

"Does anyone else have any major secrets to share today?" Avery asked. Heads shook. "OK, then. Let's keep digging. These papers are due Wednesday."

With everyone's attention turned to their computers, I sank into thought and anger fired in my gut. *Gregg picked this topic on purpose to make me look bad. There are no grand arguments to refute his stance, only subtle suggestions and supposed inevitabilities. What if Gregg is right! No! It can't be! I have to make a case for myself, Johnny, and the rest of us.*

"You look intense," Inaya noted, drawing me out of my brooding.

"I'm frustrated. There is nothing here I can use to make a solid argument that people with differing sexual orientations belong in the church and in ministry."

"I'm just thankful we live in today's world rather than back then. At least you've made it this far," Shani said. "Doors are opening, even if slowly. God is progressively steering humanity toward love and liberation."

The light came on in my head, and I wrote my opening sentence. "As certain as the movement of time, God guides humanity forward in our understanding of God's liberating love."

Thursday, February 15, 2024

The corners of Alecs's mouth lifted ever so slightly as I walked toward her. *Could that be a smile?*

"Hey, Alecs."

"Hey."

"You look happy today."

"You haven't heard?"

"Heard what?"

"You need to pay attention to what's going on around you."

"I've been busy writing an important paper. What did I miss?" I sat down and rubbed my tired eyes. Long nights on papers were taking their toll.

"You look tired," Alecs observed.

"I am."

"What was this big paper about?"

"I had to defend the place of people with different sexual orientations in the church based on past theologians' writings. There wasn't much there to draw on, so it was hard to write."

"Did you succeed?"

"I don't know. The only thing I could come up with is the idea that we have gradually improved our understanding of God and God's ways and that we continue to do so today."

"Life would be easier without God and the Bible."

"Maybe. You haven't told me what I missed."

"A judge put a temporary ban on the law that denied my treatment. I get to resume it next week."

"Wow! I did miss a biggie! I'm glad, Alecs. That's a big deal."

"Yeah."

Friday, February 16, 2024

Excitement pulsed in my veins. The time before a tennis match always brought an adrenaline rush. Fortunately, I didn't have to miss a class since the match was in the afternoon. I walked onto the court, and Mellie greeted me.

"Brenau is not that good, so don't worry," she said.

"You're dressed out and have a racquet," I observed. It was the first time since her ankle injury.

"The doc says I can begin light practices, so I thought I'd warm you up."

"Thanks!"

I crossed the court and hit her a lob.

"I see you're playing first slot," she said, returning the ball. "That's impressive for a walk-on."

"Thanks! I'm surprised the coach put me there since I haven't been able to make all of the practices."

"She knows talent when she sees it."

After a few volleys, I asked, "How's the ankle?"

"I don't want to go full steam, but it's doing OK for this."

"I need to hit a few serves to finish warming up." She retrieved the balls as I served.

The coach called us in, and Mellie gave me a hug. I hugged her back, enjoying the closeness. *Stop that!*

"You've got this! If you don't have plans after the match, we should do something to celebrate," she suggested.

"You're pretty confident we're going to win."

"I'm sure of it!"

"OK, then. Let's do something after we win this match!"

We won 7-2, and I was quite satisfied with my victory.

"I'm feeling Mexican. How about it?" Mellie asked.

"Sounds great! Which place?" I gathered my racquet bag.

"I like Los Niños. It's my fav!" She grinned widely. *She is so cute! Stop it!*

"Los Niños it is! Do you want to meet there?"

"No, I'll pick you up. Text me your address."

She gave me her number, and I sent the address. "It's right across the street from the bookstore."

Checking her watch, she said, "Does six forty-five work?"

"Perfect."

I hustled to my apartment to get ready. *It's nice to make a new friend. I just wish I didn't feel attracted to her. That complicates matters. I haven't had these kinds of feelings since Liia.*

A cold wind was blowing when I walked to Mellie's car. Over tacos, she shared how she had come to the decision to go to nursing school at Emory. *Her blue eyes are mesmerizing!*

I shared how I ended up at Emory, not mentioning the gay part. *I should quit hiding who I really am!*

We finished dinner, and I still hadn't summoned the nerve to tell her I'm gay.

"I don't want to study tonight," I said on the way back. "Do you want to come in for hot chocolate?"

"You're so cute! Do you have anything stronger to put in it?"

"No, I'm afraid not."

"Well plain will have to do, then."

I heated the water and made the hot chocolate while Mellie was in the bathroom. Taking mine, I sat on the couch. I was surprised when she sat right next to me.

"I hope we get some snow this year," she said. "It's certainly cold enough."

"I love snow!"

She sat her mug on the coffee table and leaned into me. I tensed and nearly choked on the sip I had just taken. *What is she doing?*

She turned sideways and looked into my eyes. "You didn't know, did you?"

"Know what?"

"We really have to work on your gaydar," she said with a laugh. She snuggled back.

"You mean you're lesbian?"

Sitting back up, she said, "Duh, yeah."

"How did you know about me?"

"It was obvious to me when you caught me on the court and held on a little too long. I could tell you were attracted, too."

"I can't believe I missed that."

"I'm hoping for a little more than hot chocolate," she said and pulled me close.

Chapter 18

Friday, March 8, 2024

Mellie looked dejected as I approached the court. Coming back from her ankle injury hadn't gone as well as the doctor thought. She was still unable to compete. As I opened the fence, she came running and grabbed me in an awkward hug, my tennis bag flopping around.

"Hey, good looking!" she said.

"Hey, Mellie!" I hugged her back.

"I hope you're on top of your game today. This team destroyed us last year, eight to one."

"I'm feeling good! I like playing when it's cloudy. The sun's not a problem."

"I just hope it doesn't rain us out."

"Yeah. That would be a wasted effort."

"Where do you want to go for supper?"

"Let's go back to Los Niños. I feel the need for tacos!"

"Yeah, that would be fun!"

"Maybe you'll be back on the court in a couple of weeks. It can't be too much longer," I said, trying to give her some comfort.

"I hope so. I'm doing my exercises religiously."

"I know. You'll get there." I gave her another quick, reassuring hug. "Now get me warmed up." She grinned. I couldn't help but grin back. "On the court, Mellie."

It was a tough match, but I won. In the end, our team lost five to four. "That was better than last year," Mellie said. "I'll pick you up at six thirty?"

"I'll be happy to pick you up this time."

"I like your place better than my dorm."

"OK, but someday you have to show me your room."

"Sure, but it's just a dorm room."

"But it's *your* dorm room."

After dinner, we went back to my apartment. This was our third date, and I was enjoying getting close to her. We cuddled on the couch with hot chocolate.

"I'm going to miss you over spring break," I said.

"Me, too. Are you worried about the meeting?"

"I am. I have to decide whether or not to keep going with the 'don't ask don't tell' strategy or to tell them the truth."

"That's a big decision. I'm glad it's not as big an issue for nurses. What are you going to do?"

"I think I'm going to tell them." I felt my heart rate speed up.

"Are you sure?"

"No, I'm not sure. It's such a complicated game. As long as they don't know, I'm acceptable. If they know, they will probably shut the door on my ordination. I'm sick of hiding who I really am though. It's been going on for five years now." I plopped my mug on the coffee table too hard, and some sloshed out.

"Ugh!" I went for a paper towel to clean up the mess. "What do you think I should do?"

"I don't think I can tell you that. You're whole future may rest on the decision you make."

"Yeah, that's the problem."

Saturday, March 9, 2024

The meeting was scheduled for Thursday. On the drive home I went back and forth in my mind. *What do I do? Life will be easier if I don't tell. But I want to tell. I'm sick of hiding, like my true self is not OK. Maybe I'm not acceptable. But God wouldn't have called me if God didn't want me. Grace said it was time. Was that prophetic? God, please give me direction. I need you to guide me in this.*

Nothing. No voice from heaven. No sensation in my heart. I drove in silence for ten minutes. I was just about to turn the music back on when it hit. "I need to talk to Pastor Stephens!"

Somehow that realization put my heart at ease, and I finished the drive singing along with the radio.

Will had beat me home and came charging out to the car. I jumped into him for mutual bear hugs.

"Hey, Sis, it's great to see you!"

"You, too!"

"Any more dates with Mellie?"

"Yeah, we went out last night."

"Um hm. Does that make three now?"

"You've learned to count!"

He punched me in the shoulder. Mom and Dad came out. Mom grabbed me in a hug. Dad opened the back and hauled a suitcase into the house. Will signaled he wanted to talk more about Mellie later.

It felt good to be home. *I've gotten used to Dad's stand-off behavior, but it still digs a small hole in my heart.*

"Do you still have your big meeting this week?" Mom asked.

"Yeah, it's on Thursday."

"I hope that goes well."

"Thanks! Me, too."

Tuesday, March 12, 2024

I knocked on Pastor Stevens' door at eleven o'clock.

"Come in!" sounded through the door.

"Good morning," I said, walking into the office.

"Good morning to you, too. How is seminary going?"

"So far so good. I'm making As and Bs. I've been able to help out the tennis team, too."

"Sounds like good times." She brushed her brown hair over her shoulder. "You go back before the committee this week. It shouldn't be a big deal. They'll just be checking on your progress with seminary and if you still feel called."

"That's what I wanted to talk about. I'm thinking about telling them the truth."

"I see." Her hands tensed on the desk. There was a long pause. "I'm not sure that's a good idea. Why not just let it ride until you're ordained?"

"I think that's the problem. I'm tired of hiding who I am. I'm tired of letting things ride. They're going to find out eventually. Wouldn't it be better if I come clean now?"

She rested her chin in her hands. "To be honest, I have no idea. At this point, I don't see how you're going to get ordained. It's so frustrating. I do understand you're feeling the need to be true to who you are."

"It's just so irritating! If God accepts me, why can't they?" I tugged at my hair. "Sometimes I just want to pull my hair out!"

"OK. Maybe we need to consider options if you decide to come out to the committee. If they say your candidacy is ended, then what?"

"I don't know. Is there a way to appeal the decision?"

"Not that I'm aware of."

"Who made them all-powerful?"

"It's the way we're structured."

"So my only option would be to change denominations?"

"That's the only option I can see."

Her brow furrowed. I could tell she was hurting with me. "Knowing that you care helps a lot. I don't feel so alone."

"Thanks. I do care and wish this wasn't such an unfair process."

I stood to leave, and Pastor Stevens came around the desk. "Let's have a prayer before you go." She put her hand around my shoulder and prayed.

"Dear God, you created us and love us. I'm grateful for Willow and your call on her life. I pray you will guide her in this difficult decision and open the doors that need to be opened for her. Amen."

"Amen," I echoed.

Chapter 19

Thursday, March 14, 2024

Will poked his head inside my room. "Nervous?"

"Oh, yeah!"

"Have you decided what you're going to do?"

"I keep going back and forth. I wish God would give me a sign or something."

"It's got to be a hard decision."

"What do you think I should do?"

"I was afraid you'd ask that." He slumped against the door frame.

"Well? What do you think?"

"I think it would be best to address it now. If I were me, I wouldn't want to minister in a church where I had to keep my identity a secret. It's not a good long-term plan."

"You're right! That's what I've been missing! I can't keep going like this. They have to either accept me as I am, or I go somewhere else."

"Now you're talking!"

"OK, that settles it. I'm coming out this morning!"

I took a deep breath and let it out slowly. Relief and terror swirled inside. Steeling my nerves, I walked into the building to meet with the committee. I was ten minutes early.

"They're finishing up with another candidate. Please have a seat and they'll be with you in a few minutes," the secretary said.

Great! My nerves will have time to simmer.

The door opened and a young man stepped out with a big smile. "Thank you so much," he said, shaking hands with one of the committee members.

"We'll be with you in a minute, Willow," the committee member said, closing the door.

"It sounds like the meeting went well for you," I said to the young man.

"They approved me as a candidate! Good luck!" With excitement flowing in his wake, he left.

I remember that feeling. When they first approved me, I was floating on a cloud. But it wasn't me they approved. It was someone who conformed to their image of what a pastor should be. That's about to change.

Cold moved down my fingers when the door opened and Rev. Johnson called me to come in. I took my seat in the circle of six.

"Today is mainly a check-in meeting for you. We'll be looking at how seminary is going and how you've grown in your sense of calling," Rev. Johnson, who chaired the committee, began. "I trust you are passing your classes."

"I made As and Bs first semester, so I have a three point four GPA so far," I offered.

"That's great!" he said with a smile. "You're going to be a great addition to our church!"

"How are you feeling about your calling?" Rev. Hampton asked.

"I still feel certain that God wants me to be a pastor." I swallowed hard. *It's time. I have to do this.* "I have something I need to share with you."

They looked at each other before Rev. Johnson asked, "What is it, Willow?"

"You need to know that I'm homosexual."

Silence. Awkward expressions flowed around the circle. Rev. Hampton looked at her feet. I started to speak, but something told me to wait.

"Yes, that is something you needed to share with us," Rev. Johnson recovered. "I'm sure you are aware of the church's position that people living an active homosexual lifestyle are not ordained."

"What does that even mean?" *I can't believe I said that.* "If I'm homosexual but abstinent, that's OK? That doesn't make sense to me. If we can accept part of a person, why not the whole person?" I wiped my sweaty palms on my thighs.

"I understand that we are all sinners," Rev. Hampton began, removing her glasses. "We wouldn't ordain a person who made their living by thievery. We wouldn't ordain a heterosexual person who was promiscuous with many lovers, either. A person has to be at least trying to fight their sinful nature to be a pastor to others."

"But what if a gay person lives a dedicated life that is not promiscuous? What if homosexuality is not the sin?" I countered, somehow summoning boldness.

"This is a delicate matter for the church. I personally agree with you and believe people with a variety of sexual orientations can live faithful lives and be effective pastors. But that's not the position of the church, and I have to respect that," Rev. Myers said, crossing his arms.

"Does anyone have questions for Willow?" Rev. Johnson asked.

"I do," Rev. Roper said. "Do you intend to live a celibate life?" He leaned forward.

"I can't say that is my plan. I do hope to be married someday." He sat back with his brow knitting.

"Any further questions?" Rev. Johnson asked. No one said anything. "Willow, I believe we need some time to confer on this matter. I'm going to ask you to wait outside. We'll call you back in a bit."

Come on, knees! Don't buckle! My legs felt stiff, and I hoped I didn't look as awkward as I felt while walking out of the room. *Five people have control of my future!* I made it to a chair in the waiting area. The secretary gave me a kind but knowing look as I sat down.

Automatically, I pulled my phone from my pocket and opened the social media app. I scrolled but didn't take in anything I was seeing. I could tell they were talking, some of it even sounded heated, but I couldn't understand anything being said.

I wish I knew what they were saying! I have a feeling my candidacy is over. What's my next step? I sat the phone down long enough to wipe the sweat from my cold palms.

"Would you like some water?" The secretary asked. I could tell from her expression she had noticed my distress.

"No, thanks."

"Waiting is the hardest part."

"Yeah."

I sank back into my thoughts. *Lord, please help me get through this. You have a plan, and I'll have to trust that plan to work out. Maybe that's what I can tell them.*

I'll have to control my anger and not snap at them. I'll just accept their decision and move on.

The opening of the door snapped my nerves into high alert. "Miss Grier, will you please come back in?"

I walked back into the room a little more steadily than when I had left.

"We appreciate your honesty and being willing to tell us about your sexual orientation. That was a brave thing to do," Rev. Johnson said. "Unfortunately, we have come to the conclusion that we can no longer continue your candidacy. We wish you the best in your life and trust that you will find an outlet for serving God in a capacity other than as a minister."

"Thank you for considering me. God is the one who called me, and I will have to trust that God will open the doors needed for me to become the pastor I've been called to be. It may or may not be with this denomination, but I will continue to pursue the calling God has laid on my heart." *I got that out without breaking down! Thank you Lord!*

Rev. Johnson led us in a prayer and sent me on my way. It was when I closed the car door that I was flooded with emotions. *Now what do I do?* I laid my forehead on the steering wheel. *I can't believe they terminated me just like that! They're going against God's will for my life! There has to be something I can do. Don't I get a chance to defend myself?*

A tear dripped onto the center of the steering wheel. *Should I just drop out of seminary? Is there any point in continuing? What am I going to do, Lord? The river keeps flowing, but I don't know where it's going.*

Chapter 20

Saturday, March 17, 2024

I put the last bag down and plopped onto my bed. It was dark. "We should have waited till tomorrow to come back," I said to Romeo and Sophie, who had hopped onto the bed with me.

I had elected to return to Atlanta Saturday rather than Sunday because I didn't want to have to deal with church after my meeting with the committee. *I should turn more lights on.* I remained on the bed with only the light in the kitchen. My body felt heavy. I couldn't seem to lift it.

Tears appeared, and I wiped my cheeks. *Why am I here? I should be working toward a master's degree in psychology instead of going to seminary. Dad is right. I'm just fooling myself. I'll never be ordained. I've wasted nearly a year of my life. Maybe I should go back and tell them I plan to live a celibate life and will not be a practicing homosexual. Is that what you want, God? Do you want me to live a half-life?*

In the quiet darkness, there was no answer. Romeo startled me when he rubbed his chin on my elbow. "Thanks for the comfort. You're a sweet kitty." He pushed onto my lap, and a tear dropped on the top of his head. I wiped it away. He purred anyway.

I have to stop this! Crying will not help at all. I moved Romeo off my lap and walked to the kitchen, where I sat down.

Elbows on the table and head in my hands, I tried to think through what to do with my life. *That's too big of a decision for now. I can't figure out my future while my heart is so down. OK, let's think short term. What's my next step? Supper. I should eat, but I'm not hungry. I don't feel like going out or cooking. Maybe I'll just have cereal.*

I started to get up when my heart heard plain as day, "I'm using you here."

I froze halfway up from my chair and listened. Alecs came to mind. "I do seem to be helping Alecs. Is that what you mean?"

My thighs started to burn in the half-standing position, so I sat back down. "Is helping one person worth a whole year of my life? Do you want me to finish seminary?"

My questions seemed to land on the floor rather than rising to heaven. *Maybe that's it. God brought me here to make a difference in Alecs's life.* "I'll just have to trust you to lead me to the next step."

Feeling more composed, I got up and poured a bowl of Honey Nut Cheerios.

Sunday, March 18, 2024

The Musketeers and Mellie all returned to campus Sunday afternoon, and we planned to get together for supper at Athens Pizza. Mellie came over early.

Hearing her knock, I slung open the door. She grabbed me in a hug. "I'm so sorry about the committee's decision. How are you holding up?"

Hugging her tightly, I said, "I feel better after last night. I felt God told me I'm supposed to be doing what I'm doing even if it's only to help Alecs."

"You met me, too," she said with a grin.

"That's true! And I'm glad!" I looked into her eyes and pulled her in for a kiss. "I did miss you!"

"I missed you, too. I say we skip the pizza and stay here."

"You're a temptress!"

"Maybe. I can see you're tempted!"

"Yeah, but we told everyone we'd be there."

Mellie did manage to make us a few minutes late. We found the table, and Shani said, "Glad you two could make it! I can't imagine what held you up!"

"Hey, everybody! I'm sure you've probably guessed, but this is Mellie,"

"It's nice to meet the person we've heard so much about!" Inaya chirped.

We took our seats and ordered, then Glenn said, "Our first order of business is to find out how you're handling the committee's rejection."

I knew this was coming, but I didn't expect them to jump right on it! OK, you can do this. No tears! "Fair to terrible is the honest answer. Last night I was wondering why I should even finish seminary. I sensed God saying that God put me here to help Alecs if nothing else. Today I feel like finishing seminary is the right thing for me, even if there is no future in it. I don't know. I'm such a messed up human!" I willed the tears not to start.

Mellie put her hand on my thigh, and Inaya said, "The committee's decision was just a setback. I feel confident in that. We will help you fight this thing. You are going to be a great minister. The worst case scenario is that you have to change to a denomination that will welcome you."

Mellie squeezed my thigh. Her eyes betrayed that she was near tears, which turned on mine. "Thanks," I managed, using the napkin to wipe my face.

"One for all and all for one! Isn't that the Musketeers' saying?" Glenn offered.

"All we need is swords!" Avery laughed, holding up her hand like she had a sword. We all reached to the middle of the table, putting our hands together.

The waiter arched an eyebrow as she waited for us to lower our hands so she could put the pizza on the table.

"Y'all do know how to make a gal feel better," I said.

With me feeling totally supported, the chit-chat moved to what everyone did over spring break. I noticed Johhny hadn't said a word, which wasn't unusual, but his face seemed tense.

"Are you OK, Johnny?" I asked.

"Yes." Under the scrutiny of everyone watching him, he recanted. "No. I met with my committee over break, too. I didn't tell them I'm gay. I'm afraid the same thing will happen to me. I feel like a fake."

My heart went out to him. "I certainly understand how you feel. We each have to make our own path. You have to trust that you are doing the right thing for you."

"Yeah," Shani said. "Personally, I don't think our sexual orientation is any of their business, anyway. What should matter is our ability to minister in the church."

"Amen! Preach it, sister!" Glenn responded. The waiter happened by and arched the other eyebrow.

"Our waiter thinks we're nuts!" I observed.

"She may be right," Inaya laughed.

"All you people are precious in God's eyes, and that's what counts. We're going to need strength to battle on, so let's eat!" Glenn said.

Thursday, May 2, 2024

"Hey Alecs," I said, sitting down across from her.

"Hey."

I was feeling sad. This was my last day to visit before summer break. *I hope Alecs doesn't pick up on my sadness.*

"Any news on the appeal?"

"Yeah."

I waited. We had gotten past the waiting game over the year. I finally caved. "Well? What's the news?"

"They're going to appeal."

"That's great! You don't seem happy, though."

"It doesn't matter."

"What do you mean, 'It doesn't matter?'" I was confused. I propped my chin in my hand and waited. She seemed uncomfortable, so I looked away. *I'm going to wait you out this time. I need an answer here.*

She looked down to the floor. Instead of joy or hope, her eyes seemed filled with sorrow. I squirmed, feeling a desire to know what was going on. *I wish she would hurry up and explain!*

After what seemed an hour, she looked up and a tear escaped down her cheek. I fought the need to ask what was wrong and waited.

"You're leaving."

My tears jumped to join hers. I reached across the table and she took my hand. "I'm sad, too. I should be able to get this placement next year, though. Let's focus on that." I wiped tears with my other hand. "We should see each other again in twelve weeks."

She looked into my eyes. *Is that a glimmer of hope?* Letting go of my hand, she reached into her pocket. After a hesitation, she slid a paper across the table.

Mountain of Valleys

Down
Pulls always
To darkness

Time
Crushes on
To change

Light
Flickers briefly
To hope

Life
Lifts once
To joy.

-Alecs Taylor
4/30/24

I was stunned. No words came. I reached and took her hand again as my tears cranked back up. She smiled. She actually smiled! I finally found words.

"That's beautiful, Alecs. I'm glad we found a moment of joy in these dark valleys." I handed the paper back across the table. Alecs didn't take it.

"For you."

"Thank you." I hugged the paper to my chest. *Should I take a photo of it and leave Alecs the original? I don't want to.* I realized the poem meant a lot to me.

"You have dark valleys."

"But you have been my joy." I answered.

Alecs squeezed my hand. "Me, too."

Michelle signaled it was time to leave.

"I'll write to you over the summer," I said and squeezed her hand.

"Thanks. I hope I see you again."

"You will."

Michelle gathered our group in the conference room for a farewell.

"Thank you all so much for your service here this year. You have had a great impact on these inmates' lives. I am grateful for the ways you have reached out and shown compassion and caring. That gives them hope for the future.

"I want to give a special shout out to Willow. The relationship you were able to build with Alecs may have saved her life. You will make a great pastor, Willow.

"Once again, thank all of you for your work here. I hope to see all of you back next year."

I hadn't told Michelle about the committee's rejection. Apparently Alex hadn't either. I walked out with dejection and joy swirling in my soul. *I'm so happy I was able to have an impact in Alecs's life. That makes me want to go on and be a pastor. But the committee is going to block that path for me.*

The words of Grace's letter surfaced. "You have chosen a difficult path... People will stomp on you as hard as they can." *You were right, Grace. This path is hard.*

That's how my first year of seminary ended. I felt God's call on my life. I felt a drive to minister to people. My work with Alecs had cemented that drive. If only the church could see that I have potential. *I have no idea what the future holds.*

Chapter 21

Saturday, August 17, 2024

Will pulled me into a hug before getting into his car. "I had a blast this summer! Thanks for housing me!"

"It was fun. I'm glad you stayed with me," I said, feeling sad that he was leaving. Since I had to pay for my apartment to keep it, we elected to spend most of the summer in Atlanta, exploring the sites. One of my favorites had been a show at the Fox Theater.

"You take care of yourself and keep the faith."

"You, too," I said. He got into his car and headed back to Hawksville. I stretched and walked back into my apartment. "It's Saturday afternoon. What shall we do?" I asked Romeo and Sophie.

"Meow."

"Are treats all you think about?"

"Meow."

I put five little morsels apiece on the floor. "It's ninety-five degrees! Too hot to sit outside and read, even in the shade," I explained to my kitties. I tidied up the apartment, including deflating the air mattress on which Will had slept.

I'm feeling antsy. It took a while before I could put my finger on what was making me jittery. *I'm all alone until next week.* I hadn't realized that having several days on my own would make me anxious. Classes would start next week, and everyone but me was still away for the summer. Mellie, being from Fort Smith, Arkansas, was too far away for us to see each other. We had texted and chatted a lot, though.

I thought about Central Congregational United Church of Christ. I had dragged Will to visit a few times to see how it felt in case I decided to change denominations. They were super nice folks, and I felt totally welcome there. Not that I told anyone I was lesbian, but I believe they would have been supportive.

I continued to wrestle with what to do with my life after being rejected by the committee in March. I sat on the couch to ponder this for the millionth time. *Changing to the United Church of Christ would probably be the easiest route. But that just doesn't feel right, like it's a cop-out. Why can't my own denomination accept me? I should be able to find a path forward with them.*

And so went my thoughts, round and round and round. *I wish my heart would settle on something! This churning in circles is getting tiresome.*

I jumped when a knock startled me from my thoughts. *Who could that be?*

"Surprise!" Mellie yelled as I opened the door.

"Wow! You're a site for sore eyes! I was just dreading being alone for the next few days."

"I decided to sneak in and surprise you! I'm glad you didn't go back to Hawksville for the weekend. That would have been a crusher!"

"Don't just stand there, come in! You're looking good! How'd you get so tan?" I asked as she walked through the door.

"I spent a lot of time at the pool, remember?"

"Oh, yeah. I've been so wrapped up in my little crisis I forgot. You must be tired! Did you drive all the way from Fort Smith today?"

"No, I have an aunt in Memphis. I stayed there last night. So how's your soul today?"

"Spinning in circles. I'm tempted to go ahead and change denominations, but that just doesn't feel right. I don't know what to do."

"I know exactly what to do. We're going to have dinner, come back her for a movie and dessert, and you're going to forget all about that for a while."

I loved the mischievous grin when she said dessert! "That sounds marvelous!"

We settled into a booth at Los Niños and were so busy chatting about our summer that we didn't notice the waiter until he cleared his throat. "Sorry, we haven't even looked at the menu," I said.

"Can I get you anything to drink?" he asked.

"I'll have sweet tea," I said.

"Do you mind if I order a beer?" Mellie asked. She had never drunk alcohol in front of me before.

"No, that's fine."

"Do you want to try one?"

I gave her an exasperated look. "I've had beer before, silly."

"You have? Well, why don't you join me?"

"You're a bad influence!" I couldn't resist her mischievous grin and changed my tea order for an IPA.

"I missed being with you over the summer," I said, sinking into those blue eyes.

Thursday, August 22, 2024

"I didn't think today would ever get here! I can't wait to see Alecs!" I explained to Romeo and Sophie as I got ready to go to my Contextual Education placement. I had written to her every week during the summer, and she had written back. After much encouragement, she had agreed to let her lawyer file an appeal. I was still baffled at why she resisted the idea.

After helping get the juniors oriented to the facility, I entered the room to find Alecs sitting in her usual spot. "Hey, Alecs! It's good to see you! How are you feeling?"

"Hey. It's good to see you, too."

"Have you heard any more about the appeal?"

"Yeah."

"Well?"

"They're filing it next week."

"That's great! Do they think there's a good chance you'll win?"

"It doesn't matter." *I thought she seemed down.*

"What do you mean? This is a big deal. You might get out of here."

"Here or not, I'm still in prison. It doesn't matter."

"Why do you say that?"

Silence. *The old waiting game.*

"You need to pay attention." *I'm paying attention! What is she talking about?*

"I'm paying attention. I've heard everything you've said."

"To the world around you."

"OK, I'm confused. What have I missed this time?"

"They ended the hold."

The hold? What is she talking about? I searched my mind till the light came on. "You mean the ban on your medications is back in place?"

"You don't pay attention."

"When did that happen?"

"Last week." *I didn't miss it by long!*

"I'm so sorry. I'm sorry I didn't know, too." I could feel the heaviness settling in Alecs's heart. A dark cloud shrouded my soul, too. *This is going to be hard. I have to fish for hope.* "Have you heard any more from the ACLU? Aren't they still challenging this?"

"It won't matter."

"Why not? We have to fight this."

"It will be too late."

The urgency hit me in the heart. *Alecs needs those medications now. She can't wait another year or two while the legal wheels grind.* "I understand. You need the medicine now. There has to be a way to fight this. Have you asked your lawyer about it?"

"I haven't seen the lawyer."

"OK. That's where I'm going to start. Maybe we can file a petition or something to have you exempted from the law. There has to be something we can do!" My heart raced as I battled the sense of panic rising in my mind.

Friday, August 23, 2024

It didn't matter how many times I looked at my watch, class just wouldn't end! Class started at nine. I had called before class, but Alecs's lawyer's office wasn't open till nine.

As soon as the professor said class was over, I bolted out the door and found a quiet place to call. *Ugh! I had to leave a message! She couldn't say when I would hear back, even though I told her it was urgent.* So the waiting began.

Our last class ended at two.

"Something wrong with your phone?" Inaya asked.

She caught me standing in the hall staring at it, willing it to ring.

"You sure seem antsy today," Shani said.

"I'm waiting on a call back from Alecs's lawyer. The state is stopping her medicine again, and I want to find out if there is anything we can do."

"Aren't they appealing her case?" Glenn asked.

"Yeah, but she's more worried about the medicine than getting out."

"But if she gets out, maybe she can get the medicine in another state," he explained.

"Glenn, you're brilliant! I have to go see Alecs. Now!"

Not thinking, I dashed over to the Youth Detention Center. "I need to see Alecs," I told Michelle.

"I'm afraid you can't. She's still in class."

My heart sank. *I really want to get Glenn's idea to her.* "OK, I can wait."

"Can I ask what is so important?"

"A friend had the idea that if her appeal works she could get the medicine she needs in another state."

"That might be just what she needs to get her interested in getting out of here! If you don't mind waiting about thirty minutes, I think you should be the one to tell her."

"I don't mind. I have plenty of reading to do."

Chapter 22

Saturday, September 21, 2024

They'll just have to live with a dirty apartment! The Musketeers were coming for our usual study session, and with the papers and major test next week, I didn't take the time to clean as usual. I was deep into researching my paper on the Gospel of Luke when I heard a knock.

"Someone's early," I told Romeo, who was nestled in my lap. "You have to get up." Grudgingly, he jumped down. I could see Johnny through the screen since I had left the door open to the nice fall weather.

"Hey, Johnny! You're early." *I hope that didn't sound like I didn't want him here yet!*

Johnny came through the door with a heavy cloud following.

"What's wrong?" I asked.

"Is it that obvious?"

"Yep."

"I'm worried."

"Do you care to explain?" I was stressed and a bit testy.

"What if I meet someone?"

"I'm guessing that would be a good thing?"

"Would it?"

"Johnny, please get to the point!... I'm sorry, I'm stressed with all we have due next week." I took a deep breath. "Have a seat." He sat at his usual spot around the table.

"So how could meeting someone be a bad thing?"

"It would be harder to keep my… gayness from the church."

I started putting up the dishes that were sitting beside the sink. *I don't know what to say to help.* I finally went with curiosity. "Have you met a guy?"

"No… Well, I think this guy was flirting with me at the grocery store."

"Are you going to ask him out?"

"No way. I can't risk being outed."

"I can't tell you what to do. I've made my choice, and I'm going to have to live with it. I think you will have to decide what is most important to you. Do you want to please the church or yourself?"

"It sounds like an existential crisis brewing," Shani said, letting herself in.

Johnny's face turned bright red, and he went silent.

"It's OK, Johnny. I'm on your side," Shani consoled. "This is ridiculous!"

"Me?" Johnny asked.

"No, I mean people feeling they have to choose between their calling and being who they were created to be. We have to change the system. That's just all there is to it!"

"I wish we could," I said.

"I don't think there is any wishing to it. It is something we need to start planning for. We have two years to change a centuries old position!" Shani plopped her backpack onto the table.

"How could we do that?" I asked, feeling hope stirring.

"I have no idea," Shani laughed. "But we have to try. Not just for you two, but for everybody out there who is being called into the ministry but the doors just won't open."

"Preach on!" Glenn called as he opened the door. Avery and Inaya followed right behind. *Shani's always a bit loud. I'm not surprised Glenn heard her from the parking area.*

"Who are we busting open doors for?" Inaya asked as she took her usual seat at the table.

"Willow, Johnny, and everyone else who is called but the church refuses to ordain," Shani said.

"That's a great idea, but we have two major papers and a serious test next week. I think studying has to take priority today," Avery pointed out.

"Agreed," Glenn said. "Let's let this simmer over the week and see what kind of ideas we can come up with. We can have a brainstorming session next Saturday, assuming we still have brains to storm with."

With that we drifted into our own worlds, either studying for the test or working on the papers.

Thursday, September 26, 2024

"It's two weeks till your appeal hearing. Are you excited?" I asked Alecs.

"I guess," she said flatly.

"You don't sound excited." I looked into her eyes and saw a troubled soul. "What's wrong, Alecs?"

Silence. *This must be big. She hasn't done this in a while.* I waited. I had begun thinking about what I would say at the hearing since Michelle had asked if I would be willing to testify as a character witness.

"I think I deserve to be here," she finally said.

"No you don't. You acted in self-defense. They were attacking you."

"I shouldn't have hit the guy so hard."

"That may be true, but at the time you were in danger. You were trying to save yourself from being beaten."

"Yeah. … But still… I wanted to hurt him for what he said about me."

"I see. You feel guilty for reacting with violence, and you're having trouble getting past that."

"Yeah."

"Alecs, that doesn't mean you need to be stuck in prison. What you need is to work on forgiving yourself so you can move on. That was an ugly day, but it was only one moment in one day. You are a wonderful, sensitive person. The world needs people like you. We need to get you back on track so the world can reap the benefits of what you have to offer."

She looked at me like I had lost my mind. I waited to see if my words would register.

"That's kind of you, but the world sees me as a freak."

"Why do you say that?"

"They are even banning books about people like me… about people like us."

"What are you talking about?" My eyes scrunched in confusion.

"You really need to pay attention."

"You're right. I keep my nose stuck in books all the time for school. So enlighten me."

"People have started a crusade to ban books that reference trans and homosexual people. They are having them removed from libraries. It's just like the rise of Nazi Germany."

How could she know about the beginning of the Nazis? This is one smart cookie! "That is scary. How do you know all of this stuff?"

"I pay attention and read." She looked exasperated, like I should have known that.

"Where is that happening?"

"In conservative areas all over the state. Certain people have decided they know what is right for everyone and plan to force us to live like they want."

"Yeah, I'm living that nightmare, too, when it comes to my ordination."

"I may be safer in prison."

"How can you say that? Remember the broken rib?"

"Yeah. I guess it's not safe anywhere."

I searched my soul for a lifeline for Alecs to cling to. "All I know is that we need to get you ought of here so you can resume your medication, even if it means traveling out of state to get it. Then we can worry about the rest of the world."

Alecs looked at the floor. I sensed sadness. "What is it?" I asked.

"If I get out, I won't see you anymore."

That hit like a ton of bricks. *What can I say to that? I don't want to lose contact with her.* "We will just have to find a way to stay connected. I don't want to lose touch with you, either." *I really meant that.*

She reached for my hand and squeezed it.

Saturday, September 28, 2024

Whew! What a week! I had survived two major papers and a test. I stretched and took my coffee out to the patio. It was a beautiful fall morning.

I took that wonderful first sip and sat back. *I have to come up with some ideas to convince the committee to consider me for ordination. Today is the day!*

I scoured my mind looking for ideas. *A letter? They have already rejected me in person. I don't think a letter will impress them. I didn't get a chance to plead my case, though. Maybe more of a paper discussing scriptural references?*

That's a possibility. I could talk about the things Grace taught me and help them see that the Bible is more against licentious behavior than homosexuality itself.

I relaxed and watched a gentle breeze rustle the leaves, satisfied I had a contribution to make this afternoon. After finishing my coffee, I lingered a moment and said a prayer for Will, Mellie, and for the members of the Musketeers. *I can't put off housecleaning any longer.* I willed my body into motion and tackled cleaning.

Our little group gathered at two. "Have you ever wondered why we always sit in the same spots?" Avery asked.

"We're creatures of habit," Glenn replied.

"I think it cuts down on decision making so we can concentrate on more important things," Inaya offered.

"People do the same thing in church. I think it's comforting to know we have a place in the world," Shani said.

"I wish I had a place in the world," Johnny grumped. "Did anyone come up with a strategy to get us ordained?"

"I think I'll write a paper to the head of the committee explaining how the scriptures don't refer to homosexual people living faithful lives. Maybe it will get them to reconsider," I offered.

"I was thinking the same thing," Glenn said. "If we all write letters, maybe it will get their attention!"

I noticed Shani smiling. "What is it?" I asked her.

"Those are good starting ideas, but you're setting your sites too low. This is a denominational issue. If we're going to make a change, we have to tackle the denominational leadership, and they won't cave with a few papers."

"What would you suggest, then?" Inaya asked.

"If you want liberation, we're going to have to fight. It will take demonstrations and protests at the denominational level. We will have to show up in numbers and demand change."

Silence fell over the group. *I had never considered protesting the way Shani was suggesting.*

"I believe you are right," Glenn said. "They're not going to listen to papers from seminary students. We'll have to get in their faces and insist they change their policy."

"How can six people do that? They will just brush us off," Avery replied.

"We'll have to recruit and organize," Shani answered. "We also have to be prepared for a long fight. It probably won't happen the first time. Just like we all like the same place at your table, leaders like to keep things the same. It's more comfortable that way."

"Are you saying we'll have to go to the national meeting?" Johnny asked.

"That's exactly what I'm saying. We probably need to show up at any state level meetings, too," Shani said.

"All over the country?" Inaya asked.

"Just Georgia and Tennessee, since that's where our two friends are fighting for ordination," Shani answered.

"That sounds like a lot of work," I said, trying to wrap my mind around all that it would involve.

"Most of the time, the right thing to do is difficult," Inaya responded. "I believe this is the right thing to do, the right time to do it, and we are the people to make it happen!

"Amen, sister!" Glenn said. "All for one and one for all!" We put our "sword" hands together.

Chapter 23

I arrived at the courthouse fifteen minutes early. I saw a woman who looked really nervous sitting on the front row. *That must be Alecs's mom.*

I introduced myself. "Hi, I'm Willow…"

A smile spread and before I could say anything else, she jumped up and held out her hand." Willow! I'm so glad to meet you! Alecs talks about you all the time. I'm Janet, her mother."

"I'm so glad to meet you, too. I've been praying that this will go well."

"Thanks."

I took my seat in the second row, just behind Janet. A guard ushered Alecs in. Seeing her in handcuffs sent a sharp pain zinging through my heart. I waved to make sure she knew I was there. She acknowledged me with a nod.

I rehearsed my answers to the lawyer's questions while waiting and watching the proceeding begin. *I have come to know Alecs over the last year through my placement at the Detention Center for theology school. I have learned that Alecs is a sensitive and compassionate person. She continues to feel remorse for her actions. In fact, she initially refused to appeal because she believed she deserved the punishment. Since Alecs acted in self-defense, I believe the sentence is too harsh, and she should be released with time served.*

The lawyer had coached me on how to say what I believed in a way that would give Alecs the best chance. My mouth was dry, and I was terribly nervous by the time Mr. Clarkson, the lawyer, called me to the stand. I stumbled over a few words but managed to get out most of what I had rehearsed.

I watched Alecs's face as I testified. She was unreadable, a stoic mask. *I wonder what she is feeling.* I smiled at her as I walked back to my seat but saw no response.

Mr. Clarkson called Alecs to the stand and asked her to tell the three judges exactly what happened that day. The stoic mask remained as she began.

"I took a bag of trash to the dumpster for the coach. As I came back around the fieldhouse, Darin, Jason, and Tom were waiting. They started taunting me. 'Look at the queer! He doesn't know if he's a boy or girl! Let's help him figure it out!' Darin said.

"They started pushing me, knocking me against the wall. 'She must be a girl because she won't fight back,' Tom said. Darin punched me in the stomach, and I doubled over. Tom set his bag down, and I saw the bat.

"Darin backed up and took a kick at my nose. I moved just in time, grabbed the bat, and swung just as hard as I could. I hit Darin right in the head, and he hit the ground. Tom and Jason ran. Darin was bleeding.

"I didn't know if Tom or Jason would call an ambulance, so I left him there and ran into the fieldhouse, yelling for the coach to call an ambulance.

"Darin was badly wounded and was hospitalized. I understand he has brain damage. I feel terrible about what I did. I didn't mean to hurt him so badly, but they were going to hurt me."

Tears had broken through the mask, and Alecs wiped them away. At the end of the hearing, the judge in the center, Judge Jackson, announced that they would issue a verdict a week from today.

My heart sank. *I was hoping Alecs would be released today! We have to wait a whole week to find out!*

Friday, October 11, 2024

I sat on the patio, armed with a computer and note pad. It was an amazing day. The dogwood leaves had begun to change color, and the air was crisp and clear. The sun was dropping low in the sky. I went back in for a light jacket.

Last Saturday we had divided up tasks to begin planning our movement to get ordination opened up to people with different sexual orientations and gender identities. My task was to identify when and where the various meetings would be held.

The state meetings for Georgia and Tennessee were both scheduled for the summer. *That's good! They won't conflict with school.* I couldn't believe that the denominational meeting was scheduled the week of spring break. *That's got to be a sign!*

I started reading over news articles covering last year's meeting. "Among other legislation, the leaders expect to field proposals to change the denomination's stance against ordaining homosexual people. 'This comes up every year, and it's just a distraction. We will defeat it again and move on,' one leader said, who requested to remain anonymous."

I jotted a note on my paper. "Need to identify who is bringing proposals to change stance. Could be allies."

I heard a car pulling in as I sat my pen down. *Mellie!*

"Hey! I'm glad to see you!" I said as she opened the car door. She had started her clinical rotations, and we didn't get to see each other as often as I would like. She had gone by her room to change before coming over.

"Hey to you, too!" she said as I grabbed her in a hug. "We should probably move this party inside, away from prying eyes. What are you working on?"

"We're planning to organize protests against the denomination's stance against ordaining homosexuals and anyone else who is 'different.'" I said, making air quotes.

"That's ambitious! Don't you think it would be easier just to change denominations?"

"It might be easier, but I don't think it's the right thing to do. I keep thinking back to how Grace said, 'It might be time.' She was a prophetic soul. I feel it's time to try to change things."

"You go, girl! And I'll help any way I can."

"How do you feel about joining a protest?"

"I've never done that before, but I'm willing to give it a shot."

"If I promise to behave, do you want to sit on the patio?"

"I'd rather you didn't behave," she said with her signature mischievous grin.

Saturday, October 12, 2024

A weak knock drew my attention. *That has to be Johnny!* My prediction was confirmed when I opened the door.

"Hey, Johnny!" He walked in looking sad. "You look down today. What's wrong?"

"I don't think there's any use in continuing."

"In continuing what?"

"Seminary. Ministry. Life."

"That's dismal." *I wish I hadn't said that!* "I mean, that's no way to talk. Why would you say such a thing?"

"I don't see how anything we do will make a difference. The church is a big organization and is set on its position. They're not going to listen to little peons like us."

"That may be true, but if there are enough of us demanding change they will eventually *have* to listen. Look, Johnny, nobody said this would be easy. There are already petitions being brought before the general meeting about reversing the denomination's stance. We aren't the only ones protesting this."

"I wish I had your confidence." We were still standing in the living area.

"Come on in and take off your backpack. Maybe you'll catch the spirit when you hear what everybody has to say today."

We moved to the kitchen and Johnny plopped down at the table. He seemed heavy, like lead was flowing through his veins. *Something else is going on.*

"There's something else going on... Did you meet someone?"

He looked at me with wide eyes. "Uh... How could you tell?"

"Woman's intuition, I guess. Tell me about it."

"I was eating at the cafeteria, sitting by myself as usual. This gorgeous guy sat down across from me, and we got to talking. We're going out to dinner tonight."

"That's great! We get to meet him!"

He looked down at the table. "No, we're going to a different restaurant."

"I see. Well, I hope you have a good time, but we'll miss you. Next time you either have to bring him with you or tell him it will have to be another night."

He looked up and grinned. "OK." He seemed to sink even lower in the chair.

"Now what?" I asked.

"I'm afraid I will like him."

"And that's bad because?"

"It will end my chance of ordination if I fall in love. I need to stay single."

I ran my fingers through my hair and tugged. *This is such a hard position to be in. Why does it have to be this way? What can I say to that? Faith! It's a matter of faith!*

"It's scary to pursue a calling that we may not be able to fulfill. Knowing our fate lies in the hands of a conference of traditionalists is daunting. I think it's a matter of faith. We have to keep the faith and press on, trusting God will open the doors for us. This is a lot bigger than the two of us. If God wants us in the ministry, then I believe it will happen."

I had trouble reading Johnny's face. He started laughing. *Now I'm really confused.* I waited and watched. He laughed so hard tears started to flow. I couldn't help but join in.

Finally I recovered enough to ask, "Do you mind telling me what we are laughing about?"

"I have no idea!" he managed.

"You two are having fun!" Glenn said as he led the others through the door.

"What's so funny? We want in on it!" Inaya asked.

I wiped my tears and answered, "I think we're having a cathartic moment." I looked at Johnny, hoping he would explain. He shook his head.

"The stress of being gay and trying to get ordained is getting to us. The next thing I knew, we couldn't stop laughing," I offered.

"OK, then. We have a mission to plan," Shani said, opening her computer. "This is what we have so far: sending letters to the local committees and state leaders and picketing at the national meeting."

"Picketing? I don't remember any one mentioning picketing," Avery said. She looked nervous.

"How else will we get their attention?" Shani answered. "To create change, we're going to have to put some real pressure on the leadership. We'll need national news coverage with enough attention to make them rethink keeping the status quo."

"Do you think we'll get arrested?" Avery asked.

"No, I don't. We have to keep this protest peaceful. We want the moral high ground so they have to take us seriously," Shani said.

"You seem to know a lot about protests," Inaya observed.

"Our people have been doing this for a long time," Shani answered.

"I've been thinking about the letters," Inaya said. "I think it's going to take more than six. What if we recruit other people to help us?"

"I want to ask Gregg!" Glenn joked.

"That's a great idea, Inaya," Shani replied.

"Hey, I know someone who's at Duke. Maybe he could get a campaign going there!" Avery offered.

"I have a friend at Columbia," Inaya said. "I'm sure she would be willing to help."

"I have a friend at Vanderbilt. She's not in the divinity school, but she might could recruit some folks."

"Now we're talking! If we could get hundreds of letters coming in, they might pay attention," Glenn responded.

"What we need are the names and addresses of everyone we want to send letters to. Then we can give out that information so people can write one letter and send it to each person," Inaya said.

"So efficient!" Glenn observed. "You've thought a lot about this."

We continued brainstorming and making plans. I actually felt hopeful we could make a difference. *I hope Johnny feels the same.*

Chapter 24

The hearing to receive the appeal verdict was set at 3:00pm. I had arranged to skip out on being at the Detention Center so I could go to the hearing. Once again, my heart sank when Alecs entered in handcuffs.

I rubbed my sweaty palms on my thighs. *I'm so nervous! Lord, please let Alecs go free. She needs this desperately.* The prayer helped a little, but I was still anxious.

It seemed like forever before the judges came in. After the preliminaries, Judge Jackson began to speak.

"We have considered the arguments in this case carefully. The defendant committed a violent act that severely injured another student. That is a serious matter.

"On the other hand, it is the court's opinion that the defendant was acting in self-defense. Because we believe this young man acted in self-defense, our ruling is that he be released with time served and continue under probation for two years."

I nearly clapped.

"Young man," (*I noticed Alecs cringe when the judge referred to him as male*) "I expect you to refrain from violence during your probation. Another incident will land you back in prison. Do you understand?"

Alecs nodded her head.

"The prosecution has the right to appeal, if they feel the need to, but I wouldn't advise it. I believe the original verdict was an error, and I don't believe an appeal has any chance to succeed."

I love the way the judge glared at the prosecuting attorney when he said that.

As soon as he struck the gavel, I raced toward Alecs. I hit the brakes when I realized her mother should get the first opportunity to congratulate her.

Tears flowed down Janet's cheeks. "I'm so thankful that you're coming home," she sobbed.

"Me, too," Alecs said.

Michelle touched my shoulder. "You helped make this happen. I'm proud of you."

"Thanks. Alecs is special, and I'm glad she is getting freed."

Janet turned but kept her arm around Alecs's shoulder. They took a couple of steps in our direction. "Thank you so much for what you did to get Alecs set free. This would never have happened without the two of you."

"You're quiet welcome," Michelle said.

I nodded, having difficulty controlling my emotions. I choked down a sob and said, "Can I have a hug?"

Alecs lifted her arms. "The only sad thing about today is I won't see you anymore."

"You can't get rid of me that easily," I said as the tears spilled out. "I plan to stay in touch all the time. Your mom might even let me come visit."

"That would be wonderful," Janet said. "Alecs has told me all about your visits. She really likes you."

"I really like her, too."

We walked out of the courtroom with Alecs in the middle and Janet's and my arms around her shoulders.

Saturday, October 19, 2024

I walked out onto the patio with my coffee and computer. It was too chilly, even with my long sleeved t-shirt, so I went back for a jacket. The sun filtered through the leaves, giving a stained glass effect with the fall colors.

I sat and admired God's handiwork. *Thank you for this beauty!* The first sip of coffee was delicious. *Thank you for coffee, too!*

We had agreed to have the letter we would send ready today. The week had been so busy I hadn't had a chance to think about it until this morning. I leaned back to ponder.

I have to justify my existence yet again. This time, my ordination depends on what I say. Lord, please give me ideas!

How can I communicate that the stance of the church needs to be changed in a way that they will hear and understand? My argument needs to be forceful but not condemning. Hmmm.

I sipped coffee and centered my mind, listening for the Spirit's guidance. I remembered scenes from my life, milestones along the way that led me to this moment. "It might be time." I heard Grace's words almost as if she were sitting beside me. *I wish you were here. I could use your guidance. I wonder if you can hear my thoughts when they are directed to you. OK, that last thought was random.*

I decided to start with Grace's words and began typing. "It might be time." *No, erase that.* "It is time. The church has reached a point in our understanding of humanity that we can no longer stick our heads in the sand and ignore the fact that God is calling people with a variety of sexual orientations and gender identities into the ministry.

"I am one of those people. God's call to go into the ordained ministry is very clear in my life. I have no doubts about it. Unfortunately, my church does. My local committee shut the door in my face."

Does that sound angry? Yeah, definitely. I need to rephrase that.

"Unfortunately, my church does. My local committee terminated my candidacy. Their reasoning was that there was no point in pursuing it further since the church's position is to not ordain 'practicing homosexuals.'

"I believe it is time to face the irrationality of that position. How can it be acceptable to ordain a homosexual person who does not admit they are homosexual and not one who does?

"I believe that God created every single human being on the planet. God gave some of us different sexual orientations and different gender identities, but we are all part of the created order. I believe that God does not view our sexual orientation or gender identity as evil. What is important for us, just as for heterosexual people, is to live a life of faith and love.

"If a homosexual, bi, trans, or any other person can believe in Jesus and strive to love our neighbor as ourselves, we can be just as effective witnesses for God as anyone else. If God has blessed us with gifts for ministry, why would the church turn its back and refuse to let us share those gifts?

"It is time. It is time for the church to look beyond one's sexual orientation or gender identity. It is time for the church to focus on the person and her/his/their gifts. It is time for the church to listen to God and follow. It is time for us to change church policy and catch up to what God is doing.

"It is my sincere hope and prayer that you will listen to God and open the doors of ministry to people like me."

I sat back and read through what I had written. I got goose bumps. *I think that will do!* I saved the letter on the computer and to a flash drive so I wouldn't risk losing it. *Now it's time to hunt down names and addresses for the people I'll send this to!*

Sunday, October 27, 2024

I went to worship at Cannon Chapel with the Musketeers. The free lunch afterward was always a perk.

"Are you still going to see Alecs today?" Inaya asked as we stood in line to build our sandwiches.

"I am, and I can't wait!"

"Where does she live?"

"In Smyrna. The map says it's about half an hour away, so that's not bad."

"I wish we could meet her," Avery said. "She sounds like such a neat person." *This from the person who wanted to help 'fix' my homosexuality last year!*

"Maybe we can arrange that. She's quite shy, but I'll ask in a few weeks. I think I need to give her time to settle into being back at home first."

After lunch, I drove to Alecs's home. It was a small, older home with tan siding that was loose in a few spots. I gathered my purse and looked up to find Alecs standing beside the car. A big smile lit her face.

"Hey!" I said, getting out of the car.

"You actually came!" She grabbed me in a hug.

"Of course I came. Did you think I wouldn't?"

"I am surprised. People usually prefer to stay away from me."

"Well, I'm happy to see you. How does it feel to be home?"

"A lot better! Come on in."

I noticed there was no silent hesitation in her responses. I think she's genuinely happy.

Janet met me at the door. "Thank you so much for coming. Alecs has been worried all morning."

"Alecs, you don't have to worry. You're important to me, and I want us to stay in touch."

"OK. Thanks." She gave me another hug.

"Are you sure this is the same Alecs I saw at the detention center? You seem happy."

She grinned.

"Have a seat. Can I get you something to drink?" Janet asked.

"Sure. What are the options?"

"Iced tea or coke."

"Iced tea sounds great." Alecs and I sat on the couch. "So tell me what you've been up to this week."

"Watching TV and playing video games."

"You're living the good life!"

She laughed. "Yeah."

"She also made a trip to North Carolina," Janet said coming in with three glasses of tea on a tray.

"Oh? Why did you go to North Carolina?" I asked, suspecting I knew the answer.

"I got my medicine," she said.

"This has been a good week, then!"

"Yeah."

"Wait, you also took a whole week off from school?"

"Yeah."

"When will you go back?"

"I'm not."

She's not going back to school? That can't be good.

"We're going to do home schooling," Janet said.

"I see. What do you think about that?" I asked.

She shrugged her shoulders.

"I'm afraid to put her back in the same environment," Janet explained.

"That makes sense," I replied, realizing that the kids who attacked her would still be there. "Are there any friends you'll miss?" *I feel like she needs some social interaction.*

"Not really," she answered.

An idea hit. "I wonder if there is a network of homeschooled kids who are trans."

                                    D. R. CASSADY

Janet's face lit up. "That's a great idea. What do you think, Alecs?"

"Yeah."

"Why don't you help me research that this week?" I asked, hoping to get her to buy into the idea.

"OK."

I could tell she wasn't sold on the idea. *With how long it took for her to open up to me, I can understand that.* "I realize that it's hard for you to open up to people. They haven't been exactly kind. But look what happened when we got to know each other. If you could make some friends that support you, that would be great."

"Yeah."

Chapter 25

Saturday, November 2, 2024

Doubt is a sneaky foe. It creeps in when least expected and subtly dismantles one's spirit, pulling out supports one by one.

I had been feeling so positive about our plan to protest our way to ordination. But this morning, doubt has been doing its work. *We can't change a system as large and set in its ways as the church. They won't listen to us. Ugh! This is all pointless.*

It was about time for the Musketeers to show up. *I have to pull myself together. I have to at least be strong for Johnny.* I jumped at the knock, jolted from my deep thoughts. "Come in, Johnny," I called. *He's always the one who's early.*

Johnny oozed through the door looking gloomy.

"Leave the cloud outside. I don't want it to rain in here," I joked, trying to lighten his mood. His expression told me he didn't get it and he wasn't in the mood for jokes. "OK, what's wrong."

"We're wasting our time with this protest idea. It'll never work."

I'm supposed to stay strong, but I don't think I can. "I was just thinking the same thing, to be honest. I don't see how this can possibly succeed. The church is too entrenched to change just because we say it's time."

"Do you think we should give up?"

The words "give up" sparked something in me. *I never give up! That's not in my DNA. I have to see this through. There's too much at stake!*

"No, we can't give up!" I barked and Johnny jumped. "There is too much at stake. We have to try as hard as we can. We have to knock on those doors until we can knock no more. This isn't just for you and me. It's for everyone being denied their calling."

Johnny's eyes were wide. *Maybe I came on a little strong.*

"Well, OK then. Whether there is hope or not, we have to keep pushing forward. But it's hard to live with the uncertainty. I want to know that I'm going to get to be a minister," Johnny replied.

"I wish I could have some certainty, too. Maybe that's what living by faith is about."

Johnny grinned. "You do know how to put a good spin on things."

I laughed.

"What's so funny?" Glenn asked as he and the others walked in. *He and Inaya are holding hands.*

"We have thrown in the towel and picked it back up again," I answered.

"Throwing in the towel is not allowed. We have to keep the faith," Inaya said. "With God on our side, all things are possible."

We settled down to take stock of where we were.

"Back to business, please. Twenty-seven people have signed up to write letters from Candler. Has anyone heard from the other seminaries?" Avery asked.

"Myra said she put up the message at Vanderbilt, but hasn't gone back to check it yet," I said.

"Sixteen from Columbia so far," Inaya stated.

"That's not exactly overwhelming," Glenn observed.

"But it's better than we had a month ago," Shani said. "I wonder if it would be better for people to get all the letters at once or have them come in over a period of time. What do y'all think?"

"My first thought is that if they come in all at once, the people will be overwhelmed and not bother to read them," Inaya responded.

"That's a good point," Shani said.

"Let's just let people send the letters in their own time and maybe it will cause a trickle effect," Glenn suggested.

We all looked at Shani like she was our resident expert.

Shani rested her chin on her hand. "That sounds good to me. It will be a lot easier than trying to time the mailing of so many letters."

"That's one issue down. Now we need to think about the protest." Glenn's practicality kicked in as he sought to keep us moving forward.

"Road trip!" Inaya exclaimed. "I've never been to St. Louis! We have to see the arch while we're there!"

"Absolutely," Avery replied. "I've never been there, either. Can we get there in one day?"

"I checked, and it should take about eight hours to drive," Glenn answered.

Inaya's enthusiasm is contagious. Our group is ready to take off right now! "We'll need two cars. I'll be glad to drive."

"I can drive, too," Inaya added.

"Great! We have the easy part settled." Shani called us back to task. "Now we need to think about the protest. Were you able to find who is sponsoring the proposal to allow ordination of homosexuals?"

"Not yet," I answered. "They haven't released the proposals that will come up. I'm sure there will be one, though."

"See if you can find out who sponsored it at the last general meeting," Shani directed.

"OK."

"We need to identify gay rights groups in St. Louis and try to get them to join us. I think it will take more than six folks to make an impression." Glenn jotted down a note.

"Ya'll, I just want you to know how much I appreciate this group. Our time together means so much to me," I said, feeling sentimental. "Your friendship is wonderful. Then you go above and beyond with helping Johnny and me fight for ordination. I can't imagine a better group of folks."

A moment of silence settled. Johnny broke it with, "Me, too." *He is a man of few words.*

Inaya held up her empty sword hand, and we all put our hands together.

Sunday, November 10, 2024

Alecs was waiting for me on the little front porch. I hurried from the car over to her. *She looks happy!*

"Hey, Alecs! How are you?"

"I'm good. How about you?"

We hugged. *I'm glad she lets me do that now.* "I'm good, too."

It was such a beautiful day that we sat on their little deck, which had a small table with two chairs. *I guess they don't have much company. Another hazard of having a trans child!*

"Your hair is growing."

"Yeah."

"What do you think about home school?" I asked as Janet brought out iced tea.

"I'll get you a chair, Mom," Alecs offered. She disappeared into the house and returned with a folding chair.

I caught myself before telling her that was mighty gentlemanly. "That was kind of you. How is school going?"

"It's boring, but I'm surviving."

"It's been quite a learning curve to get this set up," Janet said. "I think I'm working harder than Alecs!"

Alecs grinned, and I could tell she had something on her mind. "What is it?"

"I'm sure you haven't paid attention."

"Guilty! What did I miss this time?"

"There's going to be a protest against the book bans. I'm going to be there!" she said with the biggest grin I've seen to date.

"Now, Alecs, I haven't agreed to that yet. It might be dangerous."

"But you will. Willow's going to be there, too."

"I am?"

"You have to be! You can't let them ban books about us without telling them what you think. It's at the capitol on November nineteenth."

"I guess you're right. I do need to be there," I replied, hoping I could fit it into my schedule.

"There's been angry backlash at some of these protests," Janet said. "I don't want any of us to get hurt."

"Mom, I have to take that chance. I need to help make the statement that it's not OK to control what everyone reads. It's not OK to impose their values on the whole country."

"She does make a forceful argument," Janet responded, still looking concerned.

"That she does, but if there's a chance of violence, maybe we should sit this one out," I offered, trying to support Janet.

"You're a bunch of wimps! I'm going if I have to sneak out."

I watched anger and concern knit together on Janet's face. I thought she might explode at Alecs. Instead I saw a battle to gain control of her emotions.

"Alecs," she said firmly, "I expect you to obey my decisions. I will consider the protest, and if it looks safe enough as we get closer to it, we'll go."

"Yes!" Alecs shouted.

"But, if there are reports of bad people counter-protesting, I expect you not to go."

"Yes, ma'am."

I decided to change the subject. "Did anything interesting happen this week?"

Alecs reached to her back pocket without a word.

DILEMMA

Created being
Living and growing

One says
Beautiful and good

one says
Hideous and trash

Created being
Believing which?

-Alecs Taylor
11/6/23

I wish she could get past the pain. I have to ask. "Have you decided yet?"

"Have you?"

I wasn't expecting that. Do I give her the easy answer or the truth? "You present a hard question. The easy answer is I've decided to believe the capital One. But that's not the honest answer. I want to believe the beautiful and good, but I find myself falling back into believing the hideous and trash. I think coming to fully believe in beautiful and good is a life-long process."

"Yeah."

Chapter 26

Nervous excitement pulled me awake before my alarm went off. Alecs's mom had agreed to let her go, so I assume there weren't any reports of dangerous groups coming. But still I was uneasy.

Why am I nervous? I hope nothing happens to mess up Alecs's probation. Maybe it's because I'm skipping class. I'm not the only one who will be there. Shani, Inaya, and Glenn are coming. There are probably others from seminary who will be there. I lay there stewing until the alarm jolted me out of bed.

Sophie and Romeo had learned to flee the bed before the alarm went off a long time ago. I had knocked one of them sailing when I jerked the covers off. They were waiting in the kitchen in treat position. I dutifully complied then got ready to go.

"I brought rainbow shirts for everyone!" Inaya said, pulling shirts out of a bag and handing them around.

"Nice!" I responded. "Thanks." I pulled mine over the shirt I was wearing. I navigated the four of us to the Lindberg MARTA rail station. We were meeting Alecs and Janet at the Five Points station.

"I hope they remembered the picket signs," Glenn said.

"Trust me. Alecs won't forget. She insisted on being the one to bring them just in case we backed out," I answered. Alecs and I had spent last Sunday afternoon making signs for the protest.

"There are more folks here than I expected," Shani observed as we got off the subway train.

"That's a good sign. Maybe the lawmakers will pay attention," Inaya said.

I scanned the crowd. "I don't see them."

"We can't help you," Glenn replied, having never met them.

I looked carefully away from the exit and didn't see them. "Maybe they went outside." We moved with the crowd up the escalator and there they were. Alecs had a smile on her face, and I introduced everyone.

"Let's go," Alecs urged. "We're going to miss everything if we just stand around."

We funneled through some barricades and approached the capitol. There was a mass of people gathered near the front steps. The gold dome gleamed in the sun.

"I want to get closer," Alecs said as she began pushing through the crowd. We followed, battling our signs and offering a constant stream of, "Excuse me."

"I think we're close enough," Janet stated.

"OK," Alecs agreed. She had walked us all the way to the far side of the crowd, and we were about a hundred feet from the steps. She waved her sign, which read, "FREEDOM MEANS READING WHAT I CHOOSE!"

I noticed a group of men gathering just beyond the barricades. They wore shirts that said, "This Is MY Country." There was an American flag. Underneath, in small letters, the shirts read, "WNA."

I did a search on my phone for WNA and cringed when I read, "White Nationalists of America." *Oh, no.* I looked up at my sign. *Maybe that wasn't such a good idea. What was I thinking?* It read, "CENSORSHIP IS A NAZI THING!" *I hope they stay behind the barricade.*

A tall, slender African American woman appeared on the top step, and the crowd applauded. She waved her hands to quieten us. "Thank you. Thank you. I'm Pat Swanson, and I'm the librarian at Morehouse College. Thank you so much for being here today to let our lawmakers know that we disagree with the level of censorship going on in our state."

The crowd erupted in applause. As the noise died down, she resumed. "While lawmakers think they are protecting people by banning books, they are actually enslaving us! They are enslaving us to their ideas and perceptions of reality. They are enslaving us to think only as they think and believe only as they believe.

"This is supposed to be a free country, open to all sorts of people and all sorts of ideas. Banning books is the banning of ideas. Banning books is the banning of people who do not fit the mold of the lawmakers. Banning books is a way to coerce conformity."

It was hard to hear her over the crowd. People were clapping and shouting. I heard something in the background. It sounded like a chant. The crowd quietened a moment, and I could make out the words. "My country. My country. My country."

Dread spread in my gut. *They have the right to protest just as much as we do. I just hope they stay where they are.*

Another speaker took the stand, and the chant behind me changed. "You do not belong. You do not belong. You do not belong." They sounded angry. *We need to get Alecs out of here.*

I worked my way over to Janet. "Have you noticed the men behind us?"

"Oh yeah. I'm keeping my eye on them."

"I think we need to get Alecs out of here."

"Good luck with that. We'd have to pick her up and carry her."

I knew she was right. Wait, is she starting a chant? Alecs was encouraging people to join her in shouting, "No bans on trans. No bans on trans."

She had an infectious spirit, and people were joining her. She came by our little group, waving her palms up to encourage us. I joined in but kept glancing back at the group of men. Their number had swelled. Their chanting was louder. *Are they trying to drown us out? That's not going to happen!*

I joined Alecs in recruiting people to chant along with us. It was working, and I got lost in the moment until I noticed something missing. The men's chanting had stopped. I looked around, and they weren't where they had been. I tensed when I saw one of their shirts moving through the crowd. *What are they up to?*

One of the men came up behind Alecs. *I've drifted too far away from her!* Alecs had moved off, too, in her quest to get the chant going. I started pushing through the crowd to get back. The man said something, and she span around. I could see she was responding.

Stay cool, Alecs. Don't make him mad. I tried to will my thoughts into her head. I caught Glenn's eye and pointed in Alecs's direction. He moved toward her.

The man pushed Alecs, and she bumped into people behind her. He grabbed her sign, broke the stick, and shredded the posterboard. Time seemed to stop. I could have moved faster through a sea of molasses.

A couple of the women whom Alecs had bumped into saw what was going on and turned on the man. I could tell they were shouting. I was getting closer.

The man shoved the women and picked Alecs up by the front of her jacket. I got there just as he drew back a fist. I launched myself into him, hitting the arm that held Alecs as hard as I could.

He stumbled and banged into people in the crowd. That prevented him from falling. Alecs picked up the broken end of her stick and charged the man. I caught her. "No, Alecs! We have to let it go. If you attack, you might end up back in prison."

She paused, her wide eyes searching mine. My temple exploded with the smash of a fist, and I went sprawling to the ground, catching myself with a nasty crack to my left wrist. He kicked me in the ribs with his boot. I rolled into a ball, clutching my wrist and readying myself for the next blow.

A blue uniform whizzed by. A police officer, gun drawn, ordered the man onto the ground. My wrist hurt more than my ribs. I got back to my feet, and my wrist was already swelling. I sent the man an angry glare as the officer cuffed him.

"Are you OK?" sounded from Glenn and Alecs. I looked down at my wrist.

"Ma'am, do you need an ambulance?" the officer asked, preparing to lead my attacker away.

"I don't think so."

"We'll take her," Glenn responded.

Alecs looked worried. "Your wrist is huge."

"I hate to leave this party, but we need to get you to a doctor. Do you think you can walk back to MARTA and then ride to your car? I could go get the car and come back for you," Glenn said. He looked worried, too.

Alecs tenderly put an arm on my shoulder. "I didn't mean for you to get hurt."

"It's OK. I'm glad it was me and not you," I answered, trying to reassure her.

"You're going to have a serious black eye," she observed.

Two uniformed men came rushing up. "Ma'am we're going to assess you," the taller of the two said. I gleaned they were paramedics.

"Look straight ahead please. I'm going to shine a light into your eyes." He aimed a penlight at my eyes and moved it from one eye to the other."

"Man! That looks nasty," the shorter one said. *What is he talking about?* The man with the light was eyeing my cheek. "Her wrist looks broken."

The taller one looked down. "Yep. We'll be happy to transport you to the hospital, or you can go by car. Either way, you need to get that wrist tended to pronto."

"My friends will take me to the clinic at school," I said.

"Alecs, we're leaving now," Janet ordered. I was surprised Alecs didn't argue.

Glenn got in front and helped open the crowd while Shani and Inaya walked on each side of me with Alecs and Janet behind. I cradled my left wrist with my right hand. *This really hurts.*

We made it to the MARTA station. "I think I'm going to throw up," I said as we were going down the escalator. Descending was such a tedious ride. I hurried to the restroom and hovered over the toilet. *I'm glad I don't have long hair.* The wave of nausea passed without me vomiting, and I rejoined the others.

Back at my car, Glenn took my keys, opened the door, made sure I was seated OK, and closed it. As he slid into the driver's seat, I said, "You're quite the mother hen." Shani and Inaya laughed.

"Behave or I'll make you walk back," he snarked.

I leaned back and closed my eyes. We made it to the clinic without me passing out. The doctor set my wrist, put it in a splint, and said, "I don't think you'll need surgery." *I'd rather it was a certainty.* "You'll need to follow up with an orthopedist to make sure. I expect they will just cast it though."

The front office staff set up an appointment for me, and we were on our way.

"Thanks for taking care of me."

"No problem, sister," Glenn said. The others agreed. It was 1:25, so they whipped up a quick lunch. After making sure I took a pain pill, they headed to class.

Romeo and Sophie snuggled up when I lay down in bed. *I hope Alecs and Janet got home OK. I'll have to call and check.* My brain began to get fuzzy, and I felt sleep coming. *I hope the protest does some good. How am I going to get my backpack on tomorrow? Why does life have to be so hard?*

Chapter 27

That's my phone. The sound dragged me from my drugged sleep. I got my eyes pried open enough to see that it was Will.

"Hey, brother."

"Are you OK?" *He sounds worried.*

"What you mean, 'I OK?'" I didn't connect his question to my injury.

"I heard you got beat up at the protest and broke your wrist."

"Oh! Wait, how you know that?"

"Inaya texted me while you were in the clinic."

The phoned sounded another call coming in. "Hold on second. It's Mellie. I'll right back."

"Hey, Mellie."

"Good."

"Good?"

"Yeah. You've taken your pain medicine."

"How you tell?"

"You sound drunk," she laughed. "Are you hurting a lot?"

"Not now but was before the pai' pill."

"Don't worry about supper. I'm coming over as soon as I finish my clinical shift."

"Thanks. Will on, too. Can call you back?"

"I have to get back to work, anyway. I'll see you about four."

"Look forward it."

"Hey, Will. I'm back." There was no sound. *I guess I hung up on him. I have to try not to sound drunk!* I punched his speed dial icon.

"I'm back. Sorry cut you off."

"No problem. Does it hurt a lot?"

"Not anymo'. I've had pain pill."

"That explains the slurred words."

"Is that obvious? Mellie noticed, too."

"You're a cute drunk! Anyway, do you need me to come down and take care of you?"

"You can't miss classes. Besides, I be OK. Mellie and Musketeers will help."

"OK, but I'm coming this weekend whether you like it or not."

My phone rang again. "It's Mom. Thanks calling. I'll talk you later." *Inaya was busy!*

"Hey, Mom."

"Hey, Honey. I'll be down this evening. I'll leave as soon as I get off work." *She hasn't called me honey since I came out.*

"Thanks, you don't need. It's just a wrist. Thankful, it's my left one."

"Are you sure? I can work from there."

"My friends take care of me." *I hadn't told her about Mellie yet. Maybe it's time.* "Mellie's coming over right after her nursing shift." *That came out as a whole sentence.*

"I haven't heard about Mellie."

I'm going to do it. "I met her playing tennis. She's the one whose place I took after she sprained her ankle."

"And y'all are still friends. That's nice."

"Actually, we're dating."

"Oh." Silence. *She's going to be mad I'm dating someone.* I braced myself.

"You've been dating all this time? And you haven't told me? I can't believe it!" *I wasn't expecting that.*

"Um, I wasn't sure how you'd take it."

"Willow, I want to be a part of your life, your whole life. I'm OK with you being gay now, and I'm glad you're dating someone. I can't wait to meet her."

"Thanks, Mom. That means a lot."

We chatted for another fifteen minutes. I told her all about what happened at the protest and more about Mellie. After hanging up, happiness flooded my heart. *I am loved. Thank you, Lord.* I lay down and fell asleep.

Look at that. It was an old, rusty metal box. I picked it up, and it turned new and shiny, so I brought it back and put it on my kitchen table. I kept walking around and finding old rusty things. Each one transformed into a new piece. Then the kitchen table was covered with these objects. Am I supposed to make something out of these?

My eyes opened at the sound of the door. Mellie came flying into the bedroom.

"How are you? Can I get you anything? Is it hurting? Great Scott! Look at your face!" She didn't slow down for me to answer any of those questions.

"What's wrong with my face?" I hadn't looked in a mirror since this morning. I touched my temple where the blow had landed. It felt swollen.

"You look like you lost the boxing match."

"Oh, that's lovely," I remarked, looking into the mirror.

"It'll heal. Let me see your hand. Your fingers are really swollen. I want you to keep that hand propped up so gravity can move the swelling out. The more it swells, the more it'll hurt."

"That's good news," I snarked.

She led me to the kitchen, ordered me into a chair, and positioned my forearm on a pillow. "I was so worried when I got the text from Inaya. It was hard to concentrate."

"I think you like me," I grinned.

"I think I love you." My heart filled even more with joy.

"I think I love you, too." She kissed me so gently.

"Now, let me see your ribs. Yep, another bad bruise. I wish I could get my hands on that jerk!"

"I'm glad you can't. I don't want to have to visit you in prison!" I laughed. "Oh! I told Mom about us today."

"You're getting brave. How did she take it." She sat down.

"She was happy for me. She wants to meet you."

"Well, alright then. I guess I'll have to go to Hawksville with you some day."

"OK, but that will really push Dad's buttons. You'll have to be ready to get the cold shoulder."

"Bring it on!" she said with a grin.

Sunday, November 24, 2023

"Thanks for driving me. I'm sure I could have managed, though."

"This way I get to spend time with you and meet this mysterious person who nearly got you killed," Mellie said as we neared Alecs's home.

"I'm surprised she was OK with you coming. She tends not to do well with new people."

Mellie parked and reached for my hand. There was a cast there, so she moved to my upper arm and gave it a squeeze. "I'll try to behave today," she grinned.

Alecs came bounding out the door, charging the driver's door. She stopped, apparently realizing I wasn't in the driver's seat and bolted to the passenger side. Wide-eyed, she looked me over as I got out.

"Your face is awful!"

I reached out my right hand. "Gentle on the ribs, please." We hugged, and I said, "Alecs, this is Mellie. Mellie, Alecs." To my surprise, Alecs ran around the car and hugged her.

"Thanks for taking care of Willow!"

"Taking care of her is my pleasure, and it's nice to meet you."

Alecs stepped back and looked Mellie over. "I think she'll do." I broke out laughing, which sent zingers through my bruised ribs.

Janet came hustling toward the car. "Let's see the damage." Looking me over, she said, "That jerk really did a number on you. I can never thank you enough for protecting Alecs. And you must be Mellie. We've heard a lot about you."

"Uh, oh! You didn't tell them the truth did you?"

"Don't make me laugh!" I snickered, trying to keep the pain down.

It was a cloudy, chilly day, so we sat in the den. My fanny had barely hit the sofa when Alecs asked, "How did you get to be so brave?"

"I have never considered myself brave."

"But you attacked that man even though he could easily beat you up."

"That wasn't bravery. I was just trying to keep him from hurting you. I guess you do crazy things like that when you care about someone."

"You're going to seminary and facing off with a committee of people who refuse to accept your calling. Your planning to do battle with a nationwide church to change their whole policy toward sexual orientation. Sounds pretty brave to me," Mellie added.

"I agree," Janet said. "Here's to the bravest person I know!" She raised her iced tea glass. Alecs and Mellie joined her.

I was touched. "Thanks. Y'all are too kind. I'm glad we all got out of there when we did."

"Yeah," Alecs said. "The 'My Country' men injured forty-nine people before the police caught them."

"I'm sorry you were almost number fifty," I said.

"That's only because of you," Janet choked out, near tears.

"Yeah. That's the nicest thing anyone has ever done for me."

"I can't imagine why. You're such a wonderful person."

"Being different is challenging," Mellie observed. "People are so eager to reject those they don't understand."

"That's enough about our hard-knock lives," I said, trying to lighten the mood. "Has anything good happened this week?"

"We found a small group of trans kids who are being homeschooled in the Atlanta area. They do a social outing every week."

"That's great!"

"We're going this week," Alecs said.

"Are you excited?" I asked.

"Maybe. I'm mostly nervous."

"I hope it's a fun group," Mellie added. "Maybe you all can get up to mischief."

Alecs grinned.

"Remember, I'll be gone for Thanksgiving next week, so I won't see you."

"Yeah. I hope you have a good visit."

Driving back to my apartment, Mellie said, "I see why you spend so much time with Alecs. She's really special."

"That she is. I just wish the rest of the world could see her for who she really is."

Chapter 28

Friday, December 13, 2024

Guilt greeted me with the morning light. Mellie had slept at my apartment last night. Again. *This is the third time. Lord, forgive me my weakness. Having her here is just so delicious! I can't resist.* She moved, and I rolled over to face her.

"Hey, beautiful."

"Good morning," she murmured. "Can't we sleep a while longer?" Her eyes closed. I checked my watch. It was only 7:15, so I snuggled up and lay there enjoying listening to her breathe.

At 7:35 I got up, covered my hot pink cast with a trash bag, slipped into the shower, and got ready. *Now let's see if I can get sleepy head up.*

Mellie was such a heavy sleeper that prying her out of bed could be a challenge. I rubbed her shoulder, rocked her back and forth, then shook her. "Good morning!" I chirped. "It's time to rise and shine!" *Oh, dear. Dad used to say that.*

Her eyes opened. "Hey."

"We have a trip to make. Time to get up!"

A sleepy smile formed. "I'm going to meet your parents today. You know what that means."

"No. What does it mean?"

"We're serious."

"I'm glad you figured that out." I leaned in for a kiss. "OK, Mellie. Up and into the shower. It's time to get moving."

While she was showering, nervousness crawled into my spirit. *I hope Dad behaves. I'm glad Will's going to be there.* Will and Mellie became fast friends when he came down the weekend after the book banning protest. They got me to laughing so much I had to close the bedroom door and leave them to it to keep my ribs from killing me. I took that as a good sign.

Mellie came out with a concerned look. "You're not going to tell your dad that we're just friends, are you? Because I don't want to have to live a lie with you. I want the whole world to know the truth about us."

That thought had crossed my mind, but no, I won't do that. "That's what I want, too. So Dad's going to have to live with the truth whether he likes it or not."

"Good! No more hiding in the closet. People have to accept us for who we are. If they can't, that's their loss!"

"You're such a good influence on me."

"Last night you said I was a bad influence," she countered with her signature grin.

"That, too."

The sun shone brightly, lighting the leaves left on the oak trees as I pulled into the driveway. The familiar nativity scene in the front yard warmed my heart with feelings of home. Will came bouncing out and charged the car. Mellie parked behind me.

I jumped out and grabbed Will in a hug, banging him harder than I meant to with the cast. Mellie knocked me out of the way. "My turn!"

"Nice cast! It's… subtle. So this is meet the parents weekend," Will said. "Mom's been working on Dad, but I don't know if it's going to stick."

Mom came out with a smile on her face. "You must be Mellie. I'm so happy to meet you." She held out her hand, but Mellie grabbed her in a hug.

"I'm glad to finally meet you, too."

I knocked her out of the way. "My turn." I was more careful with the cast.

"Dad's still at work." Mom said. "We'll help you with your bags." "Will, you grab Mellie's, and I'll help Willow."

"On it, boss!"

"We'll put Mellie in the guest bedroom," Mom said, stating the obvious. *I guess she just wants to make sure.*

"Good grief! Look at the suitcases!" Will announced.

"Hey! A woman needs a lot of stuff. Besides, it's for the whole holiday," Mellie responded, punching him in the arm. *It's like they've known each other their whole lives.*

Mom bustled around, making sure Willow had towels and showing her where things were. Then we converged on the kitchen for iced tea.

Mom peppered Mellie with questions. "Are you enjoying your clinicals? Where are you from? Do you know what kind of nursing you want to do yet?"

I studied Mom while they talked. *She seems genuinely interested. I don't think she's putting on airs. I relaxed.* "OK, Mom. That's enough interrogation for now."

"Yeah, it's my turn," Mellie said. "Where did you grow up? How is your job going? What made you want to go into graphic designing? Can I see some of your work?"

Mom smiled as she answered Mellie's questions. *I think they're going to like each other.*

After Mom showed us some of her current projects, one of which was designing a book cover, I summoned up the courage to ask, "How is Dad taking the idea of meeting Mellie?"

"Mostly he just grunts," Mom laughed. "I told him he had better behave."

I heard a car pull up.

"He must have gotten off work early," Mom noted. "That's a good sign."

We converged in the kitchen just as Dad came in with his work satchel. "Hello, everybody. I was hoping to get home before you got here," he said, then put his satchel in a chair. I noticed him stiffen.

"Dad, this is Mellie. Mellie, Dad."

"It's nice to meet you," Mellie said, offering her hand.

"You, too," Dad said, offering his. *So far so good. Maybe Mom's threats worked.* "Welcome to Hawksville. It's not much, but it's home. I need to put this up before I get in trouble." He picked up the satchel and headed to the office.

As he walked down the hall, Mom grinned and held up crossed fingers. I had to stifle my laugh. Will gave a thumbs up then whispered, "What did you say to him?"

"Not now," Mom whispered. "I'm planning spaghetti for supper. I hope that's OK."

"That sounds wonderful!" Mellie approved. "I haven't had homemade spaghetti in forever."

Dad popped back into the kitchen. "I forgot my hug," he said, reaching for me. I leaned in and hugged him tightly, trying to fight back tears. *That's the first hug since I came out.* The tears worked their way out, anyway.

"What's wrong?" Dad asked, pulling back.

"I've missed those hugs," I managed.

We moved to the den and chatted for a while. I told the story of the protest and how I was attacked, leaving out that Alecs is trans. *It's probably best Dad doesn't have to deal with that, too.*

Will showed up with a Sharpie. "Signature time!" I dutifully held up the cast, and he signed, "Will, the best brother in the world!"

"Someone thinks a lot of himself," I teased.

"The truth is the truth," he responded.

"I have to agree that it's true," Mellie observed.

"Don't make his head swell," I laughed.

"I need to get supper started," Mom said, getting up to head to the kitchen.

"I'll help," I offered.

"You might do more damage than good with one hand," she answered. I got up and followed anyway. Mom turned on the eye under the spaghetti sauce. Mellie and I sat down at the table while she opened the fridge.

"Oh, no! I don't have enough lettuce for salad. Will, would you mind running to the store?"

"Sure. What do you need?" he asked as he popped into the kitchen.

"Get us two salad packs."

"I'm on it! Just let me get a jacket."

"I'll go with you," Dad called.

With them gone, I seized the opportunity. "OK, Mom, spill the beans. What did you say to Dad to get him to be nice?"

She brandished her long stirring spoon. "If you tell him I told you I'll beat you to a pulp with this." She paused.

"I promise I won't tell."

"I explained to him that he had to make a choice. He can either accept you being lesbian and be a part of your life or stay stuck where he is and lose you altogether. I believe he has chosen you."

"Do you realize today is the first time he's hugged me since I came out?"

"I do. It's been a painful six years. I think our family is on the mend now."

Monday, December 16, 2024

We said our goodbyes and left early Monday morning, determined to make the drive to Mellie's in one day. *I've never driven nine hours in one day. At least I'm armed with a thermos full of coffee.*

I had the directions in my GPS app but planned to stick with Mellie. We talked by phone off and on throughout the trip and stopped about every three hours for breaks. I was worn out when we arrived at Mellie's home. It was a small white clapboard house. I parked behind Mellie in the gravel drive.

A white deer and tree decorated the yard. Mellie's mom walked onto the front stoop and down the three steps to greet us. I battled stiffness getting out of the car and stretched when I stood up.

"Hello, dear," she said to Mellie as Mellie climbed from her car.

"Hey, Mom! It's so good to see you. I've missed you."

"I've missed you, too," she responded as they hugged. She reached a hand toward me while hugging Mellie with the other. "It's nice to meet you, Willow."

I took her hand and squeezed. "The same here."

"This is Misty, my mom," Mellie said. "I've told her all about you!" Mellie pulled away and stretched. "That was a long drive."

"You should have stopped in Memphis like you usually do," Misty scolded.

"Yeah, I know. But I wanted to get here so you could meet Willow. Besides, she has to go back in a couple of days, unless we can persuade her to stay." She wiggled and grinned.

"You're welcome for as long as you like," Misty said. "Now, let's get you in. It's too cold to stand out here."

A beautiful sunset graced the sky as we lugged suitcases inside. The smell of hot cider greeted me. "Yum! That smells delicious!"

"Mom's famous for her hot cider," Mellie informed me. "She's also been known to spike it on occasion."

"Hush, Mellie," Misty chided. "She's going to be a minister."

That's the first time anyone's said something like that to me. I hope I need to get used to it. "I hope that's the case. So far, my denomination is unwilling to ordain me."

"Oh? Why is that?" Misty asked.

"Because she's queer like me!" Mellie chirped. "Look at her. How could anyone refuse to ordain such a cutie!"

"I see you're smitten," Misty grinned.

Mellie through an arm around me. "Is it that obvious? I think it's cider time!"

"It's sad we live in a society that won't affirm people for who they are. It's gotten better, but there will always be problems, I'm afraid," Misty observed.

"If you keep talking like that, we're going to have to spike the cider to drown our sorrows," Millie scolded. "I want this to be a happy time." She started pulling mugs from the cabinet, and we joined in pouring up the cider.

"I hope you like spaghetti," Misty said. Mellie and I laughed. "What?"

"That's what Willow's mom served our first night," Mellie explained.

Later that night, Misty said, "I have to work tomorrow, so I'm going on to bed." We both hugged her good night then cuddled up on the couch. *I knew Mellie's mom was divorced but hadn't heard her mention her dad, so I asked.*

"Do you see your dad over Christmas?" I felt her tense.

"No, I haven't seen him in years. I never saw him much, but once I came out, he totally disappeared."

"I'm sorry."

"Thanks. I've accepted it now. It's just me and Mom."

Chapter 29

Wednesday, December 18, 2024

Mellie gave me an exaggerated pouty face after plopping onto the bed while I began packing. "Don't go. I'll miss you too badly!"

"I know. I don't want to go." I couldn't imagine the corners of her mouth turning down any more, but they did. I leaned over and kissed her.

"It will be almost a month before I see you again," she complained.

"That is a long time." *She does have a point. But I told my family I would drive back tomorrow.*

"I know!" Her face lit up. "You stay a couple of more days, and I'll leave early and come to your house before school starts back." *How can I resist that face!* "We can go Christmas shopping! We can go hiking at Lake Fort Smith State Park. You just have to stay!"

"You do make a compelling case. You're a bad influence on me!"

"So you'll stay?"

"Yes."

"I love being a bad influence!"

"And I love your grin!"

Tuesday, December 24. 2024

Dad had hugged me again when I came back from Mellie's. Tonight's Christmas Eve service was going to be special. It's the first one since I came out that I haven't been stressed out by the tension between Dad and me.

He even knows Mellie is coming back for a week. Thank you, Lord, for helping to bring Dad around. Thanks for helping Mom to help him along. With that prayer, it dawned on me that I haven't written in my diary in a long time. *I guess life is so good I don't need to write about my troubles.*

I pulled on a red Christmas sweater with a nativity scene and black pants. I brushed my hair and checked my make up.

"Come on, people! I don't want to be late," Dad called from the kitchen. The hallway came alive as Will, Mom, and I rushed through.

Myra and her family were walking toward the church when we pulled in. I jumped out of the car. "Myra! Hey!" I charged to hug her.

"Hey, girl! It's good to see you! How are you doing?"

"I'm on top of the world!"

"I see that. Tell me about it."

I checked to make sure Mom and Dad were out of earshot. "I think I'm in love."

"Based on your grin, I'd say it's more than a think! Congratulations. I assume the lucky girl is Mellie."

"Yep. And there's more."

"Do tell."

"Dad is thawing."

"No way!"

"Yep. Mom laid down the law before I brought Mellie to visit and told him if he didn't accept that I'm gay he was going to lose me altogether. Thankfully, he's accepting."

"You *are* on top of the world. Good for you."

"Uh, oh! We're the last ones in the parking lot!"

"Late as usual," Myra giggled.

We parted to sit with our families. I scrunched in beside Will. The Christmas tree, Advent wreath, poinsettias, and candles around the sanctuary were magical. My heart was so full I was on the verge of tears. *Thank you, Lord, for this beautiful evening. Thank you for loving us enough to send your son. Thank you for bringing Dad back to me.*

Pastor Stephens began the service. A family went up to light the Advent candles. *The only thing missing tonight is Mellie. I wish she were here.*

When we went up to receive Communion, I pulled Will ahead of me so I could kneel next to Dad. Our shoulders were touching, and he didn't pull away. I thought my heart would burst with joy.

At the end of the service as we sang, "Silent Night," to candlelight, tears warmed my cheeks. I was helping Will hold the hymnal with one hand and my candle with the other, so I had to let them run free. The warm light of the candles spoke to my heart.

I sensed in my heart more than hearing with my ears, "You are my precious child. Trust and follow. I will lead you to abundant life."

Saturday, January 25, 2025

"It's letter time, people," Shani grinned. "We need to bombard these people with our calls for change."

We had gathered at my apartment for a strategy meeting. I had found a list of the delegates to the national meeting, and we had hunted down most of their addresses. We had each secured the addresses of our local committees and leaders.

"That's going to be a lot of letters," Avery observed.

I pulled out the six rolls of stamps I had purchased. "This should cover the postage. I also have envelopes and two reams of paper."

"You didn't have to do that," Inaya said. "We'll help you pay for it."

"Since you are doing this for Johnny and me, it's the least I could do."

"I'll pay for copying!" Inaya offered.

"Thanks, but I've already printed mine," Avery said.

"Me, too," Glenn added.

"Ok, has anyone but me not printed their letters?" Avery asked.

"I haven't," Johnny almost whispered. He glanced to the floor. "I have to be honest. I'm not sure I want to send them. I'm afraid it will put me on their radar."

"Look, Johnny, you're going to be on the radar sooner or later anyway. Come on and make a stand. You have to fight for your right to exist in this world." Shani replied.

"Preach it, sister!" Glenn responded. "I agree. I know it's scary, but you have to put the real you out there or you're condemned to living a false life."

"They're right," Inaya added.

I could see the turmoil in Johnny's eyes. An idea came to mind. "Johnny, sit back and close your eyes." He looked at me like I was loony. "Come on, try it. Trust me."

"OK, but I reserve the right to run if you get crazy." Everyone laughed.

"Picture in your mind the path ahead of you for ordination. Try to think it all the way through. Imagine what you will tell each committee and how they'll respond. When you finish, tell us what you see," I directed.

After about thirty seconds, Johnny grimaced. "Well?" I asked.

"I lied all the way."

"And now, what's ahead for you?"

"I have to keep my identity secret. If I ever do fall in love, that will have to remain secret, too."

"And it will never work," Inaya offered. "You can't live a lie for the rest of your life and not expect to get caught."

"Guys, I think we're pressuring Johnny to do something he's not ready to do," Glenn observed.

"I agree," Avery said. "Johnny needs to make this decision without our prodding."

"No. You are right. I tried envisioning it the other way. It's better to come clean and be who I really am. I'm sending the letters."

I stretched the cramp out of my hand and looked at the clock: 6:12. "I'm not sure I can address any more envelopes. My hand is worn out."

Everyone but Shani put down their pens and stretched.

"I have to finish this one," she stated as she kept writing.

"I only have four more to go," Avery said. "I think I can. I think I can."

I looked at my list and discovered there were only six left. "You're right Avery. I only have six left. I think I can, too."

The door opened and Mellie popped in. "This looks serious."

"Grab a pen and help us finish," Glenn ordered.

"Yes, sir! So this is the great letter writing campaign in action." She sat down and we started passing her envelopes and addresses.

"Pizza. Pizza. Pizza." Glenn started chanting after sealing his last envelope. We piled into two cars and headed to Athens Pizza.

We had the same waiter who had asked me out a while back. I noticed him eyeing Mellie while taking our order.

"Be ready. The waiter might ask you out."

Mellie laughed. "Yeah, right."

"She's right," Shani confirmed. "I saw him looking. He asked Willow out once."

"Bring it on," Mellie answered, generating laughs all around.

"Willow's going to drop the letters by the post office tomorrow. Now we need to start focusing on the convention," Shani said. *She's always so focused.* "How many LGBTQ+ groups have we identified in the St. Louis area?"

"I found five that have contacts. There were four others, but I didn't find any way to contact them," I replied.

"Great. If they can get twenty people each to turn out, that's a hundred. Any other ideas for getting people to show up?" Shani asked.

"Just make sure they're on our side," Glenn quipped.

The waiter brought our pizza and slipped Mellie a note.

"You were right. He's asking me out. Sneaky fellow, isn't he."

When he brought our check, the waiter paused, looking at Mellie. She put her arm around me and leaned toward him. "Do you want to make it a threesome? We're a couple and do everything together."

His face flushed fiery red, and he backed off wide-eyed, tripping on a chair from the next table.

"Mellie, I think you just scarred him for life," Inaya laughed.

"Come on, folks. We have a protest to plan," Shani directed.

Chapter 30

While driving to see Alecs, worries over my systematic theology paper kept circling. *It's due in a week from tomorrow. I have to get this thing organized.* The assignment was to write our own systematic theology. *How can I put on paper everything I believe? What do I believe? This may just break my brain!*

I pulled into the driveway and saw Alecs on the front porch, bundled in a coat. She smiled and waved. *She is doing so much better than when I first met her. I'm glad I've kept in touch.*

I zipped my coat against the cold wind. "Hey, Alecs! Why are you standing out in the cold?"

"Waiting on you."

"You seem extra happy today."

"I have a friend." Her grin grew even bigger.

"Wow! That's great. Let's go in, and you can tell me about this friend."

Janet greeted me as we walked into the house. "How about some hot chocolate since it's a cold day?"

"That sounds wonderful, especially if you have marshmallows."

"Of course, we do. Alecs wouldn't have it any other way."

Janet went to prepare hot chocolate, and I prompted Alecs. "So, tell me about this friend."

She sat up a little straighter. "I met her at a homeschool thing Mom took me to. We're both sixteen and transitioning to female. She's a Swiftie and likes to write poetry, just like me."

"You two have a lot in common. I like Taylor Swift, too. What's your new friend's name?"

"Lynn. We're going to get together…." She stopped and her eyes widened.

"What's wrong?"

"We're planning to get back together next Sunday. Um, I forgot that you would be coming."

I could see the anxiety building. "It's OK, Alecs. I'll miss you, but we can see each other the next week. I think you need to work on building this new relationship. It will be good for you."

I watched as the anxiety morphed into peace. "Thanks. I'm sorry that I didn't think about you coming. I was just so excited when I met Lynn. She's a redhead."

"I'm glad you've found a new friend. Your life seems to have gotten a lot better since I first met you."

"Yeah."

We chatted over hot chocolates, then I left to drive back to my apartment. On the way, I resumed stressing over the upcoming paper.

OK, I need a starting point. That will help. Where to start? The naked trees drew my attention. *They look so bleak in the winter. I wonder if they feel cold. They'll be so alive come spring, like a resurrection. That's the way life goes. Abundant, bleak, abundant. Life! Maybe that's my starting point.*

What about life? Where did life come from? God. Hmmm. I have to start with God. Who is God? How do we know God exists? That's a tough one. I actually don't know that God exists. It's a matter of experience shaped by faith. In the living of life, I discover love, and that love is greater than anything I can imagine or understand. God is love! I couldn't wait to get home and start writing!

I booted up my computer and opened a new document to begin my paper:

God is a being that exists beyond, in, and through all life, matter, and space. God is the creative source of life and all that exists. God's existence is not a matter of scientific fact but of experience-derived discovery. That discovery reveals an infinite being whose primary attribute is love. Once discovered, this infinite love that powers the universe becomes the guiding principle that shapes all human life.

I sat back and reread the paragraph. *Seems like a good start to me.* I then began to work out the outline that would grow from this opening. Discussing the nature of God would come first followed by describing the human condition. The last section would discuss how living in relationship with God fulfills humanity, results in the existence of the church, and empowers human beings to be agents of love.

Whew! That's a load off my mind! I think writing it will be easier than coming up with the outline. A quick knock and the opening of the door signaled I had finished just in time.

"Hey, good looking!"

"Hey, yourself."

"You look mighty happy," Mellie said walking over for a quick kiss."

"I just got my Systematic Theology paper outlined. It's a relief. You look happy, too."

"I am."

"What are you so happy about?"

"I can't tell you, yet," she grinned, sitting down.

"Keeping secrets, are we?"

"I have a surprise for you."

"I'm all ears."

"You actually need to be all feet right now. I have a place I want to show you."

"Sounds intriguing! Do I need anything special?"

"Just a warm coat," she said getting up all wiggly with excitement. "Let's go!"

I grabbed my coat, and we hurried off.

Mellie drove us to a park and pulled out a picnic basket.

"Oh boy! A picnic!" I was excited. She led me to a beautiful spot where the river ran over rocks, creating small waterfalls and a beautiful sound. We scampered out onto a large rock in the middle and sat down to eat.

Mellie produced fried chicken and potato salad. "There's something extra special for dessert."

"Oh? Can we start with that?"

"You don't like the chicken?"

"I love the chicken. But you know I love, love, love dessert!"

"Patience. Nutrition first."

I looked deeply into her eyes. "That's one of the hazards of dating a nurse."

"Not to mention the bad influence."

"That, too," I laughed. "What are the hazards of dating a potential preacher?"

"I have to only partially misbehave."

After I behaved and ate the chicken and potato salad, Mellie asked, "Are you ready for surprise number one?"

"You mean there are two surprises?"

"Maybe," she grinned wider.

"Did I do something special to deserve two of them?"

"You sure did."

Mellie leaned tantalizingly close.

"And what did I do?" I stole a quick kiss.

"You are you."

"You being you is quite special, too."

I didn't even look to see if anyone was watching before pulling her in for a long, delicious kiss. "That was a nice surprise."

"Now there are three surprises. Here's the next one," she said, pulling out a plastic container with something chocolate in it.

"Yum! What is it?"

"It's a dark chocolate torte. I found it at Publix and thought you would like it."

"You're so good to me."

"I am, aren't I."

She looked so happy opening the container. My heart was as full as my belly was about to be. I took a bite. "I think the rapture just hit. This is delicious!"

"Yum! It is! Have another bite," she said, feeding me with her fork.

"Thanks, Mellie. This was a super-special evening."

"We're not done yet." The sun was setting and firing the sky with pinks and oranges. It was beautifully romantic.

"Oh? That's right. Surprise number three. I can't wait."

Mellie moved even closer, sitting cross-legged. She pulled me so that my hip nestled into the V of her legs. I looked deeply into her blue eyes.

"I could swim in the ocean of your eyes," I said.

"Willow, I have never met anyone like you. You have filled my life with joy, and I love you so much."

"I love you, too."

"Hush and let me finish."

"Yes, ma'am." I had trouble reading the emotions mixing on her face.

"I can't even remember what life was like before you caught me on the court. I think you have saved me from a life of emptiness. Now my life is full of hope and wonder, and I have you to thank for that."

I started to say something, but she put her finger to my lips and continued. "I want to spend every moment of my life with you." My heart did a flip. "Will you marry me?"

Looking deeply into her eyes, I paused. "Yes" wanted to rush out and embrace her proposal, but the ordination monstered reared its head. *If I'm married, they really won't consider me for ordination. But I do want to marry Mellie. That would be the greatest joy I can imagine.* I could see the hope and joy drain with every second of my hesitation.

Finally my heart asserted itself. "Yes, Mellie. I would absolutely love to marry you. I can't imagine my life without you, either." I pulled her in for a hug and a long kiss.

The grin I adore so much appeared. "You had me worried for a minute there."

"The ugly ordination monster tried to get in the way. It tried to tell me that if I'm married, they will never ordain me. But spending my life with you is the most important thing. I had rather have you first, whether or not I'm ever ordained."

Mellie opened her hand to reveal a ring box.

"You didn't!" I took the box, opening it eagerly. It was a beautiful opal ring.

"The stone has many colors, like your many facets."

"It's gorgeous," I noted, putting it on my finger.

"I was thinking we could go together to get engagement rings or just decide on wedding bands."

"We should get you one to match this. I love it!"

"I love you." Mellie hugged me so tightly.

My heart overflowed with joy spreading warmth all over my body and spilling out of my eyes. Mellie pulled back and wiped the tear that had landed on her cheek.

"You're crying."

"I've never been this happy in my whole life," I choked out.

"Me, either."

"You do a great proposal. I feel so totally loved."

By the time we let go of the hug, the sunset had turned to darkness. "How are we going to get back across the rocks?" I asked, dread slapping the beauty of the moment. I didn't want to break another wrist.

"That's what cell phones are for," Mellie reminded me.

We turned on the flashlights and worked our way back to land. I held Mellie's hand on the straight-a-ways as she drove us back to my apartment.

"We have to call everybody and tell them the news!" I said, the thought striking me with a jolt of joy. We sat on the couch as close together as two humans could possibly get. I called Will first and put the phone on speaker.

"Hey, Willow. What's up?"

"I've got news!"

"You sound excited."

I leaned into Mellie a little more. "We're getting married!"

"Wow! Congratulations! When's the big date?"

A shot of surprise flowed through. I looked at Mellie. "I haven't even thought about a date!"

Mellie added, "We just got engaged a few minutes ago. Give us a chance to process that first."

"I will be there with bells on whenever it is. Have you told the parents yet?"

I stiffened. "No, not yet. I wonder what their reaction will be."

"You should go ahead and do it. I think it will go OK. I know Mom will be happy."

"OK, I'll suck it up and make the call."

Mellie called her Mom next. Misty was thrilled with the news. "I'm so happy for you. Willow is such a joy. It will be great having her in the family."

I took a deep breath. "OK. Let's do this."

I called Mom's cell phone and asked her to get Dad and put the phone on speaker.

"OK. Should I be excited or worried?"

"Patience is a virtue."

"It's Willow calling," I heard her tell Dad. "We're ready."

"I have some big news." I forced the joy to override the nerves. "Mellie and I just got engaged. We're getting married!"

"Congratulations!" Mom said. "Mellie seems like such a sweet person. I think you make a good couple."

Dad's silence seemed loud over the phone. Mom paused, and I pictured her eyes pleading for him to say something.

"Congratulations. I'm happy for you," he finally said. I tried to gauge the level of sincerity, but I couldn't over the phone.

"Thanks. We haven't set a date yet. I couldn't wait to tell you till we figured that out."

With the calls over, we snuggled into each other's arms. Mellie eventually said, "I guess I need to go. I have clinical in the morning."

"You're not going anywhere tonight."

Chapter 31

I peeked out the window to see rain-washed trees in the back. It was a chilly morning but not cold enough to freeze. "I'm going to miss you two this week," I explained, giving Romeo and Sophie a long scratch behind their ears. "But don't worry. Johnny's going to stay with you."

I looked at my watch and jumped into hurry mode. *I only have twenty minutes to finish packing.* Flinging my bag into the back of the Rav4, I took off to pick up the others.

"Road trip!" Inaya exclaimed, placing her bag in the back. With her collected, Shani, Avery, Glenn, Inaya and I set off to St. Louis. The national meeting would begin tomorrow, and we had preparations to make.

"OK, people," Shani said once we were out of Atlanta's heavy traffic. "We need slogans."

"How about, 'Sin is how one lives. Not who one is!'" Glenn offered.

"I like it," Avery replied. "I've been thinking of using, 'Gays for Jesus. Jesus for Gays.'"

"I know," Inaya began. "We could say, 'Ordain Willow or we will come for you!'"

After we stopped laughing, I said, "Inaya, you're nuts."

"How about this one, 'The LGBTQ+ Zombies are here. Be prepared.'" Glenn laughed.

"This is going to be a long ride," Avery groaned.

We checked into the Last Hotel at 6:30pm. I was tired from driving so long but not tired enough to miss the wow factor of the hotel.

"Y'all, this is an amazing place!" I observed.

"Yeah. I'm not sure I'm well-heeled enough to stay here. They might throw me out," Glenn joked.

We originally planned to book one room, with Glenn sleeping on the floor. I thought about how cramped that would be and sprang for the extra room, figuring Grace would approve. *It's nice that you are still with me, Grace.* The group decided Glenn and I would take the second room.

We gobbled down pizza, which Glenn had ordered on the way, then headed to a hardware store and office supply store for the things we would need to make picket signs. With five people and luggage, we couldn't bring them with us.

Arriving back at the hotel, we got to work. I saw Avery scrunch up her face and realized she was looking at Glenn's poster.

"Surrender the marker, Glenn," she said.

"What?" he asked.

"I can hardly read that from here, much less on the picket line."

He surveyed his work. "Looks good to me."

"Nope," Shani commanded. "You are in charge of putting the posters onto the dowels. Leave the writing to folks with some fine motor skills.

"Fine. But that's discrimination against the handwriting challenged."

Tuesday, March 11, 2025

We arrived at the convention center at 8:00 since it started at 9:00. People were already arriving.

"We need to find the main entrance where the most people will pass through," Shani said.

Walking around a corner, Glenn stated, "I think we found it."

There were at least a hundred people already marching.

"Wow!" I remarked, tears popping instantly.

"I believe our recruiting efforts paid off," Avery noted.

We joined in the line of protesters. I introduced myself to the person in front of me. "Hi, I'm Willow. I am so grateful for your being here."

"Hey! You're the one I got the email from," the low voice revealing a man dressed in drag. "I'm Jack, the president of Queers for Christ. I'm so happy to meet you and grateful to be a part of this. Darling, we would have never known about it if you hadn't contacted me."

"I'm amazed at how many people are here marching."

"You haven't seen anything yet, darling. We have some late sleepers in our crew. They'll be here."

True to his word, more and more protesters joined till there were about two hundred of us. The delegates began arriving in droves. Some rolled their eyes, some told us to go home, some offered a thumbs up as they dodged us to get through the picket line.

By 10:00, I was thankful for my comfortable running shoes and the fanny pack I had stuffed with water and snacks. Jack stepped out of line and picked up a bullhorn sitting next to the building.

"Keep walking, people! You are looking marvelous today! I thank you from the bottom of my heart for being here to support LGBTQ+ rights. This is one more step toward letting the world know that we're not freaks. We're just people trying to live out our lives as God created us."

I walked past him, which put my back to him, and he continued speaking.

"Obviously, we can't all go to the bathroom at the same time, but that is necessary. Please observe the numbers leaving the line and limit the departures to no more than twenty at a time.

"If the legs are weary, there are benches along the side of the building. This is going to be a long day. Manage your energy carefully, darlings.

"Where is Willow? Willow, please come over here."

What in the world? Why does he want me? I walked over wondering what was coming.

"People, I am happy to say that we have with us one of the folks for whom we are fighting today. Willow is a lesbian who is called into the ministry and seeking ordination. Let's give her a round of applause and march on for her!"

The group clapped as best they could while holding picket signs. Someone started shouting, "For Willow! For Willow!" The group joined in, and Jack grabbed my hand and lifted it into the air.

The chanting energized me. *Maybe we really can make a change!* I took the megaphone from Jack. "Thank you! Thank you!" The chanting calmed. "Today we fight for the right to be included in the church, for the right to follow God's call on our lives, for the right to be understood as real people whom God created and whom God loves."

The crowd applauded and resumed chanting.

"You're quite the hit," Jack smiled. "We all need motivation to persevere. I appreciate you adding that motivation today."

"I'm glad I'm here." We rejoined the picket line.

On my second loop around, I noticed a news station van pulling up. *This could be good. We'll get more exposure.*

A man with a camera surveyed the scene and pointed to the spot from which he wanted to film. I passed by as the reporter began her story.

"This is Elise Summers reporting from America's Center Convention Complex where a protest is currently underway during the national meeting of the church. There are between one and two hundred people in this picket line..."

I walked far enough that I could no longer hear her. "I'm glad the news showed up."

"Yeah. That's got to be good," Glenn called from behind me.

"Maybe not," Jack added. "That is a conservative station. They may put a negative spin on this."

"There seems to always be negative spin," I grumped.

I looped around so I could see the reporter again. She had a woman from the picket line standing next to her. The woman returned to the line when I was fifty feet away. The reporter beckoned me with her finger. I stepped out of the line, my nerves tensing. *She's going to interview me. I hope I don't embarrass myself.*

"Hi, I'm Elise Summers. Could I ask you some questions?"

"Sure."

"We will be filming you for a TV report. Is that OK?"

"Yes, that's fine."

"I need your name."

"Willow Grier."

"Thanks, Willow. Now please stand here." She positioned me where she wanted me. Her demeanor transformed when she started speaking into the camera. *She's so animated.*

"Willow Grier is a participant in today's protest. Thanks for joining me, Willow. What does this protest mean to you?"

"It gives me hope that I will be able to fulfill God's calling in my life and become a minister."

"What is stopping you from fulfilling that calling?"

"I'm lesbian, and the church will not ordain me."

"Doesn't the church consider homosexuality against the teaching of the Bible?"

How do I respond to that? I need some ideas, Lord. "The understanding of homosexuality is in transition. The church is beginning to see that the quality of a person's life is more important than their sexual orientation."

"So you expect the church to go against the Bible's teaching and long-standing tradition and change their stance on ordaining gay people?"

She's aiming for that negative spin Jack mentioned. "I do. I believe it is time to understand that gay people, trans people, queer people of every stripe were created by God, loved by God, and empowered by God to live faithful lives in the church. The church needs our gifts in the ordained ministry."

That sounded pretty good.

Elise smiled into the camera. "Thank you very much, Willow."

There was an awkward pause till a man standing to the side of the camera said, "Cut."

Without another word, Elise walked over to the camera man. "Let's see what we have so far." I took that as my cue to rejoin the picket line.

I was able to hop in between Avery and Shani. I told them about the interview. They congratulated me on my comments. As we came around on the building side of the loop, Jack was handing out small pieces of paper. Mine had the number 3 on it. I scrunched up my eyes and looked at Jack.

"You'll find out in a minute, darling."

As I turned the corner toward the street side, I heard Jack on the bullhorn. "My most marvelous protesters! You look wonderful! The truth is one cannot live by picketing alone. Food is a necessity. So is a break. In order to keep the line intact, you have a number. Ones are to break for lunch at eleven, twos at twelve, and threes at one. Please try to return within the hour and please sit down to eat, people! Give those legs a break!

I see why Jack is president of this group. He's so enthusiastic and upbeat. I'm glad he's here. It would have been pitiful had it only been the five of us walking this line. I hope this makes a difference.

Chapter 32

Wednesday, March 12, 2025

Clothes bounced out when I slammed my suitcase on the bed to get out today's outfit.

"Still mad?" Glenn asked, looking over sleepily from his bed.

"I can't believe that woman twisted everything I said! The gall! How dare she say that we are trying to force our radical ideas on a solid church. Ugh!"

"I like the fire in your soul, but could you tone it down a notch. I want to sleep till you're out of the shower."

"Sorry."

We had seen the news broadcast of the story about our protest, and just as Jack predicted, the reporter had turned the report against us.

"I'm wearing a second pair of socks today," I informed Glen after showering and dressing.

"That's a good idea. My feet are weary."

I was finishing a bowl of cereal while Glenn laced his boots. I couldn't resist asking, "Are you ever going to ask Inaya out?"

"Why would I do that?"

I raised an eyebrow and waited.

"Is it that obvious?" he finally replied.

"Yep. I think you two would make a great couple."

Dressed and fed, we set out on the fifteen minute walk to the convention center. A cold breeze blew, and I was thankful for my puffy jacket. I pulled on my mittens.

"Does anyone know when they are taking the vote on our issue?" Shani asked.

"Henry Walsh, the head of the committee that is proposing it, said it would be sometime today," I answered.

"That just leaves this morning and maybe the lunchtime passersby to make our impact. I hope none of the delegates tuned into that news broadcast last night. It didn't help at all," Shani observed.

"When are you going to set a date for the wedding? You're wearing me out with this waiting," Inaya pleaded.

"We're talking about this summer sometime. It's hard to decide on a date. Plus we have to find a place to have it. I promise you'll all be invited."

Thinking about the wedding prompted me to miss Mellie even more. We talked on the phone, but that wasn't the same as having her here. She had decided to spend the week with her mother. Since Mellie was an only child, her mother was having a hard time being by herself. *I understand, but I still miss her.*

We arrived at the convention center at 7:48. The crowd was about half the size. I sought out Jack.

"Good morning, precious! You look fit as a fiddle today."

"Good morning, Jack. It looks like we have a smaller crew today."

"Yeah, the first day is always the best."

"So you've done this before?"

"Darling, we protest every chance we get. Somebody has to get the word out that queer folks aren't evil, you know."

"I'm grateful for your spirit and your commitment. Today is the day of the vote. I have my fingers crossed!"

"I hope you're prayed up, too, darling. We need help from above for this change to happen."

He looked over his protesters with a warm expression. I sensed hope in his heart. "I've been praying nonstop," I assured him.

"Great! Maybe this is the day!"

The arriving delegates increased to a steady stream. Most circled around the picket line and appeared to ignore us. One man broke through just behind me, and I heard, "Hey! Watch what you're doing! And you call yourself a Christian?" Taunts spread from the picketers, and I looked around to see Inaya on the ground. The man looked flummoxed, hesitated as if he wanted to apologize, then turned to go into the building.

I hustled back to Inaya. "Are you OK?"

"Yeah. That jerk tripped me when he charged through the line."

I offered a hand and pulled her up. "Sorry about that."

"It's not you who needs to apologize. I'm certain that guy won't be voting for us," she laughed.

I put my arm around her shoulder, and we rejoined the line.

"I think you should get married at Cannon Chapel," Inaya suggested. "It's a beautiful place, and it will be too hot to get married outside in the summer."

"You're working harder on this wedding than I am," I laughed. "That's one of the places we're considering. I'd really like to have the wedding in my home church, but they won't let us." A wave of sadness whisked by at that thought.

I heard footsteps hurrying behind me and looked around.

"Hey, Willow." It was Henry Walsh.

"Good morning. Will the proposal still come up today?" Henry kept pace with me.

"It's on the agenda for this afternoon. I hope it doesn't get delayed. Say your prayers and cross your fingers."

"You've got it."

He marched along with us till he came to the doors.

Three more news vans pulled up almost at the same time. The crews set up then caught delegates as they passed by. One by one, the crews started turning their attention to the picketers.

One reporter called for Jack by name as he passed by.

"I take it they know each other," Inaya noted.

"Jack said his group are old hands at protesting, so he's probably been interviewed before," I said.

The day dragged on and my feet protested. We found a taco place for lunch. I wanted to take my shoes off but resisted the temptation.

"My feet say they don't want to go back," Glenn griped, finishing his last bite of taco.

"Mine are with yours," Avery said. "I'm glad I brought hiking boots instead of flats."

"I hope we get some good news this afternoon," Shani said.

"Me, too," I echoed. "I'm so grateful to y'all for doing this. It means a lot."

"The Musketeers wouldn't have it any other way," Inaya smiled, holding up the empty sword hand.

"All for one and one for all," Avery said as we put our hands together.

I noticed other customers giving us odd looks. *I guess we are quite the site with our picket signs leaning against the wall and our hands in the air.*

One woman marched up to us. "You're part of the picket line against the church, aren't you?"

"Actually, we're for the church. We're trying to steer them to do the right thing," Shani answered.

"You should be ashamed of yourselves. Those kinds of people have no place in the ministry." She lifted her chin and stomped out of the restaurant.

"Well, isn't she the self-righteous queen," Glenn snarked.

Anger boiled then calmed more quickly than I expected. "People just don't understand. They're stuck in their traditional way of thinking, and it's hard to break out of that."

"That's kind of you," Inaya said. "But I'm still mad. She doesn't have to spew her thoughts all over us."

I'm surprised at how little anger I feel. "Yeah, I had a flash of anger, but for some reason it's gone. I can't explain it."

"Must be the Holy Spirit's got a hold on you," Glenn expounded in his preacher voice. That got more looks from the customers.

"Or maybe you have been battling this stuff longer and can let it roll on off easier," Avery suggested.

"That could be it," I agreed.

"OK, feet, it's time to pound the pavement for a few more hours," Shani announced.

At 3:07 a few delegates emerged from the building. I passed the door then looped around. Our line had dwindled from the morning, so I made each lap quicker.

Henry Walsh walked through the door as I was directly opposite it. He circled around to meet me. I knew what he was going to say by the look on his face, and my heart sank to my toes.

He shook his head as he approached. "We lost by a hundred and forty-nine votes. I'm sorry."

"I don't know what to say. I was so hopeful." My eyes were dry, too sad for tears. I wanted to lie down and curl into a ball and never get up.

Jack came hurrying over. "Bad news?"

Henry nodded.

"Thanks for all you've done. You're an inspiration, and we'll just have to keep fighting, darling. This is just a flat tire on the road to redemption. The fight goes on, and we'll be back next time." *How can he be positive after this defeat? I'm dying here.*

The Musketeers gathered around me, Shani and Inaya's arms around my shoulders.

"This is awful. I can't believe they turned it down," Inaya said.

"I'm not surprised. Remember, this is a long game. We have to take down the wall one brick at a time," Shani encouraged.

"If it's any consolation, we lost by over five hundred votes last time," Henry offered.

"One brick at a time," Glenn echoed.

I could see by the slumped shoulders that the word had made it around the picket line. The next thing I knew, Glenn was in the center of the circle lifting his arms and shouting, "One brick at a time! One brick at a time!"

The picketers joined in. Jack came over the bullhorn, "One brick at a time! Keep shouting, darlings! One brick at a time! We may have lost this skirmish, but we have pulled down a lot of bricks!

Jack's words and the crowd's chants brought feeling back to my numb body. My heart was still in my toes. *I don't know if I can keep marching. Each step will be a stomp on my heart.*

Jack put both hands on my cheeks. "Promise me that you will come back tomorrow. This is not a time for quitters."

Every fiber of my being wanted to say no, but the intensity in Jack's eyes moved me to say, "Yes. I'll be back." *At least tomorrow's session only goes till lunchtime.*

Walking back to the hotel, my mind kept spinning and getting nowhere. *What am I going to do? What am I going to do?* No answers came, just that infernal repetitive question.

The phone rang. "Hey, Mellie."

"That doesn't sound good. What happened?"

"They voted the proposal down," my voice as flat as my heart.

"I'm sorry. I wish I were there with you."

"Yeah, I could use you right now."

"I know you're disappointed but remember that you still have options. That other denomination will be lucky to get you." *Mellie never can remember the United Church of Christ.*

"I guess you're right. I should probably contact them soon."

"I sense a silent but."

"But I really want to minister in my own denomination."

"In that case, suck it up, buttercup. You'll have to keep on fighting."

"I don't know if there is any fight left in me. I was so hoping this would bring the change I need."

"Changing directions in a big ship like the church is labor and time intensive. But you have God on your side, so sooner or later it will happen."

"Thanks for the pep talk."

Chapter 33

Thursday, March 13, 2025

Glenn had to threaten me with a pitcher of water over my head to get me out of bed the next morning.

"Get up or I'm pouring on the count of three. One. Two."

"OK. OK. I'm up." I moved to the edge of the bed to prove it.

"You'd better hurry!"

I was soul weary as we marched, not to mention my feet being sore. Just before noon, Jack picked up the megaphone and spoke to the fifty-ish people there.

"Darlings, you have done excellent work this week! We have knocked a lot of bricks out of that wall. One day we will be accepted, appreciated, and affirmed for who we are. Until then we keep marching, we keep working, we keep pushing! The delegates will be coming out soon, so let's keep the line tight. We have one more chance to show our resolve. Thank you so much for all you've done this week, and I'll be letting you know when the next opportunity presents itself."

The delegates emerged in droves. A line formed and people began walking clockwise just outside our counterclockwise loop. They surrounded us and began to sing.

We shall not be, we shall not be moved,
We shall not be, we shall not be moved,

Just like a tree that's planted by the water
We shall not be moved.

Angry glares peered from many of the faces I passed by. *I have to keep my composure and not let them rattle me.*

I began to hear another song rising from our group.

Jesus loves me!
This I know, for the Bible tells me so.
Little ones to Him belong;
They are weak, but He is strong.

I joined in, singing as loudly as I dared since my voice isn't wonderful.

After our groups had circled each other three times, the delegates began pushing through the picket line, shoving us. I saw one woman from our group fall. A man gave me a shove as he came through. I caught my balance before falling.

The attacks stunned me. I had no voice to call them out for their behavior. *These are supposed to be leaders of the church?*

Jack sounded over the bullhorn. "We have just witnessed how people who aren't touched by the love of Jesus behave." He had it turned up full volume so the retreating delegates could hear. "In the end, the love of God will prevail and hatred will be smashed under Jesus's feet."

Our group applauded. I saw anger in the faces of the delegates who turned back to scowl at Jack. After all of the delegates had finished exiting the building, Jack called us together.

"My darlings, you did excellent work this week. We have pulled down a lot of bricks from that wall that is blocking us from fully participating in the church. We got a glimpse of what we are battling in those hostile folks who attacked us. Is everyone OK? Do we need any ambulances?" Nods followed by shaking of heads moved through the group.

"Wonderful! We battle against the forces of darkness and principalities and powers, but we must not give up. In the end love will conquer all!" More applause.

I will let you know as soon as I'm aware of the next opportunity to be the voice of the LGBTQ+ community. In the meantime, keep the faith, keep praying, and keep fighting!"

"My feet are sooo tired," Avery complained back at the hotel.

"I know what you mean. These puppies are howling," Shani added, kicking off her boots.

"I don't think I'm up for sightseeing," I grumped.

"Let's take a thirty-minute nap. We should be good to go by then," Inaya said.

"Where do you get all that energy?" Glenn joked.

"Oh, come on. We have to at least see the Arch," Inaya encouraged.

Glenn lay down on the bed and was out. For the first time in a long time I wanted to write in my diary. Not having it, I pulled out my computer to jot down my thoughts.

3/13/25

This has been quite a setback. The convention voted down the proposal to allow LGBTQ+ folks to be ordained and serve in the ministry. I don't know what to do. Mellie says to keep fighting. Jack says to keep fighting. Everybody says to keep fighting. But how long do I bang my head against an immovable wall? My heart won't climb back out of my feet.

I need some guidance. Is it time to give up the fight and change denominations, or do I continue down this soul-crushing road? Or was Dad right all along? Should I not even be pursuing ministry? I felt so certain you wanted me in the ministry. Did I just misread your call? I don't know how to move on from this mess.

A knock on the door signaled naptime was over. Shani poked Glenn to awaken him.

"I don't think I'm going." I crashed onto the bed.

"Can I see what you're writing?" Inaya asked.

I slid the computer toward her, lips drawn.

Inaya read through the entry. "We have to get your mind out of the gutter and your heart out of your shoes. You're definitely going with us. Avery..." Inaya gestured to my other side. She took one arm and Avery the other, and they literally dragged me from the room.

Sunday, March 16, 2025

"That sucks!" Alecs's eyes narrowed.

"Yeah."

"What are you going to do now?"

"I don't know," I answered, looking at the floor as if there were something interesting there.

"They're still banning books about LGBTQ+ people."

"What are you going to do now?"

"I don't know. Mom won't let me go to any more protests. We're two peas in a pod, and the pod is wilting, shriveling."

"We are bleak, aren't we."

Alecs laughed.

"What so funny about shriveling in the pod?"

"You claim there is an infinite power on your side, and here we sit moping like kids who've dropped their ice cream. Surely there's something to be happy about."

Alecs had never said a religious thing since I met her. The comment shocked me with the realization that I was placing all my hope in human beings. "You know, you're right. I've been discounting what God could do in our situations. We'll have to keep the faith and trust on."

"I like the sparkle in your eyes."

"And I like you. You've helped pull me out of the doldrums," I smiled for the first time since St. Louis handed me the defeat. "Thanks for lifting me up today. I need to get going. Mellie is coming back into town."

"When is the wedding?"

"We haven't set the date yet." I could feel accusatory vibes.

"Y'all have to get on that! Don't forget to invite me. I want to be there."

"I could never forget you! I definitely expect you to come."

"We wouldn't miss it," Janet said, coming in from the kitchen.

I drove back to my apartment, enjoying some Alecs-inspired joy. About three blocks from home the phone rang.

"Where are you?"

"I'm almost back to the apartment."

"Good, because I'm sitting here waiting for you."

"You're back early!" I forced my foot not to bare down on the accelerator. Mellie was sitting on the patio when I pulled up. I jumped out of the car and flew into her arms.

"I missed you, too," she said.

Emotions bubbled over into tears as the joy of being with her collided with the sadness I had felt since the defeat in St. Louis.

"There's something wet on my neck. Are you crying?"

I nodded, unable to speak. Mellie squeezed harder. I had no idea how long we stayed that way. It felt so good to be in her arms. My tears finally stopped.

Mellie pushed back. "Are those happy or sad tears?"

"A mixture. I'm a hot mess! I'm sure more of the tears were smiling at seeing you than frowning at the path to my ordination being blocked."

"I'm glad to hear I'm winning," she grinned.

"Hot chocolate with marshmallows?"

"That sounds almost as wonderful as you!"

Mellie plopped onto the couch while I busied with the hot chocolate. "I bet you're tired."

"I left extra early so I could get back."

"That's too long of a drive for one day. You need to go back to stopping in Memphis." I dropped some mini marshmallows in.

"It's worth it to have a little more time with my favorite human." She grinned as I handed her a mug.

"We have work to do." I returned her grin.

"Oh?"

"Yeah. I'm tired of fielding a never-ending stream of 'When's the wedding?'"

"I know. We need to set a date and a place."

"Inaya suggested Cannon Chapel. The idea is growing on me. What do you think?"

Hesitation. What is she thinking?

"I was kind of hoping for an outside wedding."

"I thought about that, too, until I remembered how hot and buggy it would be. I'm not sure I want to sweat like a pig during the ceremony."

Mellie burst out laughing.

"What's so funny?"

"I'm picturing you in a wedding dress with sweat dripping off your chin and wet stains shining through."

"Yuk!"

"I think it's cute!"

I scrunched my eyes. "You're nuts!"

"That's what you love about me."

"True."

I pulled away from a long kiss. "If you're trying to distract me, it's working."

"What were we talking about?"

My soul fell into those beautiful, half-closed blue eyes. I pulled her closer. "We were talking about that thing that would let us spend the rest of our lives together."

"Oh, yeah. The pig-sweat wedding. I'm afraid I have to agree. If we're doing it in the summer it should be indoors."

"Having it in a church feels important to me, but I guess I could look at other venues."

"Actually, I like the idea of having it here. This is where we met, and we'll always have this place in common no matter where life takes us."

"So we have a location?"

"Yes! Now all we need is a date."

Excitement surged as I opened the calendar on my phone. "I can't believe we are really doing this!"

"You still want to get married, right?"

"Of course! I just meant that it feels a lot more real to have concrete plans. Let's see. Do you want to be June brides?"

"That's only twelve weeks away."

"You don't think we can pull it off?"

"Not with finals coming. How about July or early August? We need time for a honeymoon before school starts back."

I flipped over to July. "What looks good?"

"How about the nineteenth? Of course, we'll have to check to see if the chapel is available that day."

I squealed so loudly that Mellie jumped. "We're getting married! We're getting married!"

Mellie held me tightly, and for that moment the anxiety over ordination evaporated.

Chapter 34

Johnny looked extra long-faced as he walked into my apartment for our Saturday Musketeers session.

"What's wrong?" Inaya asked.

He sat down, taking his time to respond. "I'm glad I didn't go to the protest, but I feel guilty about it. It might have blown my cover."

"Your cover?" I asked.

"Yeah."

"Do you care to explain?" Shani prompted.

"They might have found out I'm gay."

"They being…?" Glenn tugged.

"The ordination committee. Now, I can still just not tell them."

"So you've reversed your decision and gone back to trying to hide your true identity in order to be part of a church that doesn't accept you?" Shani scolded.

Johnny's shoulders slumped farther. I could see the pain in his eyes.

"Guys, this is a hard decision. It could cost Johnny his life's goal if he comes out to the denomination. I understand how hard it is. I may never be able to fulfill my calling because of my decision," I interceded.

Johnny's eyes caught mine and he sat a little straighter. "Thanks for understanding. I just don't know what to do, and I want to keep being gay secret in order to keep my options open. I can always come out, but I can never go back into the closet if I tell."

"That is true, but I hate to see you sacrifice yourself for your vocation," Glenn said. "We have to find a way for the whole you to be a minister."

"Besides, I don't think you'll survive long if you try to deny who you are," Avery added. "One thing we've learned is that ministry requires our whole selves."

Johnny slumped again.

"You don't have to do anything right now. I'm sure God will lead you in the direction that's right for you," I consoled. "I think you're doing the right thing by keeping your options open."

"Dr. Stancil won't give us options on the paper due Tuesday. We need to get to work," Glenn, always the pragmatic one, prompted. Laptops opened in unison, and we got busy on the papers.

Sunday, April 20, 2025

Alecs ditched me so she and her new friend could go bowling today. *That's OK. I'm glad she's expanding her life. Besides, we have so many decisions to make for the wedding!* I scrolled through dress options while sitting on the patio drinking coffee and waiting for Mellie. *When we set the date in July, I hadn't realized that we would still have to have all the details worked out before finals were over. We just don't have time to go to a dress store.*

My stress level was rising when Mellie pulled in. "Good morning!" She chirped as she walked to the patio.

"Good morning to you, too."

"You look stressed, and it's only nine o'clock."

I hopped up for a hug. "There's too much wedding stuff to figure out."

"Relax. We'll work it out. And if we don't, that's OK, too. All we need for sure is you, me, and a preacher."

"That's not exactly the wedding we have in mind."

"True. How did that line go?" She paused, thinking. "Plan for perfection, expect the worse, and get something in the middle. Do you have more coffee?"

"You don't think I'd forget you, do you? I was looking at dresses. After we get your coffee, I'll show you some possibilities." *I'm a bit taller than Mellie, but I think we could pull it off.* "What do you think of matching dresses?"

"Cute," she remarked, adding creamer. "I think we'd be darling!"

We pulled our chairs together on the patio, and I started scrolling to find the dresses I had liked.

"Halt!" Mellie ordered. "Go back." I scrolled. "A little further. There!" She pointed to a sleek, elegant calf-length dress with a sequined bodice.

"Wow! How did I miss that one? I like it! Do you want to look at anymore?"

"I'm happy with that one, unless there's something you like better," she grinned.

A wave or relief flowed through my soul. "That's one biggie checked off. We won't have to get married naked."

Her grin widened. "That would be fun!"

My face flushed.

"You like the idea, too! Just you and me, naked as jay birds!"

I couldn't help but laugh and pull her in for a kiss. "You make life so much fun!"

"I love to make you laugh. Now, what other momentous decisions do we need to make today?"

"We need to pick out save the date notices, invitations, flowers, plan a reception, and…"

"Don't forget the most important one of all."

"Oh? What am I forgetting?"

"The honeymoon!"

"I love it when you grin like that!"

We missed church that morning.

Thursday, May 8, 2025

My brain was in a sleep-deprived fog and my nerves jittered as I sat down for the last final. It was the church polity class. *I hope I don't crash right in the middle of the test.*

"We've got this!" Inaya chirped, taking the seat next to me.

"How do you do it?" I asked, overwhelmed by her fresh presence.

"Do what?"

"Come to the last final looking so… untired." I struggled to even find that word.

"I found that I do better if I get a full night's sleep, so I stop studying and go to bed."

I may have grunted.

Inaya laughed. "You should try that sometime."

The professor entered and handed out the tests. I got to it, willing my mind and hand to function.

After the test, the Musketeers gathered in the common area on the third floor.

"We survived our second year!" Avery whooped, charging up to the group.

"I'm not sure I did," I responded.

"You do look rough," Shani said, her eyes bleary, too.

"Same to you," I countered and got a laugh from the crew. "I hope I passed that last one. My brain was total mush."

"You know you passed. You always get good grades," Johnny corrected me.

"I hope you're right. I'm going to miss y'all over the summer." A wave of sadness washed over. *These people have been my lifeline for the last two years.* "I don't know what I would have done without y'all during our time here."

"Now don't go getting all maudlin," Glenn said, hopping next to me and hugging me around the shoulders. You won't even miss us because you have a wedding coming up."

"Y'all will be there, won't you?"

"I wouldn't miss it," Inaya assured me.

"You don't really think you can get married without us, do you?" Shani said.

"Thanks. Maybe we can plan a dinner or something beforehand so we'll have time to visit."

"Let us put that together. You'll have enough to worry about," Inaya offered.

"That would be wonderful."

"Until then, all for one and one for all!" Glen held up his sword hand, and we joined him.

I went back to my apartment and crashed onto the bed, two purring kitties settling in next to me. With those comforting sounds, I drifted to sleep.

"There's something missing! I have to find it!" I raced around a strange house, looking in closets and drawers.

"Willow, the wedding starts in five minutes! Come on!" Mellie urged.

"I can't get married without it!" I kept running from room to room to room. "Where is it?" The panic escalated with each door I opened. "I have to find it!" I shouted. I heard doors slamming behind me. Mellie was chasing me, trying to keep up.

The sound of slamming doors brought me awake. *I still hear the doors.* Then Mellie's voice registered.

"Wake up, Willow! The door's locked."

The cats didn't move, so I had to crawl around them to get out of bed. My brain felt like pudding as I unlocked the door.

"Finally," Mellie grumped.

"I'm sorry. I was dead to the world."

"I noticed. I had a nap before coming over, too."

"This was a rough finals week."

"You OK?"

"Yeah. Just tired. I was having a weird dream when you woke me up."

"Do tell!" Mellie sat on the couch and beckoned me next to her.

"It was time for our wedding, but I had lost something. I was running all over this weird house looking for it. You kept chasing me and telling me we needed to get to the service."

"They say dreams represent what's going on in our souls, and the different characters are varying parts of ourselves. It sounds like you feel something is missing in your life."

Her eyes softened to concern as I thought about what she had said. "Most likely what I am missing is a path to ordination. But what would you represent, then?"

"Maybe I'm the part of you that's pulling you to move on and put that struggle behind."

"That makes since. But since I keep running and searching, am I not ready to put it behind me?"

"Nope. Not yet. We'll have to find the path together."

"Together." I nestled my forehead into her neck and was so comfortable, I fell back asleep."

Chapter 35

Friday, May 23, 2025

I *envy Mellie. She has her life planned out, and there are no obstacles. When she graduates, employers will be lined up at her door begging her to come work for them. Her being gay won't be an issue at all. Maybe I should have gone into nursing. Ugh! I couldn't take the blood and needles.*

It was our last day with Mellie's mom before we left to visit my family for two weeks. We were originally going to part and visit our parents separately but being away from Mellie that long seemed too hard. She suggested we make the visits together. "It would save gas and cut down on separation anxiety," she reasoned.

"You look pensive," Mellie observed, walking into the kitchen after her shower.

"I was just being jealous."

"Do explain." She poured coffee, eyeing me as I hesitated.

"It's silly. I don't want to tell you."

"You know that building a relationship requires openness. Now spill the beans, Willow."

"OK. I was envying you for having no obstacles ahead. You'll be able to take your pick from a bunch of jobs, and none of the employers will even ask if you're gay."

"Yeah, nursing is a sweet career right now," she smiled, stirring creamer into her coffee.

"I, on the other hand, am in a dead-end degree program with no prospects for a job. What am I going to do?" My anxiety spiked. Again. *I wish it would quit doing that.*

"Oh, no. There you go again."

"I can't help it. Anxiety just attacks. It won't leave me alone."

"One step at a time. Remember that."

"I know. I know. You keep telling me that, but the future looks so… empty. What am I going to do with my life? I can't work as a chaplain if I'm not ordained. I'd have to get another degree to work as a counselor. I need to get things worked out so I know where I'm going."

"But you do know where you're going." Her mischievous grin calmed my nerves.

"Oh? Where?"

"Today you're going hiking at the lake and then to the grocery store to get steaks for tonight."

"That's true. I was looking a little farther down the road."

She walked around and put her arms around me. "You really can't see that far ahead, sweetheart. That's why we need to focus just on today. Leave next year to figure itself out."

I relaxed in her embrace and let the uncertainties of the future flow out with my breath. Mellie softly rubbed my back.

"There. That's better," she soothed.

I slid my chair back and pulled her into my lap. "I'm so thankful for you."

Tuesday, June 3, 2025

We had been at my house, well technically my parents' house, for ten days when Dad made his announcement. "I'm not paying for the whole wedding, you know."

"No one asked you to," I answered, tensing at this sudden return to his old self. *I bet he would if I were marrying a man. It seems a tradition has yet to develop regarding who pays when there are two brides or two grooms in the wedding. I wonder how long that will take. Seminary has trained me to think like that. I wish Will were here instead of doing that vet internship.*

I realized I had drifted off, and Dad was talking. "I'm sorry. Would you repeat that? I got lost in thought."

"I said that your expenses are getting out of control. When your mother and I married, the whole wedding cost… Joyce, do you remember how much our wedding cost?" *OK. I was expecting him to say that two women shouldn't be getting married.*

"About eight hundred dollars," Mom called from the kitchen.

"We were sensible. We had it in our church with the reception in the fellowship hall. Our Sunday School class provided the food for the reception."

"Dad, that was twenty-eight years ago. Things have changed. Prices have gone up. Besides, my church won't allow me to get married there."

Dad just grunted and walked out of the den. I noticed the worried look on Mellie's face.

"Did he really think we expected him to pay for the whole thing?"

"Probably. It's tradition that the father pays for his daughter's wedding."

"Mom doesn't really have much to contribute. I could pay for half… Well, I mean I could pay you back after I start working."

"You silly sort-osaurous. You would just be putting money into our account, then."

She smiled. "That sounds nice, but what is a sort-osaurous?"

"I have no idea, but you are one." I laughed and jumped to tickle her. She squealed and ran around the couch.

"Calm down, children," Mom called.

I fell onto the couch laughing.

"It wasn't *that* funny," Mellie crashed into me.

"Laughter is good medicine," I managed after getting the giggles under control. "This whole wedding thing is so stressful. I'll be glad when it's all nailed down."

"Yeah, me, too." Mellie sat up. "Should we just drop the reception? That's going to be the most expensive part."

"No way! I want a party."

I pulled the receipts from the folder we were using for wedding planning and opened the calculator on my phone. "So far we've spent about four thousand five hundred, and all we have left is the reception. We can do this!"

"If you say so, but that's a lot of money. Maybe we should just have finger foods at the chapel."

"We just have to find a place that will let us in for not too much money." My mind rushed around trying to think of a spot.

Mom appeared in the den and spoke softly. "Don't worry about Dad. He'll come around, and we'll help. He's always a little shell-shocked about spending money. Go ahead and plan a nice reception. We need to have time to celebrate."

"You're so precious," Mellie said. "I'm thankful you're going to be my mother-in-law."

"Thanks! I'm glad you'll be my… daughter-in-law? Is that the right term?"

"Perfect," Mellie grinned.

"It will be great to have you in the family."

Mom hustled back to the kitchen. "See, I told you it would be OK."

"You're right. Is the reception all we have left to work out?"

The thought hit like a clap of thunder. "We haven't talked about our last name!"

"We haven't, have we." Mellie searched my eyes. "You haven't even thought about it!"

I cringed. "Guilty. I've been so worried about everything else that I missed that detail."

"It's a pretty major detail."

"What are you thinking?"

"I'm for hyphenation. Do you like Waters-Grier or Grier-Waters better? I think I like Grier-Waters. It rolls off the tongue. Then if we have any kids, they would be earlier in the alphabet. I was always last for everything in school."

"Kids? We haven't talked about that, either."

"I kind of like kids. How about you?" She was reading my face before I even spoke.

"The thought has wondered around in my mind. I think I would like to have children. But would one of us get pregnant or would we adopt?" Relief washed over Mellie's face. *This is important to her. Why didn't she mention it before?*

"I'd love to get pregnant and have a baby. It sounds like fun."

"I guess we could take turns," I laughed.

"I like it! That's a great idea."

"But there would be a lot of stigma the kids would have to battle. That might be hard."

Mellie scrunched her eyebrows. "You wouldn't let that stop us, would you? Besides, things are changing. It wasn't that long ago that we couldn't have gotten married. By the time we have kids, there may be no problems."

"Having kids isn't that far away, you know."

"Oh hush. I want children. At least one."

She searched my eyes with pleading in hers. "It's OK, Mellie. We'll have children, one way or the other. We'll just have to deal with the problems as they come." I opened my arms, and she fell into them. "What other major details have we failed to cover?"

"I don't know, but I'm glad to get those two out of the way."

"Remember back in Fort Smith when you told me building a relationship requires openness?"

"Yeah. So?"

"It goes both ways. If something's on your mind, you have to tell me. I can't read it, you know."

"OK. I'm holding no more worries. Well, except for this reception. Let's get back to planning that."

I opened the computer and entered a search for wedding reception venues near Emory. "OK, here we go."

"Yum, what's that place?"

"It looks too nice." I clicked on the Miller-Ward House on Emory's campus.

"Wow! Yep, too nice." Mellie frowned when she saw the price tag."

I clicked on the next one and watched the color drain from Mellie's face.

"That's even worse," she squeaked. "How about restaurants with private dining areas?"

"At this late date, it may be hard to find a place," I warned.

"I hear moaning and groaning," Mom said, marching into the den.

"It's sticker shock from the reception venues we've looked at," I explained.

"Hold that thought and let me talk to Dad to see if we can agree on an amount to contribute." She left with an air of purpose.

Mellie smiled with relief. "What if we could get that first one and cater Bar-B-Que? That would be amazing! Check to see if it's available."

I checked. "I can't believe it! It's open that afternoon!"

"OK, but don't get your hopes up until we hear from your parents. I hope no one rents it before us!"

We were scrolling through the photo gallery and being amazed when Mom came back. "We'll put five thousand toward the wedding. You can use it however you like."

Mellie and I squealed with delight and grabbed Mom from both sides.

"Thank you so much!" Mellie and I whooped at the same time.

"I have to thank Dad, too." I took off down the hall and found him in the study.

"Hey," I said, announcing my presence.

He looked up from his book. "I assume Mom told you."

"She did, and I am so grateful. That's so generous!"

"We've been planning to pay for your wedding since you were born. I just didn't think it would be like this."

I resisted the surge of anger and strived to keep it out of my voice. "Still, I'm overwhelmed by the gift. I don't mean to be a disappointment, but I can't help who I am."

I watched as an unreadable expression took hold of Dad's face. As I searched, trying to figure out what was going on, he said, "Willow, you're not the disappointment. I am. I'm sorry it has taken me so long to accept you for how you were created. I want you to know that I'm trying to get there."

I thought my knees were going to buckle. I fell around Dad's neck, quivering as tears sprang from my eyes. Dad hugged me tightly. "I love you, too."

Chapter 36

Monday, June 9, 2025

Guilt surged when it dawned on me that Mellie had no place to stay when we get back to Atlanta. She had given up her dorm room, which wouldn't be open in the summer anyway, and we planned to live in my apartment after the wedding.

She's planning on us living together! I've been so wrapped up in wedding planning that I failed to see that coming! I hope Mom doesn't ask! I had already seen Dad on his way to work.

I slipped into Mellie's room and whispered, "Are you planning to stay with me until the wedding?"

"I thought you'd never ask," she answered with that grin I love. She read my hesitation. "I see guilt oozing out of your pores. It's OK. Everybody lives together now. Besides, in a little over five weeks you'll be legally mine!" She was bouncing with excitement.

"How can I possibly resist you?"

She oozed over to me, swinging her hips. "I happen to know that you can't resist!"

"You're right. Resistance is futile." She pulled me close.

"Umm hmm," I heard from the doorway. "Sorry to interrupt, but would you like me to make lunches for your trip?" Mom asked.

"Thanks, Mom! But we're actually going to wait and leave right after lunch."

"Yay! That will give me a couple of more hours with you! You can help me pick a place for us to stay. I don't want to end up a long ways off."

We gathered around the kitchen table with mugs of coffee and started hunting accommodations.

"Look at this place! Do you think Misty would be comfortable staying in the same house as us? It has plenty of room."

Mom had located an older, elegant home for rent on Lullwater Road about a mile from campus. She turned the computer so Mellie could see.

"Wow! That's a nice place! I'm sure Mom would love to stay there. I'm not sure she can afford it, though."

"No worries. We've got it covered. It will give us a chance to get to know each other a little better."

Mellie texted the idea to her mom. After a couple of back and forth texts, Misty agreed.

Wednesday, July 16, 2025

Guilt reared its ugly head again. *Mom and Dad are coming down today. They'll figure out Mellie and I have been living together. What am I going to do?*

"Are you going to pour that or hope it gets in by osmosis?" Mellie teased.

I observed the coffee pot frozen in midair. "It just hit me that Mom and Dad will figure out we're living together when they get here."

"And?"

"They won't approve."

"Willow, Willow, Willow. You have to quit worrying so. We're going to be wife and wife in three days! Quit fretting and get happy!"

"Yes, ma'am. I'll try." My arm got back in gear, and I poured two mugs of coffee. "What if…"

"Nope! Don't say it! We're adults, and we have made our decisions. They will just have to live with it. It's OK."

My life has been so riddled with guilt and rejection. I'll be glad when all that's behind me. Will it ever be behind me? I tried to squelch the rising worry. "Let me transition to more positive worrying, then. Is there anything we have forgotten to arrange for the wedding?"

"Not that I know of. We have a preacher, a place, dresses, and flowers."

"I'm glad Doctor Galloway was willing to do the ceremony. He's nice."

"Remind me why we picked him." Mellie sat down after adding cream and caramel flavoring to her coffee.

"He's my pastoral care professor. He can perform the wedding since he's UCC. Do you think that's a sign that I'm being led to change denominations?" I sipped my delicious coffee and watched as she responded.

"I have no idea about signs. Remember, one day at a time. Our mission today is to get parents settled into that amazing house."

"OK, I'll try to steer back to the present. Will's coming tomorrow! That will be fun."

"I like Will. He makes me wish I'd had a brother."

"After Saturday, he'll officially be yours, too."

"Yay! This is so exciting!" Mellie clapped her hands. "We're getting married!"

I smiled, and my heart warmed with joy. "I love seeing you happy and excited."

Saturday, July 19, 2025

My eyes burst open, and I flung off the covers. "We overslept!" I announced, jumping out of bed.

Mellie's sleepy voice was barely audible. "What time is it?"

"Oops. Four forty-seven." I double checked the alarm setting then slid back into bed. My eyes closed but sleep stayed out of reach. I waited till I heard Mellie's even breathing and quietly climbed out of bed.

Pulling a throw over me against the coolness of the air conditioning, I started writing in my old diary.

7/19/25: WEDDING DAY!

I'm marrying Mellie today. Life couldn't be better! Well, there is one thing that could make it better, but Mellie made me promise not to let my worries over ordination bog me down during the wedding and honeymoon. Lord, you have been so good to me. Thank you for letting Mellie fall into my life. Thank you for helping my family to accept me the way you created me. Somehow, you even brought Dad around.

As I wrote, images of a gaping hole filtered into my consciousness. I stilled my pen and closed my eyes, letting the image materialize. It was a dream I had before getting up, and it brought with it a sense of dread. I wrote it down as I remembered.

Dad was walking me down the aisle while Will walked Mellie. I was so happy. In front of the preacher, right where we were to stand, a huge hole opened. I stopped and looked into it.

There was no bottom, nothing but darkness. I began to sweat. Mellie smiled and stepped into it. I swallowed and followed her. Then I was falling.

I smiled, thinking about the dream. *I'm about to step into the unknown, and Mellie is coming with me. Maybe that's a nice dream.* My eyes got heavy, and I drifted off to sleep with that pleasant thought like a soft pillow.

Softness brushed my lips, and I awoke to Mellie's gentle kiss. "Hey. You're getting married today," she grinned.

"I hear you are, too. We have hair and make-up at ten, dressing at one-thirty, and the wedding at three. We'd better get moving!"

I told Mellie about my dream as I pulled on my jeans.

"I'll happily jump down that hole with you!" She confirmed.

"It's all set and ready! There's nothing left but to enjoy the service," Mellie announced as we waited for our cues to enter for the ceremony. I was nervous and excited.

The opening notes of "Wedding March" sounded, and Dad took my arm. *There was a time I didn't believe he would ever walk me down the aisle.* Will took Mellie's arm, and we walked in together. My bridesmaids, Inaya, Shani, and Avery, and Mellie's three teammates from tennis formed a welcoming sight.

My nerves made the ceremony a blur, but Mellie's beautiful face kept me anchored. Dr. Galloway told us what to do each step along the way. After the final prayer, he said, "You may kiss your bride." I drank in Mellie's soul through her marvelous blue eyes then enjoyed a precious kiss.

Turning us to face the congregation, Dr. Galloway announced, "You are all invited to the reception at the Miller-Ward Alumni House. Please join us there at five o'clock. I now present to you Mellie and Willow Grier-Waters."

Claps erupted as Mellie and I hustled down the aisle. *I'm actually married to the most wonderful person in the world!* People showered us with congratulations.

"My smiling muscles are getting worn out," Mellie whispered.

"Mine, too. But this sure is fun!"

By the time people finished congratulating us, we had an hour before the reception. "Let's go relax at the venue until people show up," Mellie suggested.

"Sounds good. There's not much point in going to the house."

At 5:00 people began arriving. "How could I be so tired already?" I moaned.

"You have to summon your energy reserves. It's party time! Maybe this will help!" Mellie ran her fingers up and down my ribs.

I squirmed with laughter. "I'm sure that's just what I needed."

The reception was a blast. We went through introducing the bridal party. The Bar-B-Que was delicious. Then came the father-daughter dance. Since Mellie's father wasn't there, Will filled in. That suited Mellie just fine.

I took Dad's hand, and we began to dance around the floor. *I didn't realize he was such a good dancer.* "Dad, I've envisioned this dance since I was about twelve years old. It's the one thing I've always wanted at my wedding."

"This is special," he answered.

We had the venue till 10:00, so Mellie and I planned our exit at 9:45. Since we were staying at my, oops, our apartment, we didn't bother to change. Tomorrow we were heading to Daytona for our honeymoon.

Opening the venue doors, the crowd lined the walkway, armed with bubbles. People started cheering, but I quieted them. "Mellie and I are extremely grateful to each of you for sharing this special day with us. It means a lot that you were here."

With that we started down the gauntlet of bubbles. The cheers were punctuated by horns blaring. Concern drained my joy. Gunshots echoed over the horns. Everything went blurry.

I heard Will yelling, "Everyone on the ground! Call 911." He pulled me to the ground, and I heard Mellie scream. She crashed next to us, and bright blood seeped through the shoulder of her dress.

"No! No! No!" I dragged myself to her. "Someone call an ambulance!" I yelled three times. She held her shoulder, rolling side to side. "Will! Help!"

Will whipped out his handkerchief. "This is going to hurt, but I'm putting pressure on it to slow down the bleeding." He pushed down on the wound. Mellie winced and passed out. My heart broke into a thousand pieces, and the world went dark.

"We have to get her to the hospital," I whimpered.

Will whacked me on the arm with his phone. "Call 911, just to make sure it happens. I noticed the gunshots and horns had faded.

"I need an ambulance! My wife has been shot!" I screamed into the phone. As the operator talked me through providing the address and telling her what happened, I noticed Will putting his coat over Mellie. *Please don't put that over her face!* He was just keeping her warm.

I disconnected the call and heard, "It was the same group that was at the protest. I saw their shirts." Looking up, I saw Alecs. She knelt and put her hand on my shoulder. I could see compassion flowing from her heart. Janet appeared over her shoulder, and she nodded agreement.

"Please tell the police that," I managed through my tears.

Misty cradled Mellie's head, and Mom and Dad hovered on my flanks. I watched Mellie's chest rise and fall with slow breaths as I moved hair out of her face. Time had stopped. I had no idea how long we were frozen in that position before I heard sirens.

Hands took my shoulders and moved me aside, an authoritative male voice saying, "I need to get to the victim." EMTs converged on my precious Mellie. Words and equipment whisked by.

Mellie's eyes opened, and I sobbed. "You're back," is what came out.

"We're transporting you to the hospital," the man who had moved me aside stated.

"I need to go with her," I whimpered.

"You can meet us at the hospital, ma'am," the EMT said. My soul was pulled out of my body as I watched her being loaded into the ambulance. Then the doors closed, and I crumpled to the ground.

Will and Dad lifted me. "Come on, sweetheart. We have to get to the hospital," Dad said.

Chapter 37

*W*hich hospital? Which hospital? That question kept ricocheting in my mind. I was lost, not knowing where they had taken her. *Dad seems to know where we're going.*

We had finally gotten away from the police officer who wanted to question me. Dad, Mom, Will, Misty, and I were in Dad's vehicle. My sobs had turned to numbness. Will and Misty were both patting my leg. "She's going to be OK," Misty consoled.

Dad pulled up to the emergency room entrance at Emory University Hospital. I nearly pushed Will out, trying to hurry him up. They allowed Misty and me to go back.

"Hey," Mellie croaked as we walked into the little room.

"Hey." I wanted so badly to hug her but was afraid I'd hurt her, so I touched my cheek to hers.

"They got my dress off without cutting it."

"What?" I failed to comprehend and looked to Misty for help. She burst out laughing.

"You've been shot, and you're worried about your dress!"

Mellie grinned. "It's my wedding dress."

"I think you're going to be OK," Misty added.

"These pain medicines are great! You should try them."

I gently took Mellie's hand, avoiding the IV. "We need a picture of that goofy look."

Someone pulled the curtain back. "I'm taking you to X-ray. Please tell me your name and date of birth."

Mellie paused. "I don't know my name. Well, I do. I was Melissa Waters until this afternoon. Now I'm Melissa Grier-Waters. But that hasn't been officially changed, so I guess I'm still Melissa Waters. What do you think?"

"I think you're precious," I answered. "She's right about her name," I directed to the woman who had come to take her.

With Mellie back from X-ray, we waited on the doctor.

"I do know how to ruin a beautiful day," Mellie moaned.

"You didn't ruin it, those jerks with guns did," I corrected.

"I guess that's true. But still, this wasn't how I had planned to spend our wedding night." Her cheeks reddened.

"Mellie Grier-Waters, I've never seen you blush before."

"I shouldn't say things like that with my mom present."

Misty laughed. "We'll just chalk that one up to the drugs."

"Hi, I'm Doctor Adamson. Please tell me your name and date of birth," a fit looking woman with graying hair announced, popping into the room.

"Melissa Waters. October twenty-three, two thousand two."

"We need to do surgery on that arm. The bullet passed through, but there is enough damage to the deltoid and one of the arteries that it needs some repair."

"Will I be able to use my arm again?" Mellie asked.

"You should recover fully, but you will need to be in a sling for about six weeks," Dr. Adamson answered. "We have an operating room available. Are you agreeable to the surgery?"

Mellie eyed me and Misty then nodded her head.

"Good. You're… wife and mom?" Dr. Adamson asked.

Mellie reached her hand toward me. "How did you know?"

"The dress might have been a clue," she grinned. "You are welcome to wait with her till we take her back. They will direct you to the waiting room where I'll come talk to you after the surgery. We'll keep you overnight. If everything looks good in the morning, you can go home."

"Yay!" I jumped up and clapped. It was my turn to blush. Dr. Adamson smiled. "She's going to be fine," she said before walking out.

I couldn't sit still while Mellie was in surgery. I paced the waiting room. Will walked with me for a few rounds, then sat down. All six bridesmaids walked into the waiting room, still wearing their dresses.

"Is Mellie OK?" Inaya asked.

"She's in surgery, but the doctor said she'll be fine. Hopefully, she can go home in the morning."

"That's a relief!" Shani said.

Alecs and Janet came in right after the others. *I'm glad this is a big waiting room!* Alecs hugged me. "I'm sorry about Mellie."

"Thanks, Alecs."

"The police said there are security cameras. Hopefully, they can identify who did this. I told them they were part of the White Nationalists of America."

"I sure hope they catch the creeps," Misty responded, venom in her voice.

Misty's response sent me down a dark hole filled with anger and dread. *Are we always going to face this kind of hate and rejection? Is there no way to escape it? Why can't people just let us be? I couldn't bear to bring children into this world. Those jerks have to pay for what they did to Mellie! It's just not fair! No one should hurt her. She's too precious. Lord, I need you to get Mellie through this. She has to be OK.*

A touch on my forearm brought me back. Inaya was holding a tissue out to me. I hadn't noticed the tears flowing. "Thanks."

Dr. Adamson popped into the waiting room with a smile. "The surgery went well. There was a laceration to the deltoid that I was able to repair. The artery wasn't nicked nearly as badly as it appeared to be. All in all, she's in good shape and should be able to return to playing tennis."

I raised my eyebrows. *How did she know about tennis?* I guess Dr. Adamson read my expression. "Melissa explained how she needs that arm for her backhand on the way to the OR."

"Thank you so much for helping her," Misty said.

"I don't know why people have to be so hateful," Dr. Adamson responded. "Tomorrow you should be able to get on with your new life."

Sunday, July 20, 2025

It was 2:42 in the morning, and my body was exhausted.

"Let's go to the house and get some sleep. There's an extra bed you can use, Willow," Mom suggested.

A surge of panic hit. "I'm not going anywhere! I'm staying with Mellie!"

"I'd like to stay, too," Misty said.

"And I'd like to bring a change of clothes and anything else you need," Will offered.

"That would be nice," I answered. "I'd like jeans, a t-shirt, and my lavender jacket."

"We can speed up the process if I bring your clothes," Dad offered to Misty.

Mellie was sound asleep when they rolled her into the room. She awoke briefly when they moved her to the bed. I gave her a quick kiss, and she was asleep before she could tell us how she felt.

"I'm sure it's the anesthesia," Misty observed.

As if on cue, a nurse came in and stated, "She'll sleep most of the night as the anesthesia wears off. We'll take care of her if you want to sleep in your own beds."

"Nope. I'm staying here." I stated unequivocally.

"Is this your wedding day?"

"Yes. It didn't end so well," I answered.

"I'm so sorry. We'll get her back on her feet as soon as possible." She began taking vital signs.

Will popped in with my change of clothes. "Finally," my feet rejoiced. I hadn't realized how sore they were in the heels. While I was changing, I heard Dad and Misty talking. "We're so happy to have Mellie as a daughter-in-law. We've grown to love her while she visited."

"Thank you. I feel the same about Willow."

I soaked up the joy before leaving the bathroom. *Just a few months ago I would never have believed I would here those words coming from Dad.*

"How are you holding up?" Dad asked as I walked out the bathroom door. "My feet are much happier now. I'm OK, I guess. I want Mellie to be all right. I'm so tired." The words just fell out of my mouth.

"The doctor said she will be fine," Misty pointed out. "We just have to be patient and let her heal."

"Patience is a hard task," I managed through a yawn.

"I'm going to go so you can get some sleep," Dad said with a hug.

"I'm so tired," I said again as I sat down in the chair. My body was shutting down like turning off a computer. The adrenaline had dissipated, and I was going to sleep whether I wanted to or not. I felt a blanket cover me just before sleep took over.

Whispered voices shepherded me back to consciousness. "If I can go home, that's what I want to do," I heard Mellie say, and I was suddenly awake and on my feet.

"You're awake! How do you feel!" I bumped into the side of the bed and had to catch myself from falling on her.

"Good morning, wife," she grinned.

I finally noticed Dr. Adamson standing back, smiling.

"I'm sorry. I didn't mean to interrupt."

"You're fine. It's fun to watch two people so in love," she said. "Now, I need to have a look at the incision."

The hurt shoulder was on the side of the bed where I was sitting, so I moved.

"Looks good. Someone did a great job here. Have you been to the bathroom?"

"I peed earlier," Mellie answered.

Dr. Adamson put a stethoscope to Mellie's abdomen. "Nice. Your gut is working and blood work looks good. We'll get you ready for discharge and send you home with antibiotics and pain medicine. I understand you're a nursing student."

"I am. One year to go."

"Then you know what to watch for. If you see redness, heat, or drainage around the wound I want you to call immediately. Infection is our biggest danger at this point… Well that and you misbehaving and trying to use that shoulder before it's ready. I'll have you come to the office in two weeks to remove the staples. Any questions?"

Mellie shook her head.

"Thank you so much for taking care of her, Dr. Adamson."

"You're quite welcome. That's what I'm here for."

Chapter 38

Friday, August 1, 2025

By Monday afternoon, after we brought Mellie home to the apartment on Sunday, it became apparent that other than Mellie being one-armed, things were under control. Plus, we needed some alone time. We insisted that everyone go home, and we headed to the beach Wednesday morning.

We had a sweet one-bedroom condo with an ocean view. Sunbathing on the beach, relaxing around the pool, and our little wine and cheese parties on the bed made for a scrumptious nine days. I even enjoyed cutting up Mellie's food and helping her get dressed.

"I hate to leave. This has been the perfect honeymoon, except for your shoulder, I mean."

"I'm glad I finally talked you into going."

"I was a little stubborn, wasn't I."

"You can say that again. Just look at what we would have missed."

"You're right, as usual," I agreed, rubbing her thigh as I drove.

"You realize you're going to have to help me rehab this arm when I'm released to play tennis."

"I was hoping so. We have to get you in shape for tennis season. It's your senior year."

We rode in silence for a while as we closed in on Macon. As the miles passed, the relaxed joy of the honeymoon oozed out while the realities of life crawled back in.

I have to get Mellie to her doctor's appointment Monday. Then we have three weeks before classes start. That will be nice. We can just relax and enjoy being together. I wonder if they will send her for physical therapy. I bet they will. The beach sure was nice.

I also have to figure out my life. This is the year. I have to make a decision. I need some direction, Lord. There is no more time to flounder. I either have to change denominations or pick another career. And I want your guidance in deciding.

"Aw, don't." Mellie's comment drew me out of my thoughts.

"Don't what?"

"Start stressing out. We're not even back home yet. Did you know I live at your apartment now?" She twisted in the seat to see me better, and I glimpsed her signature grin.

"I'm not stressing out."

"Yes, you are."

"How can you tell?"

"Your eyes squint just a little when you get stressed."

"Guilty. But you are wrong."

"I am?"

"Yeah. It's our apartment now, not mine."

"Touché! What are you stressing about?" Let me guess. You're worried about my arm."

"Nope."

"Traffic between here and home?"

"Nope."

"Then it has to be the usual: ordination."

"The third time's a charm! I have to make a decision about my life's direction soon. Should I even bother finishing seminary? Should I go ahead and start pursuing another career? Should I go ahead and change denominations? It's just too hard to make that big of a life-altering decision."

"Listen to you."

"I'm listening, and it's a confusing whirlwind." I tried to relax my grip on the poor steering wheel.

"No, you're talking in shoulds and oughts. You need to be thinking in terms of wants. What does your heart tell you it wants to do? That's where you'll find your answer."

Search my heart. She's right. I need to get out of my head and into my heart. What is it telling me?

I tried making the dive from head to heart. What I found surprised me. *It's still there. What I want is what I've always wanted. My heart is telling me that the ministry is where I want to be. I have to keep following that path no matter where it takes me.*

"Willow, dear." Mellie drew me back, and I looked over. "You're going thirty-five miles an hour." A honk confirmed her observation. I hit the gas and sped up.

"Mellie Grier-Waters, you're a wise soul!"

"I like hearing things like that!"

"My heart says that I want to be a minister. I have to follow that path until I get there."

"Good for you! You might have to let go of the ties to your church in order to follow that lead."

"That's true, but we'll see. I have to remember that God is in the mix, too."

We joined the throng of vehicles crawling toward Atlanta on I75, and I noticed that Mellie had gotten quiet. "Is it your turn to stress out?"

"What if the men who shot me are able to find out where we live? What if they come back for another attack? What if they've broken into the apartment and destroyed everything?"

"They can't find out where we live." *I hope I sounded confident.*

"You don't know that. They found our wedding." I could hear the panic on which those words floated.

"True. I have wondered how they knew the reception was for a gay couple. Only last names are listed on the website."

"I know. I checked, too. From the things they shouted, it was obvious they were attacking because we're homosexual."

A heavy silence drowned out the music in the car. *How could they have known?* "Somebody had to tell them we would be there."

"Somebody on staff at the venue, maybe?" Mellie wondered.

"If that's the case, then they don't know where we live." That thought was a comfort.

"I hope you're right… Wait, our address would have been listed on the application to use the site."

Music filtered through the dense silence hovering in the car. I could sense Mellie's anxiety, and I wanted to calm her. *What can I say to help?*

We both startled when Mellie's phone rang.

"Hello… I see. Thanks so much for letting me know." She disconnected. "They've arrested five people for the shooting."

"It's about time!" I didn't have to look to tell Mellie's anxiety was diminishing. "That's a good thing. We won't have to worry about them anymore."

"Unless they get out on bail."

"It hurts seeing you hurt. I wish I could fix everything."

"Life is just too complicated to fix. I think we have to trust and move on."

"You are a wise soul."

Wondering how the shooters found out about our reception kept nagging me. Finally I asked, "Mellie, could you call the officer back and ask if they could include questioning the suspects as to how they found out about our reception?"

"I'm on it." She called back and left a voicemail for the officer.

"If it's someone on staff, this could be a problem for any gay wedding. I really want to know who tipped them off."

I was tired when we got back to the apartment, more so from worrying about Mellie and who tipped off the White Nationalists of America than the drive.

"Home, sweet home," Mellie said, unfolding herself out of the car and stretching as best she could in the sling.

"The condo was nice, but it's good to be back."

Mellie tried to pick up her suitcase but winced with pain.

"Leave it, silly. I'll get it."

We ordered delivery pizza and went to bed early. I spooned Mellie, holding her close as I fell asleep.

Desperate moans awoke me in the night. *Mellie!* She wasn't in the bed. *Has someone grabbed her?*

I rushed into the den, hauling the lamp from the bedside table as a weapon. I found Mellie squirming on the couch. *A nightmare!*

I sat the lamp on the table and rubbed her back. "Mellie. Mellie. Wake up," I called softly. She finally jerked awake. "You were having a nightmare."

"I got shot again."

I pulled her close. "This is going to be harder to get over than we thought. We might need some counseling."

She pulled away. "I don't think so. I'll be fine."

Wednesday, August 20, 2025

I don't know if celebrate is exactly the right word, maybe "began" would be better. Mellie and I began the first day of class with coffee at the Starbucks across the street. She hadn't had a nightmare in two weeks, which was part of our celebration.

Excitement about seeing the Musketeers grew as we rode the elevator up.

"This is our final year as students. I can't wait to graduate and start working." Mellie was excited, too.

"I wish I could say the same, but I don't know what I'll be doing after graduation."

"There you go again. I think it's time for you to quit quivering and go on the offensive. Tonight we formulate a plan to get you out of this rut."

"I've had so many plans. I don't know what else to try. I always end up dejected when I think of the future. It's getting tiresome."

"I'm getting tired of listening to you, too. That's why we're coming up with a final plan. It has to be one that moves you forward and not deeper into the rut." Being in her sling, she waited for me to open the door.

"OK. I'll try to think of something today."

"I'm thinking, too, and you might not like what I come up with."

"That sounds drastic! I'm not good with drastic, you know."

"I've noticed that."

I gave her a quick kiss as our paths parted and headed to class.

"Look, here comes the old married woman!" Glenn teased as I walked into the classroom.

"You're just jealous," I returned.

"That's true. So how is married life?"

"It's good. Mellie's shoulder is getting better. She should be out of the sling in a couple of weeks."

"Y'all did have a rough start," Shani added.

"Hey, everybody!" Inaya said as she bounced into the classroom. "We're starting our final year! I'm excited!" *How can she be so bubbly this early in the morning?*

I heard a grunt. Gregg was sitting two rows in front of us. The sound caught all of our attention.

"You OK, Gregg?" Glenn asked.

"Just trying to wake up," he answered. Then he stretched, his arms rising over his head. His t-shirt sleeve slid up his arm, revealing a chilling sight: a tattoo of a snake circling three letters. I think my heart stopped when I read the letters: WNA.

Chapter 39

Wednesday, August 20, 2025

My mind churned along with my stomach all day. *Could he be a member of the group that shot Mellie? Could he have been in the car? Is he the one who shot her? Is he out on parole? Oh, no! Does he know where we live? Do I tell Mellie?*

The Musketeers gathered in our usual spot on the third floor.

"I'm looking forward to our preaching class," Avery said. "I hope it improves my skills."

"Your congregation does, too," Glenn quipped.

"Hellooooo," I heard Inaya say. She was talking to me. "You seem a thousand miles away."

"It's the stress of married life. Maybe we should stay single," Glenn joked.

Should I tell them? I think I have to. Inaya will keep bugging me till she finds out.

I took a deep breath, motioned for everyone to get close, then whispered, "When Gregg stretched this morning, I saw a tattoo that said, "WNA."

Glenn's face twisted with confusion. "So? A lot of people have tattoos."

"That's the initials of the group that shot Mellie and broke my wrist."

The ensuing silence was accompanied with wide eyes.

"Are you serious?" Shani asked. "I read up on that group, and they are really evil. How could someone in seminary be a part of that?"

Inaya was pecking on her phone. "There are a number of organizations that have the initials, 'WNA,' including the World Nuclear Association. Maybe he's interested in promoting safe nuclear energy."

"The initials had a snake around them that looked like the 'Don't Tread on Me' snake."

"Oh," Inaya responded. "I guess that shoots down my theory."

"Well, Gregg's a jerk, anyway," Johnny pointed out.

"Don't you see?" I continued whispering. "He could have had a part in the shooting. He might have shot Mellie!" *I said that louder than I meant to.*

"I don't think he would do anything that drastic," Avery said.

"He's quite zealous about his beliefs," Shani observed. "I wouldn't put it past him."

"This is ridiculous. We're talking about one of our classmates." Inaya pointed out. "I know Gregg is ultra conservative, but I can't believe he is violent. Maybe he was part of that group before he became a Christian."

"That makes sense," Avery replied.

"There's another issue. How would the WNA have known that a reception for gay people was happening? Someone had to have told them," I explained, expressing my long-held suspicion.

"That's a good point, but what if they were just acting like a gang? It could have been an initiation thing, and it just happened to be your wedding," Glenn pointed out.

Glenn's comment hit home. *Could I have been mistaken all this time? Could it really have been a random attack?* "I hadn't thought of that before. I had just assumed they targeted us because we're gay. The police arrested five people. I just hope they don't find out where we live while they're out on bail."

"That's a scary thought. I'm sorry you two have had to go through this," Inaya said. "It has to be hard."

"It is. The honeymoon was great. We hardly thought about it."

"I bet," Glenn grinned, drawing a flush to my cheeks.

"Since we got home, Mellie has been having nightmares."

"She might need some counseling," Avery suggested.

"She shot that idea down in a hurry," I answered.

"I have to disagree," Johnny chimed in, surprising me that he was still here. He'd been so quiet.

"Disagree with counseling?" Avery asked, scrunching her eyebrows.

"No, with the idea that it might have been a random attack."

"Why do you say that?" Shani asked.

"Because the White Nationalists of America is not a gang. It's an established group with an agenda to root out anyone they disagree with. I'd say there's a ninety-nine point nine percent chance the attack was deliberately meant to target a gay couple. That also means someone informed them of the wedding. I just looked, and there's no way to tell it was a gay marriage ceremony. All you can see is last names."

I don't believe I've ever heard Johnny say that many sentences in a row. My nerves started their jitters again.

"Look, now you've made her anxious," Inaya scolded.

"We'll get you through this," Glenn comforted. "We could take turns standing guard at the apartment."

I laughed. "You're a nut."

"That's what Musketeers do," he responded.

"What? Act like nuts or help out?" Avery asked.

"Both," Glenn answered, drawing laughs all around.

"I'm also nervous because I have to face Mellie tonight. She is demanding that I quit waffling and come up with a definite plan for getting ordained."

"You mean you're still on the fence about that?" Shani asked.

"Yeah. I just can't figure out what to do."

Glenn held up his hand with the imaginary sword. "One for all and all for one! You come up with the plan, and we'll help you execute it."

We put our hands together, and I noticed Gregg walking away shaking his head.

I was sitting at the kitchen table writing out the pros and cons of my options for ordination when Mellie got back from class.

"You'll be happy to know that I'm hard at work," I offered.

"First things first. I haven't seen my wife all day," she grinned, coming in for a hug and kiss. The kiss lingered, then progressed.

An hour later she said, "Much better. Now we can get to work. What have you come up with so far?"

I gave her one more long hug, slid into my pajamas and fetched the papers I had been writing on. "I've been writing the pros and cons of the different paths I could choose." I surrendered the papers.

"I see." She mulled over what I had written. "You've only given yourself two options, and neither is what you really want."

"There is no way forward for what I really want." I pulled my feet up, sitting cross-legged on the bed.

Mellie looked deeply into my eyes. "What do you really want?"

"I want to be a minister in the church I've been part of my entire life. I want them to quit rejecting me and embrace me. That's what I want!" Firey anger flashed through my soul.

"Those are fighting words! That's what I wanted to hear. Now we can work on a plan to make that happen."

"There's no use. I've tried everything I know to do." The fire dwindled.

"That's because you've been playing nice." Mellie raised one eyebrow. "Now it's time to play dirty." She grinned.

"What do you mean? You're getting me worried." I couldn't fathom what was going through her mind.

"I'm not sure how, but we have to find a way to put pressure on the people with the power to make a change. We have to twist their arms enough that they will give in."

"What else could we do? We've gotten a pile of people to send letters. We've protested. A proposal to ordain people regardless of their sexual orientation has been defeated for the last several years."

"What about the Civil Rights Act?"

"What about it?"

"Couldn't we sue, saying they are discriminating against you because of your sexual orientation?"

"People have tried that and been shot down."

"Well maybe it's time to try again."

"I can't afford to hire a lawyer for that. I'm sure it would be too much."

"Can you afford not to?"

Mellie's comment hit home. *If I am going to live the life I feel God is calling me to, I have to give it my all. Maybe she is right.* "But that would mean spending all of our savings."

She uncrossed her legs, leaned forward, and held me by the shoulders. "You're going to have to take chances to achieve your dream. We may end up poor as church mice, but you will regret it the rest of your life if you don't try."

"Did I ever tell you you're a wise soul?"

"I think you've said that a few times."

"Did I ever tell you that I love you?"

"Yep. I love you, too." She leaned in and kissed me. "You're not going to get away with changing the subject. Let's research lawyers who might be good at this kind of case." She hopped off the bed, heading for her computer.

"Oh, I forgot to tell you something creepy."

"What's that?"

"There is a guy in my class that has a White Nationalists of America tattoo on his arm."

Mellie froze in her tracks. "That is creepy. Do you think he had something to do with the shooting?"

"I don't know. That's what I first suspected, but the other Musketeers didn't think so."

When Mellie turned back to me, I knew I shouldn't have told her. I could see the anxiety in her eyes. "I'm calling the detective in the morning and telling him about this. If that guy had anything to do with me getting shot, I want him to pay. What is his name?" She sat the computer on the bed and grabbed pen and paper."

"Gregg Sanders. He's a jerk. During my first year, he cornered me with a group of friends. I was afraid he was going to get violent until Shani put him in his place."

"And he's in seminary? I don't think the ministerial training is working on him."

"He seems to consider himself a defender of the way things have always been."

She just grunted and opened her laptop. "Let's find a lawyer."

Chapter 40

Wednesday, October 1, 2025

The classroom was buzzing as I approached on a cloudy, chilly Wednesday. The buzz fizzled to silence as I walked in. *That's weird. Were they talking about me?* Inaya came up to me with an unusual somber expression.

"Did you hear the news?"

I braced myself. "No. What news?"

"They arrested Gregg. We assume it had something to do with the attack at your wedding." She whispered the last part.

A shock surged through my veins. "Wow. I guess I shouldn't be surprised. I have to let Mellie know." I whipped out my phone and sent her a text.

"It appears you were right," Glenn said. "Gregg must have had something to do with the attack. I knew he was a jerk, but I didn't think he was that low."

"Right," I agreed. My mind was still trying to process the shock. A text from Mellie pinged my phone.

"I can't believe someone in seminary could be so wicked. I hope he gets a long sentence!"

"Mellie's mad that someone in seminary would stoop to such sorry depths. I don't understand how he could hold to such views and still claim to be Christian."

"Maybe someone cut out the parts about loving your neighbor from his Bible," Glenn quipped.

"We are shaped by our tradition. If he grew up in an atmosphere that promoted hatred, then that's what he thinks is right, normal," Shani explained.

Our preaching professor, Dr. Fred Cranston, walked in and put materials on the desk. "I can see by your faces that you have heard. One of our own was arrested yesterday afternoon. Though we don't know, the buzz on campus is that it was due to his involvement in an attack at the wedding of another of our students. I'm going to ask that we take a moment to pray for Gregg, even if he feels like your enemy." He looked at me when he said that last bit.

I closed my eyes. *Dear Lord, I am hurt and angry that a fellow student might have had something to do with Mellie being shot. I know I'm supposed to love him, forgive him, and pray for him, but that might take a minute. I will ask that you be with him during this time. Amen.*

Wednesday, October 1, 2025

"Hurry up! We have to be there at three!" Mellie was trying to move me along to get ready for our meeting with the lawyer.

"I think I'm dragging my feet because I'm still not sure about this."

"We have to at least find out what he has to say. Come on!"

I put on the hustle, and we pulled into the parking lot at 2:55. "Made it," I observed.

The secretary directed us to sit down. We waited about five minutes, and she announced, "Mr. Lawrence will see you now."

Adam Lawrence was a bean pole of a man with graying at the temples of his short-cropped curly black hair. "Good afternoon. I'm Adam Lawrence. It's nice to meet you." He extended his hand.

"I'm Willow Grier-Waters, and this is my wife, Mellie."

"Please sit down."

"I love your desk." I couldn't help touching the carved mahogany.

"I see you have an eye for fine furniture. This was my grandfather's. He was a master woodworker and made it by hand seventy-five years ago."

"Wow! It's gorgeous," Mellie chimed in.

"What can I do for you today?" Mr. Lawrence asked.

I explained my situation.

"Your denomination states that it will not ordain self-avowed practicing homosexuals. Since you two are married, you won't be able to fly under their radar, so that's not an option. There have been suits filed before, but they didn't succeed."

I'm surprised that he knows so much. And that's just off the top of his head.

Mr. Lawrence opened his computer. "Let me look up something." A combination of clicks and typing followed.

Minutes stretched on. I looked at Mellie, and she lifted her eyebrows. *I wonder what she is thinking.*

Finally he looked up with sadness in his eyes. "I'm sorry, but I don't think there is anything I can do for you. I don't see any chance that we could win this case, and I don't want to take your money knowing that. The precedent cases are quite clear that the church has the right to determine whom it will ordain."

"What about this," Mellie spoke up. "I was shot by an anti-gay group coming out of our reception. It turns out that one of Willow's fellow seminarians is a part of that group and informed them when the wedding would take place. Can there be some sort of liability there?" *She's grasping at straws.*

Mr. Lawrence creased his brow, put a hand to his face and rested that elbow on the desk. He drifted off for a few seconds. "Has this seminarian been found guilty?"

"No, the trial hasn't even started."

"I see what you're saying. If this person is found guilty, we could claim the church was complicit in an act of violence. But in that case, we would be suing for monetary compensation. It's a longshot and still won't help with your ordination. Well… it might raise public awareness, which could put some pressure on the church."

My heart was sinking. *Who knows how long it will be until the trial… Probably too late.* Mellie and Mr. Lawrence sounded a long way off.

"So there is nothing we can do?"

"I'm afraid I can't help you. But definitely keep pushing them to make the right decision. If the seminarian is found guilty, and you want to sue, please call me."

He stood, and I gathered it was time to leave. My legs felt weak walking to the car. Mellie must have sensed my distress. She kept her arm around me all the way.

"You want me to drive?"

I handed her the keys, and she opened the passenger door. "I'm sorry," she said, settling into the driver's seat. "We'll have to come up with plan B, or C, or D, or whatever we're on now."

"I don't know if I have any fight left."

"Willow Grier-Waters! I will have no talk of giving up. We are going to keep fighting for you. You're also fighting for everyone who comes after you, you know."

Guilt pinged my conscience as I remembered telling Johnny the same thing. "You're right. I have to keep fighting. Like Shani said, this is a long game. I may not get to the promised land, but I could help pave the way for someone after me."

"That's the spirit! We just have to think of what to do next. Any ideas?"

Parking behind the apartment, Mellie looked at me with a wicked grin.

"You've had an idea."

"I have."

"Let's hear it."

"You're going to use me."

"What do you mean?" I had my hand on the door latch.

"Tell the story of me getting shot. Make the point that the church is helping perpetuate violence against us by standing against people of differing sexual orientations. They can either help continue the wrong or stand for what is right."

"Yeah. I could send out letters to people stating that."

"You have to think bigger than that."

"Oh?"

She grinned again. "We're going to contact reporters from newspapers and television. It's going to take some serious egg on the face to get the church to change."

Now I understood the wicked grin. I pondered what she had said. "What if they won't listen?"

"What if they will?"

Mellie sees hope in the bleakest situation. But I don't want to get my hopes crushed again. My heart is so tired of getting stomped on. I don't know what to do.

"Are you getting out?" I hadn't noticed Mellie coming around and opening my door. "You have to pull yourself together and hit the tennis court with me before it gets dark."

"I can do that." Thankful for a different focus, I got out of the car.

With Mellie ten weeks out from her gunshot wound, we were starting to build up her backhand. "Don't try to kill it. Just ease into it," I instructed.

"Got it."

After a few volleys I asked, "How does it feel?"

"Hit one more, and let's see."

I aimed the ball toward her backhand side, and she ripped a zinger down the line. "That's how it feels." A big smile adorned her reply.

"I take it the·shoulder is feeling good."

"Yep! And I just had a thought."

"What might that be?"

"I wonder if any of the newspapers reported on the shooting when it happened."

"That's a good thought. We were so busy at the hospital and honeymooning that I never thought to check."

"That's our first mission when we get back."

Chapter 41

Monday, October 13, 2025

lass dragged on. It was preaching, well technically homiletics. I was having trouble focusing to provide feedback. *My turn's coming up next week.* Gregg was back, and he wore an even deeper scowl than usual. Finally Dr. Cranston dismissed us, and I hustled to the apartment to meet Mellie.

"Are you as nervous as I am?" I asked when she walked through the door.

She looked me up and down. "I don't think so. I haven't been dancing a jig."

"I'm not dancing a jig." Mellie raised one eyebrow. "OK, maybe I am." I tried to calm the jitters. "What if the story causes the WNA to come after us again?"

"Do you want to be ordained or not? I think it's a chance we have to take."

"OK. But I'm still worried."

Mellie wrapped me in a comforting hug. "We'll get through this together."

I leaned in, soaking up her confidence. "OK, let's do this." With that we were off to meet the Atlanta Journal-Constitution reporter who had written an article about Mellie's attack at our reception after it first happened.

Zachary Lyons greeted us with kind blue eyes and unkempt blond hair. He looked like a person who always worked too hard. He extended his hand. "Welcome. Welcome. I'm Zachary Lyons. Just call me Zach." He gestured to the two chairs in his cubicle. "Have a seat. Can I get you some water?"

"I could use some, thanks." My throat was nervous-dry.

"I'll be right back." He returned with three waters, pulled out a notepad, and sat in his desk chair. "I remember the shooting. I tried to get an interview with you, but the hospital wouldn't let me near you. My editor insisted the story go out the next day, so I had to give up. What brings you in today?"

My tongue went on strike, and I sat there frozen. Mellie picked up the ball.

"We want to provide more context to the story, and there has been a new development."

"I'm all ears! Which one are you?" His pen was paused on the notepad.

"I'm Mellie, the one who was shot."

Zach wrote, keeping his eyes on Mellie. "How are you now? Fully recovered?"

"I'm still working on my backhand for tennis, but other than that I'm back."

Zach directed a questioning look at me.

"Her nightmares are getting farther and farther apart. She's coming along nicely." *Thanks for getting in gear, tongue.*

"I see. You're having ongoing issues from the shooting. Have the police arrested anyone in connection with the attack?"

"That's part of the new development. They arrested the men that they believe to be the shooters, and they have also arrested a person believed to have informed them about the place and time of the reception."

Zach kept jotting notes. "That's odd. Why would they be looking for an informant."

"I'm in seminary at Emory. One of my classmates is apparently a member of the WNA. I believe he is the one who told them when and where to attack," I offered.

"That's an odd turn of events. And you say the police arrested this person?"

"Yes," Mellie and I responded together.

"So… in a sense the church is complicit in the attack. It's one of their own who initiated it."

My mouth dropped open. *I can't believe he made the connection we were hoping for on his own! I thought we were going to have to convince him.*

"How do you feel about that, Willow?"

"Angry and hurt." *I wanted to say that someone associated with that group shouldn't even be part of the church, but I knew that the church being open to a variety of people is what Jesus wants. It's what I'm seeking to convince the church to do. Zach's looking at me. I need to say more.* "It hurts that someone who is in class with me to become a minister could foster such violence. It seems totally against Jesus's teachings."

"It just hit me that you are studying to become a minister in a denomination that won't ordain you. Is that correct?"

"Yes, that's their current position. But we hope to change that."

"You're not trying to use the court of public opinion to push for that change, are you?"

I froze. *I don't want to lie to him, but will he write the story if he knows that's what we want?* In my hesitation, Mellie took over.

"That's exactly what we are hoping to do."

Zach paused, tapping his pen on the notepad. "I like it," he grinned. "We could use this situation to try nudging the church to affirm the value of queer people. I'll have to get my editor on board, of course."

Mellie was smiling, and I smiled back. Zach scribbled some more notes. "Do you mind telling me the name of the seminary student responsible for the attack? I can get it from the police records, but it's easier this way."

"Gregg Sanders." *It felt good to give his name. I shouldn't feel that way, but I do.*

"Do you have any idea how the police figured out he was involved?"

"I told them," Mellie replied. "Willow saw a tattoo on his arm with the WNA initials."

He jotted down some more notes. "All right, then. Is there anything else you want to tell me?"

I looked at Mellie, and she shook her head. "Not that I can think of right now."

"If you don't mind, could I have your phone numbers in case I need to follow up with you?"

"Of course," I replied, and we gave him our numbers.

"This gives me plenty to get started with. Thanks for reaching out. I'll be in touch."

On the way out of the building Mellie asked, "What are you grinning about?"

"My gaydar is working better."

"You noticed did you?"

"Yep. Zach is one of us. I don't think it could have worked out any better."

Monday, October 20, 2025

"I'm petrified," I responded to Mellie's question as I poured coffee.

"You'll do fine. You always do."

"But I haven't given a sermon since my senior year in high school. And that wasn't actually a sermon."

"Suck it up, buttercup. This is what you want to do the rest of your life. Seize the moment and enjoy it."

"That's easier said than done. I'm thankful we are limited to ten minutes."

Fortified with coffee, breakfast, and Mellie's encouragement, I headed to homiletics.

Shani was the first to present her sermon this morning, and I would be next. She did an excellent job, preaching from John 8:31-38. Her message focused on how Christ sets us free to be the people we were created to be and enjoy life as God intended.

I wiped my sweaty palms on my pants when Dr. Cranston called me to come up. Looking out over my classmates, including Gregg's grumpiness, I began.

"The words of I Corinthians 16:13-14 spoke to me as I prepared this sermon, and I would like to share with you what the Holy Spirit shared with me. Here the word of the Lord. 'Keep alert, stand firm in your faith, be courageous, be strong. Let all that you do be done in love.'

"This is the word of the Lord."

"Thanks be to God," the class responded.

"Mellie and I were at the beach in July. Walking in the shallow water, the outgoing waves would suck the sand out from under my feet. It was hard to stand up.

"In this passage, Paul calls us to stand firm in our faith, but it's hard to stand firm when the ground beneath you is shifting. That's where we find ourselves as Christians today.

"The waves crash and sand washes out from under us as society battles with becoming more accepting of people with a spectrum of sexual orientations and gender identities. We want to stand firm in our faith, but we need a solid foundation on which to stand, one that doesn't keep shifting on us. Where are we to find that?

"Paul offers that firm foundation in this passage, 'Let all that you do be done in love.' The one foundation that will never shift on us is love. It will never get sucked out from under our feet or leave us unbalanced.

"If we look at all that is going on around us through the lens of love, we discover a place to stand. Love opens our hearts to view the world around us as God does. We see a wonderful world full of God's beloved creations. There is not a single part of the created order that God does not value and nurture.

"Paul is inviting us to step onto that foundation of love so we can stand firm in our faith and join hands with God in nurturing the people God has created, building them up rather than tearing them down, offering a steadying hand when the ground washes out from under people, and helping all of God's people step up onto the solid rock of love.

"Love is the greatest power in the universe. It is the force God used to bring creation into existence. It is that same force that you and I can use to bring people into God's Kingdom. Love is the rock on which we can stand firm in our faith. Love is the one thing that will never lead us astray."

I returned to my seat in a blur. *I'm exhausted!* It dawned on me that the class was clapping. *Maybe they liked it.* Dr. Cranston calmed everyone down then called Avery to come up. *She looks as nervous as I felt.*

Avery did a great job on her sermon, then Dr. Cranston reminded us that our critiques of the sermons were due the next class session. *I dread seeing what people have to say about mine.*

Chapter 42

Tuesday, November 11, 2025

The bedroom door opened, and Mellie came out all sleepy, hair tussled. My heart warmed. *I love the way she looks when she just wakes up.*

"Good morning!" I chirped as I put my cereal bowl in the dishwasher. "I wish I had a late class today."

"Morning," she replied.

I rushed over and hugged her. "You're still nice and warm from the bed. Coffee's in the pot." I hustled to the bathroom to brush my teeth. "Do you think we need to call him?"

"Call who?" she called back.

"Zach. It's been almost a month." I started brushing.

"He said he had research to do and would get back with us. I trust him."

"Wha mmm got dismmm?" I tried with toothpaste in my mouth.

"Have you learned a new language?"

I gave up trying to talk till I rinsed. "What if he got distracted with another story. It couldn't hurt to check in with him."

Mellie was sitting at the table with coffee when I came out. "That's true. Maybe we should give him a call."

"What time do you get out of class today?"

"About three thirty."

"I should be home about that time, too. Let's call him this afternoon."

"OK."

I hurried to class, running four minutes late. Pushing myself to move fast, I got to class just as the professor began. I was breathing hard as I took my seat.

"Glad you could make it," Glenn whispered.

Just before class ended, I heard my phone vibrating in my purse. *It's Zach! I have to answer.* I slid out of the classroom as quickly and quietly as I could. "Hello."

"Hi, Willow. Zach Lyons. How are you today?"

"I'm fine. How about you?"

"Doing well, thanks. Did I catch you at a bad time?"

"No, it's perfect. Class is just about to end."

"Good. I have uncovered a lot of serious stuff about the WNA. This story will be a lot bigger than we thought. We're planning to publish it this Sunday. Is there any way you and Mellie can come in and go over some things with me before it runs?"

"I'm sure we can find a time. Let me coordinate with her and get back with you."

"Sounds great. I'll look forward to seeing you again."

"Thanks for calling. Bye." I texted Mellie, knowing she wouldn't look at her phone until she was in between classes.

Thursday, November 13, 2025

Zach already had water bottles set out for us when we sat down in his cubicle.

"Thanks for coming in. I need a little corroboration on parts of the story." He clicked his mouse a couple of times. "Is this the image you saw on the tattoo?" he asked, turning the computer so I could see.

"Yes. That's exactly what it looked like." A surprising flare of anger surged.

"That's what I expected. OK, let me tell you a bit about what we have uncovered. The WNA has a charter in which they lay out their goals. The goals include 'ridding the United States of unwelcome foreigners and LGBTQ trash.' I'm quoting there, so don't hit me.

"The charter goes on to say, 'We envision a pure America, free of these unholy influences and ruled by God.' They see their mission as purging America until it becomes a theocracy for white straight people only.

"We have uncovered a string of terror attacks perpetrated by them across the country, which we have forwarded on to the Justice Department. For some reason they aren't posting their exploits. Usually this type of group wants the world to know what they're up to.

"A contact at the FBI said he believes they are playing a long game, wanting to get the groups they want out of the country sufficiently terrified so that when they gain power these groups will be clamoring to escape the country. So far they are targeting Latinos, African Americans, and LGBTQ+ people."

"When they gain power?" Mellie asked.

"Yes. The FBI believes that sometime soon they will have candidates running for offices all over the country, including president. God help us if they do actually gain control of the government."

"How could that happen? Won't they all be in jail for the crimes they're doing?" I wondered.

"The group is growing rapidly, and only a small portion are committing the crimes. It appears they recruit people who are willing to go to jail for the cause to do the attacks while the leaders groom others for becoming candidates for public office."

"Unbelievable," Mellie observed.

Zach sat back in his chair, drawing his lips thin. *I wonder what he is thinking.*

"When we run this story, I'm afraid you will be in danger. Even without our mentioning your names, the context of the story will make it possible for them to identify you."

I searched Mellie's expression. "What have we done?" I asked, my world shaken.

"We have done what needed to be done. I told you that we would have to face consequences to bring this story to light."

"I never thought it would be this bad, though."

"I think you need to start carrying stun guns." Zach's comment shocked me even more.

"That's a scary thought. Besides, if they are using firearms what good will a stun gun do?" Mellie replied.

Zach was silent. He scrunched his eyebrows together. "This is the part of my job I hate. I have tried to word the story in order to keep you insulated. Since it begins with the context of your attack, they could decide to seek revenge on the paper by going after you. Or they might come after me. Hence…" Zach opened the top drawer of his desk to reveal a handgun and stun gun. "I stay as prepared as I can."

"I like that combination," Mellie said. "How long does it take to get a concealed carry license?"

"Actually, you no longer need a license in Georgia. If you're going to carry it out of state, the state will have to have reciprocity with Georgia, and you'll need a license then."

"I guess our next stop will be a gun store." Mellie replied.

"I'm glad to hear that."

My heart was pounding. *I don't want to own a gun. I don't think I could shoot a person. I don't even want one in the house. What am I going to do?*

"Willow. Willow. Earth to Willow…" filtered into my consciousness. I turned toward Mellie.

"Are you OK? I didn't mean to scare you that badly. I just want you to take precautions," Zach said.

"I don't want to own a gun. I don't believe that's how God wants me to live," I stated, ignoring Zach. I watched Mellie's eyes narrow and knew she was angry.

"If you don't carry a gun you may not live," she responded tersely.

"We'll talk about it later," I answered, not wanting an argument in front of Zach.

"I understand your religious objections. Please at least consider the stun gun. That won't kill anyone but could save your life," Zach pleaded.

I pulled myself out of my inner conflict and said, "I really appreciate your hard work on this story. Is there anything else we need to know or do?"

"I want you to have a chance to read the story before it's printed." He pulled it up on his computer. "But I do have to ask that you not say a word about it to anyone until it comes out."

"Agreed," Mellie answered.

"Wow! That's great. It does sound like the church's equivocation on LGBTQ+ people helps justify these attacks," I observed.

"Thanks. I'm glad you like it. I am grateful that you brought this story to me. I hope it will get picked up around the country."

"Me, too," Mellie replied.

Wednesday, November 19, 2025

"Do you have your stun gun?" Mellie asked as I loaded my backpack for class. That question was now part of our morning ritual.

"Yep. It's in my purse," I answered, trying to hide the irritation.

"You know I ask only because I love you and want you to be safe."

I see I didn't do a good enough job hiding my irritation. "I know. I'm just still uncomfortable carrying a weapon."

Mellie left the table and pulled me into a hug. "You're carrying it for me. Just think how broken I would be if I lost you."

I pulled back and looked deeply into those wonderful blue eyes. "It's nice to be loved so much." I gave her a long kiss.

"Are you sure we have to go to class," Mellie grinned.

"Don't tempt me." I pulled away and slid my backpack on.

"You be careful. That creepy Gregg will be there."

"You be careful, too. I couldn't bear losing you, either." I hurried out the door.

I was never late until I got married. Now the pull to spend time with her makes it hard to get out the door.

Gregg glared at me as I walked into the classroom, looking angrier than usual. *I can't resist.* "I take it you read the paper." He didn't respond, which left me feeling nervous. *I'd rather know what he was thinking than face a silent enemy, so I prodded.* "The WNA is a dangerous organization. They are doing terrible things and needed to be exposed."

"You underestimate whom you are dealing with. Plus, you are the one doing dangerous things to our country. We are just trying to set things right."

The others in the class had gone silent. All eyes were on Gregg and me.

So he is a member of the WNA. "You have a strange perception of right and wrong. I think you need to read your Bible."

"I think you need to read *your* Bible. Leviticus eighteen says you should be banished, cut off from your people," he said standing up.

Anger hit like a hammer. I glared back at him. "Leviticus nineteen warns against people with tattoos." It was as if I had poked a hole in him and all the air rushed out. His head dropped, and he sat down, eyes glued to the floor. Strangely, I felt compassion for him. *Where did that come from?*

"The good news is that Jesus came to do away with the old ways and usher in a new covenant based on loving God and loving our neighbors. So we both stand as forgiven sinners whom God loves," I offered.

Gregg looked up with soft eyes. "I have been so wrong. I'm sorry."

Professor Cranston walked in, "Please take your seats. We have a lot to cover today."

The anger left and joy filled its place as I sat down. *Maybe he will have a change of heart.*

Chapter 43

Tuesday, December 2, 2025

My phone vibrated at 2:33pm. I glanced at my watch and got excited. It was hard to resist pulling out my phone to read the whole text, but I didn't want to disturb class. I half listened, half willed my hand not to reach into my purse until class ended.

I whipped out my phone and opened the text. "Good news! The story has been picked up by a dozen papers across the country, including the New York Times! The word is spreading!"

I noticed Zach had sent the text to Mellie, too. I replied, "That's great! Congratulations on the success of your story!" *At least I assume it's a big deal for a reporter to have his story go all over the country.*

I texted Mellie separately. "Make sure you check out Zach's text."

"What's more important than hanging out with us?" Glenn called from the doorway.

"I got a text from the reporter that the story about the WNA attack is being run in papers around the country."

"Wow! That's big news!"

I followed Glenn to the third floor sitting area where Shani, Inaya, Avery, and Johnny had captured our usual couch and chairs.

"I can't believe finals are next week. Then we only have one more semester!" Avery said.

"It's going to be sad when this is over," Inaya lamented. "I'm going to miss all of you."

"I'll miss all of y'all, too," I replied.

My phone vibrated again. "I saw it. That's wonderful! I'll see you at the apartment. We have work to do!" *I wonder what she means by that.*

"Mellie just saw the reporter's text," I explained.

"Maybe that's one more step toward ordination," Shani observed.

A flutter of jealousy stirred in my heart. They all had only one more step to be fully approved for ordination. As long as they passed their courses it was a done deal. *I wish I were in their shoes. Even Johnny is set. I hope hiding his true self doesn't consume him. Maybe that's what I should have done. No, that's ridiculous. I wouldn't have Mellie, and there is no way I could live in hiding. I'm just not capable of that.*

"Oh, Willow. You left us again," Glenn called.

"Sorry, I was taking a trip down 'what if' lane."

"We need to celebrate the end of classes and were talking about keeping the tradition and going to Athens Pizza," Inaya explained.

"Sounds good to me!"

"I trust Mellie and Douglas will be joining us," Inaya prompted. Douglas, a law student, was Shani's new beau.

"He'd better," Shani responded.

"I'm sure Mellie will be there."

"Great! A table for eight! I should be a poet," Inaya laughed.

"Our usual seven o'clock?" Glenn asked.

"Perfect," I answered.

"One for all," Glenn raised his hand.

"And all for one," we answered, putting our hands together. Professor Cranston laughed as he walked by.

We returned from the pizza party, and Mellie parked behind the apartment. "I'm glad you turned the patio light on," She noted. It was a cold, windy evening, so we hustled inside.

The work Mellie had alluded to in her earlier text was to write an open letter to all of the denominational leaders describing how their failure to affirm people of varying sexual orientations and gender identities is being used to legitimize the hate crimes perpetrated by groups like the WNA.

"Let me grab my laptop, and we'll get to work on those letters," Mellie stated, heading to the bedroom.

As I reached for my backpack, there was a knock at the door. "Who could that be?" Mellie wondered. I looked out the peephole but didn't see anyone. As soon as I unlocked the door and pulled it open, it exploded out of my hand. Two men with dark hoods and baseball bats rushed in.

The first one took a swing at my head. I ducked, and he lost his balance from the force of the swing, falling to the ground. I grabbed my backpack and slammed it onto his head as hard as I could.

"We're here to teach you sluts a lesson," The other man growled, drawing his bat back and aiming at my head. The one on the ground groaned and started to get up.

"Don't move," Mellie yelled from the doorway, gun drawn.

"Oh, look. She has a little toy gun. I bet she doesn't even know how to shoot it."

"Drop the bat, or you'll find out."

I whacked the one getting off the floor with my backpack again, and his head bounced off the floor.

The other man reached behind his back, and I saw a gun. "He has a gun, Mellie." Terror gripped my heart when I realized Mellie was frozen. She couldn't pull the trigger. I jerked the stun gun out of my backpack and charged, pushing it into his back.

He lunged forward, and I stayed with him, remembering I had to keep the stun gun on him for at least three to five seconds.

He hit the floor, and I kept the stun gun on him until he went limp. I looked back, and the other guy was moving again. Mellie still stood frozen.

"Call the police!" I yelled, jumping up to use the stun gun on the other man if needed. Mellie put the gun on the table and whipped out her phone.

I slammed the door and locked it.

"What are you doing? We're stuck in here with them!"

"What if there are others out there? Get your stun gun. We might need it." Adrenaline was surging, and I was totally in fight mode. "We have to stay away from the windows."

I checked the man whom I had hit with the backpack and found a gun in his waistband, too. I grabbed it and then wrenched the gun out of the other man's hand. Holding two pistols and a stun gun, I quipped, "Just call me Rambo."

Mellie squinted her eyes, looking puzzled, until it registered what I had said. A smile worked onto her face, and then she laughed. She went back to the 911 call.

The guy I had whacked looked dazed but was trying to get up. His eyes widened when he felt for the gun and it was gone.

"Stay on the floor and don't move," I ordered, aiming his own gun at him. His eyes swam as he tried to focus. *I might have hit him a bit too hard. No, he deserved it.*

He rolled onto his knees, and I lunged with the stun gun, zapping his back till he collapsed. Hearing movement across the room, I looked to see the other one writhing. *So far he doesn't seem coordinated enough to get up.* I stood, ready to zap whichever one needed it next.

I jumped off the ground at the knock on the door. "Atlanta Police. Open up!" I could see blue lights flashing through the window. Mellie peeked out the window anyway before opening the door.

"We had a call about a home invasion at this address." In a fluid motion, the officer pushed Mellie behind and drew his weapon. "Drop the weapons, now," he ordered. I had forgotten I was still holding one of the pistols. And a stun gun.

I almost just let go and let them fall till it dawned on me that the pistol might fire. I knelt, put them on the floor, and backed away. A second officer rushed in and scooped them up then picked up the guns on the table.

"Officer Chapman," the first one said, holstering his gun. "Do you mind telling me what happened?" He eyed the two men on the floor and the bats. "Cuff the two men, Henry. Wait, before you explain, do you have any other weapons on the premises?"

"There is another stun gun in my purse," Mellie said. Officer Chapman's jaw dropped. "Just how many weapons do two women need?"

"Two of the pistols belong to these men," I pointed out.

Mellie handed over her stun gun. "Now, please tell me what happened tonight."

I explained the attack as best I could remember, with Mellie filling in missing pieces.

I heard a beeping sound and noticed red lights flashing in the window. Paramedics soon filed into the apartment. "We're going to need to transport both of these men to the hospital, Officer Chapman instructed.

"If you check their upper arms, I suspect you'll find the White Nationalists of America symbol tattooed there," I told Officer Chapman.

Without a word, the paramedic slit the sleeve of the hoodie and opened it up, revealing the tattoo.

"Why would you suspect that group is responsible for this attack?"

Mellie explained the shooting at our wedding and the newspaper article.

"This one may have a head injury. Let's take him first," one of the paramedics directed.

As they carried him out on a gurney, Officer Chapman called, "Hit every bump you can."

After the second intruder was loaded into an ambulance and hauled off, the lecture began. "Ladies, please don't ever open your door if you don't know who's on the other side. You managed to overpower these two, but don't let that go to your head. It might not go so well next time. I'm glad you have weapons and aren't afraid to use them, but it's better to not get in a situation where you need them to start with. Please be smart."

After the officers left, Mellie and I collapsed on the couch after checking to make sure the door was locked three times. Each.

"I'm sorry I froze. I just couldn't pull the trigger." Tears seeped out of Mellie's eyes.

"That's because you're a healer. Taking a life goes against everything you stand for."

"It looks like you're right. I think I'll sell the gun."

"Let's not make a decision until tomorrow. I'm too addled right now to do anything but cuddle with you."

Chapter 44

Wednesday, December 3, 2025

The sound of clanging pots drug me from my sleep. I was still on the couch. I hadn't expected the gift of sleep, being so wound up after the invasion, but somehow around midnight Mellie and I both drifted off in each other's arms.

My eyes squinted against the light, I could see Mellie unloading the dishwasher. "Must you do that right now?" I grumped.

She slammed another pot into the cabinet. "And must you do it so loudly?" I griped.

"Get up. We have a letter to write."

"You sound angry." I sat up on the couch, keeping the blanket pulled around me.

"I am angry. How dare those people attack us! Just because we're gay doesn't give them the right to break into our home and beat us to death with bats! I'm tired of being treated like a second class citizen, like someone who is dirty. It's not right! And I'm tired of the church treating you like you're tainted."

She slammed a frying pan onto the counter. "And the only thing I know to do about it right now is to write that letter."

"OK, I'm getting up, but please give the pots a break."

She placed the frying pan in the cabinet with exaggerated gentleness. "Better?"

I just sighed and headed to make coffee. "The truth is I've been thinking about that letter ever since you mentioned the idea. I think I've about got it worded in my head, but I need nourishment and coffee first.

Fortified with a bowl of granola cereal and armed with a flat white, I opened my laptop and began writing.

December 3, 2025

An Open Letter to All Bishops.

Dear Bishops,

I am writing to share my story because I believe it is important for you to understand what is happening and how the church could make a positive difference in the world.

I am a lesbian who was called into the ministry during my senior year of high school. I was on track with my candidacy process and entered seminary at Emory University. After discovering that I'm lesbian, the committee terminated my candidacy, but I have continued to pursue my education.

On 11/19/24, I was at a book ban protest when members of the White Nationalists of America attacked a transgender friend of mine. I sought to defend her and ended up with a broken wrist from the fight. On 7/19/25 while leaving our wedding reception, my new wife was shot by the same group. We were attacked solely because we are a gay couple. One of my fellow seminary students, a member of that hate group, is alleged to have informed the group of the time and location of our wedding. On 12/2/25, two members of the WNA broke into our apartment and attempted to beat us to death with baseball bats.

"Hey, Mellie?"

"Yeah?"

"I just had a creepy thought."

"Are you going to share it?" She poked her head out of the bedroom.

"I wonder if Gregg told the WNA where we live."

"Do you think so? I need to meet this guy with my stun gun in hand."

My hands were shaky and my heart racing as I went to write the next sentence.

It is highly possible that the same seminarian informed the hate group where we live, making the last attack possible.

What is the church's position in all of this? The seminarian, who is a member of a hate group and likely responsible for two attempts on my wife and my lives, is fully approved and on track to be ordained this spring. On the other hand, I, who am seeking to live a faithful and loving life, have no path to ordination and have been rejected by the church as unworthy of the position of minister.

I hope my sharing this story will help you see that the church is indirectly sanctioning hate crimes in America. The church's ongoing, active refusal to fully affirm people with varying sexual orientations and gender identities helps legitimize the perception held by hate groups, as well as some church people, that we are to be cast out and considered filth.

In response to Jesus's teachings that life is about loving God and neighbor, the church needs to take a stand for love by ending it's conflicting message that people like me are allowed to enter the doors but not welcome to fully participate in the life of the church.

I hope you will realize the harm that is being done to LGBTQ+

people across the country and lead the church to take a stand of affirming, loving, and welcoming LGBTQ+ folks into the full life of the church. There are many of us who are seeking to be faithful disciples only to find the doors of the church closed and locked.

Yours in Christ,
  Willow Grier-Waters

I sat back and read over the letter. Mellie popped out of the bedroom. "You stopped typing."

"I think it's finished. Have a look."

She came over and read through it. "I like it! Now I'll have to write one."

"What have you been doing in there all this time?"

"Making up the bed and praying."

Friday, December 5, 2025

I walked into the Rollins building to a barrage of questions about the latest attack. Frankly, I was tired of talking about it, but I pressed on. The Musketeers greeted me with warm hugs. Thankfully, I had already told them about it.

Gregg sat with his eyes locked on his computer. Anger flared, and I couldn't resist. "Did you tell them where we live?"

He didn't even look up, just sat there and ignored me.

"That's what I thought." I was shaking with rage as I sat down for the homiletics final.

Later that afternoon, Mellie and I sat down at the kitchen table, laptops open. We had agreed to let our letters sit for a couple of days and then read them over again before mailing them. She said, "You read mine, and I'll read yours."

"OK, it's a deal."

Swapping computers, we looked over each other's letter.

"What are you grinning about? Did I make a mistake?" Mellie asked.

I looked up, filled with pride. "I'm proud of you. This is an amazing letter!"

"Thanks. Yours is quite spunky, too." She leaned over and kissed me. "Whether or not these make any difference, at least we will have had our say."

"I don't think yours needs changing at all. How about mine?"

"Nope, yours is perfect. Let's hit print."

We spent the rest of the evening addressing envelopes and stuffing them with letters. I had to stop and stretch my hand four times to deal with cramps before we finished.

"Let's send them off with a prayer," I said, taking Mellie's hand. "Dear God, please place your blessing on these letters and open people's hearts if it is your will to open the ministry to all of your people. Amen."

"Amen," Mellie responded. "Let's make a post office run then celebrate with ice cream!"

As I pushed my letters through the outgoing mail slot, I felt hope. *Maybe this will make a difference.*

Chapter 45

Monday, February 2, 2026

With numb fingers, I opened the mailbox to retrieve the mail on my way back from class that cold, cloudy Monday. On top was a letter to Mellie and me with Bishop Sterling Bradley's return address. My heart pounded, and I broke into a sweat.

Hurrying into the apartment, I laid the letter on the table and stared at it, frozen in place while my mind did the zoomies. *I wonder what it says. Should I wait for Mellie to get home? I can't wait another forty-five minutes. I should open it. It's bad news. I should wait for Mellie, then I'll have a shoulder to cry on. I have to read it now. I can't read it now.*

My mind was still doing laps when Sophie brushed against my leg, causing me to leap off the floor. She hurried under the table and scowled at me.

"Sorry. I know it's treat time." I dished out the little morsels, which seemed to please the cats immensely. *I wonder how those taste.* I resisted the temptation to try one.

I walked wide of the table, trying to resist the heavy pull of the letter, and sat on the couch. After pulling out the commentary on the Gospel of Luke, I caught myself chewing my nail. *This is serious stress. I haven't done that in a long time.*

After ten minutes of failing to focus on what I was reading, I nearly gave in. *This is ridiculous! I either have to open it or leave.* I pulled on my coat and headed to the coffee shop in the bookstore with the commentary. I had finished half of a caramel macchiato and checked my watch more times than I care to admit when it was finally almost time for Mellie to get home. I took coffee and book and walked back across the street. *I've almost made it.*

Mellie opened the door and I flew into her arms. "Hey. It's good to see you, too."

"We got a letter."

"Do you care to explain a little more?"

"We got a letter from Bishop Bradley. He's the head of the denomination."

"What did it say?" she asked pulling back with wide eyes.

"I wanted to wait till you were here to open it."

"Let's check it out!" She shrugged off her backpack and coat.

My hands were shaking so I couldn't get it open.

"Allow me," Mellie offered. She opened it and held it so we both could read.

I didn't think my heart could race any faster, but it did. "I can't believe that."

"It's terrifying."

"No, it's incredible!"

"Nope. I'm sticking with terrifying. You have to do the talking."

I read it over again to be sure. "He really is inviting us to speak at the national meeting. Do you know what this means?"

"Yeah. It means I'm going to have to buy some Depends because I will definitely wet my pants."

"You're a goose. We get to tell our story to the whole conference. If their willing to listen, maybe they're willing to change!"

Monday, March 16, 2026

"The hotel website says there's an iron in the room," Mellie offered, trying to soothe my nerves as I packed my new dress.

"OK, but I'm packing ours anyway. Just in case."

Mellie pulled me into a hug. "Remember that thing called trust? I think you need to relax and trust that what is meant to be will be."

"I know. I just can't help it. The futures of a lot of people may rest on what we say and how we come across."

"You mean what you say. I'm just there for moral support."

Mellie remained firm that she would not speak at the conference. "You at least have to introduce yourself. It will look odd if you don't say a word."

"I'll think about it and get back to you. Now finish packing. They should be here in ten minutes."

Shani, Inaya, and Glenn arrived, suitcases in hand. I noticed a ring flash on Inaya's finger.

With a big grin, she put her arm around Glenn. "We have news! We're engaged!" She announced, holding up the ring.

"Congratulations!" I threw my arms around both of them. "You'll make a great clergy couple!"

We piled into my vehicle and headed to Nashville.

The clerk at the hotel must have noticed our posterboards. As I walked up to the counter to check in, she said, "You must be part of the protest group."

"Yes, we do plan to participate," I affirmed.

"Tomorrow's my day off, so I'm planning to walk, too."

"Thank you very much."

Tuesday, March 17, 2026

Light drizzle chilled the air as we walked to the convention center.

"I'm glad we have ponchos," Shani said. "I just hope our posters don't get destroyed."

"Oh, ye of little faith," Glenn replied. "It's going to clear up soon."

"I hope you're right. Marching in cold rain is not my idea of fun," Inaya moaned.

Approaching the convention center, I saw a sight I didn't expect to see. "Jack!" I yelled and charged toward him, lunging into a hug. "I can't believe you're here!"

"Of course I'm here, darling. I believe this is the year for change!"

I took his hand and pulled him toward Mellie. "You have to meet Mellie. Mellie this is Jack. He's the president of Queers for Christ and was at the protest last year. This is Mellie, my wonderful wife."

"Well congratulations, you two. It is a pleasure to meet you, darling."

Henry Walsh, sporting a rain coat and hood, walked up and pulled me aside. "I see you're on the program for tomorrow. That's good news." He paused and looked at the sky. "I wonder if you should be out here. Maybe you should go back to your hotel to make sure you don't get sick."

I could sense that he placed a lot of importance on my speech. "Thanks, but I'm sure I'll be fine."

"I see. Tomorrow's a big day. I have a good feeling about it."

"What was that about?" Mellie asked as she and Jack joined me.

"That's Henry Walsh. He leads the campaign to get ordination for all people brought before the convention. He was worried I'll get sick before tomorrow."

Jack placed his hands on his hips. "So what is happening tomorrow that I don't know about?"

"We've been asked to address the convention," I explained.

The sun broke through the dismal drizzle. Jack shielded his eyes and looked up over my head. When he looked back, a tear rolled down his cheek. He pointed to the sky. Mellie and I turned to see a gorgeous rainbow.

Jack wiped the tears away. "If that's not a sign, I'm not standing here."

Wednesday, March 18, 2026

Nervous didn't begin to describe the jitters running through my soul as I ironed my dress. I had to brace my elbow on the counter to get my hands to stop shaking so I could apply makeup.

When I walked out of the bathroom, Mellie took me by the shoulders. "You look absolutely marvelous!"

"You do, too," I replied, observing her all dressed up. "Why do you seem so calm?"

"Because I know you've got this. You'll do a wonderful job."

"Thanks. So you'll introduce yourself, then I'll step up and give my speech, right?"

"That's the plan, darling, as Jack would say. I like him."

"He is a neat guy." I took Mellie's hand. "OK, let's do this."

"Wow! Those are some cold fingers. You're stressed."

"You can say that again."

As instructed, we arrived at the auditorium at 9:30am. Folks in the picket line clapped as we approached, and Jack ran over and hugged both of us.

"This is big, really big!" he said.

We made our way to the front of the auditorium where there were seats reserved for anyone who would be speaking. Sitting down, I leaned into Mellie so our shoulders touched, finding comfort and strength in that simple touch.

At 10:11am, Bishop Bradley took the podium. "As we have for the last several years, today we take up the issue of ordination for self-avowed practicing homosexuals and people of the whole spectrum of sexual orientations and gender identity.

"As the leading body for the church, it is our task to guide church policy in compliance with scripture, tradition, reason, and experience. As we bring these guiding principles to bear on this issue, I have asked a young couple who have been particularly impacted by current church policy to address us this morning. Willow and Mellissa Grier-Waters, will you please come forward?"

I seemed twice my weight as I rose from the chair. Mellie looked at me, smiled, and led the way.

Stepping up to the microphone, she said, "Hi, I'm Mellie Grier-Waters. Thank you so much for the opportunity to be here today." *Why doesn't she sound nervous?*

"Some of you might have heard of the group, White Nationalists of America. If not, they're a hate group of white supremacists whose aim is to rid the United States of any group they don't like. Homosexual people are among their targets.

"Willow and I became targets on the day of our wedding. As we were coming out of the reception, members of this group circled the building, firing guns. One shot hit me in the shoulder, requiring surgery and many nightmares to recover from.

"Now I'd like for you to hear from my wonderful wife, Willow."

I stepped up to the podium. Mellie squeezed my arm as I tried to recover from the fact that she had said more than her name. *I'll have to adjust my message on the fly.*

"Let me add my thanks to Bishop Bradley and this group for the opportunity to be here today. It is a great honor.

"Mellie described one incident out of many that are occurring in our nation. I suffered a broken wrist while trying to defend a transgender teenager from an attack by a member of the same group Mellie mentioned.

"We are in a season of turmoil as this country tries to grapple with the presence of people who do not fit the mold of straight heterosexuality. There are a lot of us out there, and as a church we have to bring our influence to bear on this situation.

"Let's start with reason. If we look at the science, our sexuality appears to be determined in the womb. If we accept that, then sexual orientation and identity is something human beings are born with. Those of us who aren't heterosexual are part of the created order just like straight folks. We know from Genesis that God looked on all of creation and proclaimed it good.

"Next, let's consider experience. How many of you know anyone who is not straight? If you have a relationship with a queer person, then you probably understand that we are just people trying to live the lives God has given us. If you don't have the experience of knowing someone of the LGBTQ+ community, then please remedy that. Seek out one of us and get to know us. That will make the decision you face more real. Knowing the people whom this decision affects will wrap flesh around your consideration.

"What about tradition? Our tradition has stood firmly against affirming the value of LGBTQ+ people. As a church, we equivocate, saying we want these people to come to church but not fully participate. One of the most common death knells of the church is tradition: We've always done it that way.

"Finally, there is scripture. The Leviticus texts condemn homosexual acts for men and sex with animals in the chapter right before it condemns tattoos. Relax. I don't believe the church is about to strip anyone of their ordination for having a tattoo. That is the law that Jesus came to replace. We now live under his law of love.

"The New Testament texts that refer to homosexuality always refer to behavior that is lewd, promiscuous, and raucous. The Bible never addresses the possibility that LGBTQ+ people might seek to live a faithful, responsible, loving life as disciples of Jesus.

"I'm here to suggest that it is time to follow the lead of the Holy Spirit and move beyond equivocation regarding LGBTQ+ people. It is time to affirm that we are created by God, loved by God, and gifted by God to provide valuable service to the church. I ask that you take a stand of affirmation today and vote to allow members of the LGBTQ+ community to be ordained and share our gifts with the church.

"A vote for full participation in the life of the church will also send a message to society that we do not condone acts of violence like Mellie and I shared with you this morning. Thank you very much."

I stepped away from the microphone and was surprised by the loud applause. I was also surprised by how tired I was. *How can three minutes drain me so?* Mellie took my arm, steadying me as we walked back to our seats.

Chapter 46

Thursday, May 28, 2026

Snuggling up to Mellie before getting out of bed, I whispered, "This feels like a wonderful dream."

She took my hand, "Ummm."

I lay there, enjoying the warmth and closeness. Today was ordination day. We had both been through graduation. Mellie had her pinning ceremony and had a job lined up at the hospital in Roderick Falls, Tennessee. That's the small town out from Nashville where I would pastor my first church.

I can't believe all of this is happening! Thank you so much, Lord. Your blessings are totally amazing.

I tried to get up, but Mellie held my hand and pulled me back. "Just a little longer."

I couldn't resist but kept an eye on the clock. *Ten more minutes.*

When the clock hit 6:50, I announced, "I have to get ready." Pulling away from the delicious cuddle, I crawled out of bed to get ready for the big day.

Leaving Mellie with my family and her mom to find seats in the auditorium, I made my way back to the room where the ordinands gathered for our instructions and to line up for the service. Joel Baily handed out cards with our names on them and instructed us to hold them upside down as the bishop ordains us. Susan Williams called out our names to get us lined up alphabetically and marched us into the auditorium.

As the service progressed, my mind wondered. *I can't believe this is really happening! After all of the rejections, all of the attacks, and all of the struggles, I finally get to fulfill my calling. I wonder what the church will think of me. What am I going to preach my first sermon on?*

Bishop Bradley was assisting with the ordinations and took the podium. "My fellow disciples, this is a historical day as we are about to ordain our first gay minister. I hope you will let this day register in your hearts as a day in which the church takes a giant leap forward in our calling to live out Jesus's command to love God and neighbor in all that we do.

"I would like to recognize Willow Grier-Waters as the ground-breaking individual who was willing to answer God's call upon her life and press forward in the face of adversity to bring us to this moment. Willow, will you please stand so that we can see you?"

I wasn't expecting this. I stood from my seat. The applause was definitely lacking in exuberance, but people did applaud. Sitting back down, I realized that the battle for affirmation was not finished.

It was time. My nerves tensed and heart pounded as we lined up at the altar. Bishop Bradley and Bishop Weatherford placed their hands on my head. "Receive authority to preach the Word of God, to administer the sacraments, and order the life of the church in the name of the Father, the Son, and the Holy Spirit. Amen."

Goose bumps covered me as they spoke. The voices seemed far away, as if they were coming from heaven itself. I felt a tingling closeness to God, unlike anything I had ever experienced before. As they moved to the next ordinand, I wiped the tears from my cheeks. *Thank you, God, for this powerful moment.*

After the service, Mellie launched and nearly knocked me backwards with her embrace. "I'm so proud of you! You are a trailblazer!"

Dad pulled me into one arm and Mellie into the other. "You both know how to make a Papa proud!"

Mom hugged each of us with, "Me, too."

"My turn," Misty said.

"We sure have had a lot of celebrations lately," Dad noted.

"It has been a great season," Misty added. "And now our girls are about to launch into the lives they've prepared for."

"Sorry about that," Dad quipped. "You'll be working for a long time."

As we loaded up to go to dinner I realized that this could be the last time we are all together. *With Misty in Fort Smith and my parents in Hawksville, would we ever all be in one spot? I will just have to make that happen.*

⌒

Monday, June 22, 2026

I set my laptop on the desk in the pastor's office and surveyed the still unemptied boxes of books. *Y'all will have to wait. I need to work on my first sermon. It has to be good.*

Sitting down at the old walnut desk, I ran my hands over its surface. The deep tone and the pattern of the grain were warm and inviting. It felt like home. *The river of life continues to flow and has brought me to this place.* A memory of the feather floating by in the stream behind the old factory flashed in my mind. *I'm no longer trying to swim. It's time to fly.*

I opened my Bible to the lectionary reading for this Sunday. It couldn't have been a more fitting passage. Coming from Matthew 10:40-42, it read, "Whoever welcomes you welcomes me, and whoever welcomes me welcomes the one who sent me. Whoever welcomes a prophet in the name of a prophet will receive a prophet's reward; and whoever welcomes a righteous person in the name of a righteous person will receive the reward of the righteous; and whoever gives even a cup of cold water to one of these little ones in the name of a disciple—truly I tell you, none of these will lose their reward."

Welcoming and caring. The gospel of love. That's exactly what Jesus wants us to do right here in Roderick Falls.

I continued to ponder the sermon. The sound of my phone ringing prompted a jump that sent my chair backwards a few inches. "Hello," I answered.

An obviously upset voice came over the phone. "Hi, Pastor, it's Joe. I'm sorry to bother you on a Monday morning, but they have just diagnosed Sheila with cancer. We're at the hospital now, and they have admitted her for testing. We need your prayers."

"Oh, Joe, I am so sorry to hear that. Where is the cancer?"

"They found a spot on her liver, and the biopsy came back positive."

"I'll be praying and will come by the hospital today." I disconnected the call and went back to the sermon. Instead of the sermon, my mind kept envisioning Joe and Sheila in the hospital room bearing the weight of the bad news. They had come by to introduce themselves the day Mellie and I moved in.

I gave up on the sermon, deciding to go on to the hospital. *Lord, I think it's time for some of that caring you have called us to.*

Thank you so much for letting me share Willow's story with you. The intersection of religion and LGBTQ+ issues has often been fraught with hostility. My goal in writing these novels was to bring hope and inspiration to people who have been impacted by negativity regarding Christianity, spirituality, and sexual orientation and gender identity issues. I hope these stories have been affirming and freeing, like a feather in flight!

OTHER BOOKS BY THIS AUTHOR:

NOVELS:

THE DARK WINGS TRILOGY:

**DARK WINGS RISING
DARK WINGS DARING
DARK WINGS SOARING**

ADVENT DEVOTIONALS:

**THE SOIL OF SALVATION
INSIGHTS FROM MATTHEW
PRESENCE IN THE MANGER
THE COMING LIGHT**